STORM RUNNERS

About the Author

Roland Smith has written numerous award-winning books for young readers, including *Jungle Hunters* and *Tentacles*. For more than twenty years, he worked as an animal keeper, travelling all over the world, before turning to writing full-time. Roland lives with his wife, Marie, on a small farm south of Portland, Oregon.

www.rolandsmith.com

STORM RUNNERS

ROLAND SMITH

SCHOLASTIC

Scholastic Children's Books
A division of Scholastic Ltd
Euston House, 24 Eversholt Street
London, NW1 1DB, UK
Registered office: Westfield Road, Southam, Warwickshire, CV47 0RA
SCHOLASTIC and associated logos are trademarks and/or
registered trademarks of Scholastic Inc.

First published as three separate novels
in the United States of America by Scholastic Inc.
Storm Runners, 2011
Storm Runners: The Surge, 2011
Storm Runners: Eruption, 2012

This edition published in the UK by Scholastic Ltd, 2012

ISBN 978 1407 13138 2

A CIP catalogue record for this book
is available from the British Library.

Printed and bound by CPI Group (UK) Ltd, Croydon, CR0 4YY
Papers used by Scholastic Children's Books are made from
wood grown in sustainable forests.

1 3 5 7 9 10 8 6 4 2

www.scholastic.co.uk/zone

For Niki, Chad Myers (the guy I tune into
during weather disasters), and Joan Arth and Naomi
Williamson (look for the two Ds)

PART 1

THE
STORM

ONE YEAR EARLIER...

Chase Masters decided it was time to repair the tree house in the back yard. It had been his little sister Monica's favourite place. She'd spent so much time up there they'd nicknamed her Little Monkey – a nickname Monica had liked.

He started by tearing out a couple of rotted support beams and replacing them with treated four-by-sixes. He was going to fix the roof next, but he never got to it.

The next morning, he and his father, John, were sitting in the kitchen, eating breakfast. Eggs, pancakes, bacon – a Sunday tradition since Chase had been born.

"Want some more grub, Chase?" his father asked.

Chase shook his head. He'd already eaten five eggs and a half dozen strips of bacon, and he was still working on a stack of pancakes tall enough to sit on.

His father poured himself another cup of black coffee, sat down at the table, and looked out the back window.

"Thunderstorm," he said. "After we clean up I better head out to the job site and double-check to make sure everything's tied down and covered. Want to come?"

"Sure."

Large raindrops began to splatter the back yard.

Chase's father leaned closer to the window. "Are those tools lying outside?"

What his father was really asking was, "Why in the BLANK did you leave those tools outside?"

Tools were like religious artefacts in the Masters house. After each use, they were to be cleaned, oiled if necessary, and put away in their proper place – and each tool had only one proper place.

"Sorry." Chase jumped up from the table.

"Relax. I'll get 'em. Finish your pancakes. It'll give me a chance to see what kind of job you did on those supports."

"I did it right."

Chase's father grinned. "I have no doubt. You were trained by the Master."

Chase returned the grin. And it wasn't because of his father's terrible pun. Chase was relieved that his father wasn't upset that he was fixing the tree house.

When Monica was five years old she'd wandered off, sending the whole family into a terrified panic. They had searched for hours. Chase's mother had called the police. They were about ready to issue an AMBER Alert when Chase found Monica sound asleep in the old oak tree in the back yard. If she had rolled over, she would have fallen eight metres. Chase and his father (mostly his father) had started building the tree house the next morning. Soon Monica was spending almost as much time up in the tree house as she was in their real house.

The tree house had been sitting empty for a little over a year now, and Chase had not mentioned his repair plans to his father. There was an unspoken rule in the Masters household: the deaths of his mother and sister were not to be talked about, because the subject opened sores that hurt for days.

As far as Chase knew, his father hadn't set foot in Monica's bedroom since the accident. It was almost as if he thought she was still in there and would come running out one day, filling the house with her wild, uninhibited giggling. Chase would have given almost anything to hear that laugh again.

Chase watched his father walk across the yard in the now pouring rain. John Masters hadn't bothered to put on a coat and he was getting drenched. His lightweight cowboy shirt clung to his lean, ropy muscles. His brown hair had turned black in the torrent. He climbed the slick rungs screwed into the gnarled trunk and inspected Chase's work as if he were a structural engineer, which he wasn't. He was a builder. One of the best in the city. He had built their house, and several other houses in the neighbourhood too. After he'd married Chase's mother, he'd started a construction company with her brother, Bob.

Chase's father climbed down from the tree and gave his son a thumbs-up sign, which Chase took to mean that he could continue with his renovation and maybe, just maybe, they could put the past behind them and get on with their lives.

It turned out that they did get on with their lives, but it wasn't the life Chase had been expecting.

Chase's father reached down and picked up the nail gun. He shook the rain off it, looked up at the sky...

Chase was still a little shaky about what happened next.

There was a blinding flash of white light followed by a deafening explosion that shook the house. When Chase's eyes cleared from the flash, he saw his father crumpled beneath the tree. His clothes were smoking. Chase ran out of the house, yelling. The sharp stench of ozone filled the back yard. His father wasn't breathing. The snaps on his shirt were fused to his chest. People showed up from all over the neighbourhood. A couple of them were doctors. They started giving him CPR.

Chase couldn't watch.

He looked up at the tree.

His father's left boot was dangling by its shoelace from a lower branch.

Two days later his father came out of his coma.

When Chase told him how terrible he felt about leaving the tools outside, his father laughed and said, "That bolt of lighting was waiting for me my whole life, Chase. If it hadn't nailed me in the back yard, it would have gotten me in the front yard, walking to my truck, or later at the job site. You can't hide from your fate."

On the road with his father over the past year, Chase had thought a lot about the word fate and decided that it was one of those little words with a big meaning...

01:58 PM

When my father got struck by lightning, so did I, Chase thought. *When Mom and Monica died, so did I . . . a little . . .*

"I guess you can't separate your fate from those you're with," Chase said quietly.

"What?" his father asked.

Chase jumped. He hadn't meant to say that last part out loud. "Nothing . . . uh . . . just thinking about a song."

"You want the radio on?"

"No, I'm fine."

Chase and his father were in Florida speeding down a road along the Gulf of Mexico. Chase's father had one hand on the steering wheel of their 4x4 truck. In his other he held a travel mug of black coffee. Chase's job was to replenish the mug from the Thermos at his feet, which he had filled four hours earlier in the weather-battered fifth-wheel trailer they were pulling. His father called the fifth-wheel the Shack. It was where they lived. It was nicer on the inside than the outside. The rough exterior was the result of a hailstorm in Oklahoma two weeks ago. Chase had been inside the Shack when it hit. The worst part had been the sound. His ears had rung for twenty-four hours after the ten-minute pounding. When he'd opened the door, the ground had been covered in golf-ball-size ice pellets for as far as he could see. A mile away a farmer had been killed running from his John Deere combine to his house. He should have stayed inside the combine.

"What time is it?" his father asked.

His father did not wear a watch. The perfectly running clock on the dash had been covered with black electrical tape. At the top of almost every hour (when they were together) he would ask Chase, who wore a radio-controlled atomic-time watch, that same question.

"Two o'clock," Chase said. "Exactly."

"Perfect."

The Internal Clock Game. This was just one of the games his father played during their frequent long drives. Another game was How to Get Out of Doom City. This consisted of his father picking a random street in a random city, and a disaster like a flood. The goal was for Chase to quickly find high ground, then plot a route that would get him out of town before the disaster caught up with him.

Chase wondered if Tomás played driving games. He doubted it. Tomás was behind them, driving the Shop – a thirteen-metre trailer pulled by a Mack semi tractor – by himself. Tomás's living quarters were in the front part of the trailer, with a separate entrance. The rest was filled with two mountain bikes, an all-terrain quad, and enough tools and supplies to build a three-storey home. Behind the Shop, Tomás was pulling a second 4x4 truck.

Signs on the sides of all the rigs read, m.d. emergency services, followed by a 1-800 number.

Obviously the M.D. didn't stand for *Medical Doctor*, but sometimes the authorities thought it did and Chase's father didn't correct them. M.D. stood for *Masters of*

Disaster. In his father's world, everything had a double meaning.

About a week after the lightning strike, the economy was struck by recession. The building industry tanked. Chase's father and uncle's business was on the verge of bankruptcy. Uncle Bob was on the verge of an emotional collapse.

    Chase's father wasn't worried at all. He had other plans. He sold everything they owned, including their house and their vacation cabin on Mount Hood. With the proceeds, he bought the Shack and the Shop, paid off his half of the construction company's debts, then signed the company over to a grateful but stunned Uncle Bob...

    "What are you going to do, John?"

    "Start over. See the country."

    "What about Chase?"

    "He'll go with me, of course."

    "What about school?"

    "He'll go to school."

Chase had been to three schools in the past year and was heading towards his fourth, provided it wasn't wiped off the face of the earth by Hurricane Emily, who was whirling her way anticlockwise across the Gulf of Mexico.

    Emily had started out a few weeks earlier as an innocent little thunderstorm in Ethiopia. She moved west over the Sahara Desert, picking up sand and heat, then swept out into the Atlantic, where she became a tropical storm and got her name. As the trade winds pushed her further west she gathered humidity and power. At seventy-four miles an hour she graduated from a tropical storm to a hurricane.

Which is more than I'm going to do if we don't settle down in a school for more than two months, Chase thought.

He had just got used to the school in Oklahoma when his father pulled the plug and started them towards Emily. Coincidentally, or maybe not, Emily was his mother's first name. His father still had work when they'd left Oklahoma. Chase wondered if the hurricane's name had anything to do with their leaving so quickly, but he knew better than to ask. Nothing could shift his father's mood faster than bringing up his mom or sister.

Chase looked over at his father. He used to know him face-on. Now he knew him mostly in profile from the passenger seat. About the only time they were together any more was in the truck driving to a disaster. When his father and Tomás were working, they slept in hotels, only coming back to the Shack & Shop to pick up supplies. Chase had thought that being on the road would bring him and his father closer together. In some ways it had, but right now, sitting a metre apart, they might as well have been in different solar systems.

Chase's relationship with Tomás was not much better, but theirs was a language problem. Tomás's English wasn't good and Chase's Spanish was nonexistent. Chase wasn't sure how Tomás and his father communicated so well. A combination of Spanglish and telepathy, he guessed. Tomás had worked for Chase's father for more than twenty years. When his father told Uncle Bob that he was taking Tomás with them, Uncle Bob almost wept.

"I'll have to hire three new guys to replace him," Uncle Bob had said.

"Four," his father had replied.

More like five, in Chase's opinion. Tomás was at least ten years older than his father, but he was a building machine. Tomás never walked between tasks. He jogged, like everything was an emergency. A few years before they hit the road, Uncle Bob had jokingly said that he would give Tomás a five-grand cash bonus if he could frame a two-storey house that passed building inspection in twenty-four hours. Tomás did it in twenty-two. The building inspector said it was the best framing job he'd ever seen. Uncle Bob handed over the cash.

Tomás was married and had eight kids, but Chase had never met his wife, or the rest of his family. Neither had his father. They lived someplace in Mexico. Tomás visited them once a year around Christmas, and Chase assumed he sent most of his money down south to them. In his truck he kept laminated photos of all of the kids arranged by age. On top of his dash was a plastic statue of Saint Christopher, patron saint of travellers. Saint Christopher was also invoked against lightning. Tomás had given his father a Saint Christopher's medal when he was in the hospital. So far, it had worked.

On most Sundays, Tomás put his hammer down for a few hours and went to church. Chase had gone with him a couple of times. He didn't think Tomás understood a word the priest was saying, but that wasn't the point.

Chase believed that Tomás went to church for the same reason he had left everything behind to join Chase's father.

Tomás was loyal.

02:16 PM

They had left the motorway and were now driving down a dual-carriageway. Tomás had taken the lead, which was unusual because as far as Chase knew, Tomás had never been to Florida.

They always parked the Shack & Shop on private property – high ground – at least forty miles from where his father thought he and Tomás would be working. *Thought* because they didn't really know where they'd find work. That depended on where the storm hit and the amount of damage it caused – two things nobody could predict. But Chase's father was pretty good at guessing.

As with the Internal Clock Game, Chase was not sure how his father did this. Before the lightning strike, his father hadn't been at all interested in weather. After he got out of the hospital, he had the Weather Channel on twenty-four hours a day. He read every book about weather he could get his hands on. He bought weather software for his laptop. After two weeks he could predict the weather anywhere, almost perfectly, several days out. Chase joked that he should become a meteorologist for a local television station. His father told him he had something very different in mind.

Another thing that changed after the lightning strike was his father's sleeping pattern. He'd always been an eight-hours-a-night guy. On weekends he'd sleep nine or ten hours if he could get away with it. Not any more. His father hadn't slept more than four hours a night since the strike and he never seemed to get tired. Chase thought he had more energy now than he did before the strike. It was almost as if his father had electricity in his veins instead of blood.

Ø2:31PM

Tomás stopped the semi in front of a chain-link gate. He jumped out, swung the double gate open, then jogged back to the cab. Chase wondered if maybe Tomás had lightning in his body too.

They followed Tomás through. Chase got out and closed the gate behind them, then climbed back into the cab.

"What is this place?"

"A farm," his father answered. "Tomás's brother, Arturo, works here."

Chase didn't know Tomás had a brother.

"They need some minor repairs," his father continued. "I told them that we'd fix 'em up if they let us park here for free. You're in charge of the repairs. Tomás and I will be in Saint Petersburg – Saint Pete, as they call it."

Chase hoped his father was right about the repairs being minor.

"Where's the school?"

"About ten miles away. You'll have to drive the quad down to the road to catch the bus."

"You think the storm is going to hit up here?"

"I haven't checked the satellite images since early this morning, but there's a chance it could shift north-east. Palm Breeze might get nicked, but you'll be OK. This is the highest ground in the county. You'll still need to be alert, though. You know the routine."

Chase did know the routine. Sitting at his feet, next to the Thermos, was his go bag – a daypack that each of them had within reach twenty-four hours a day. Inside was everything they needed to survive for three days: satellite phone (for when the landlines and mobile-phone signals failed), first aid kit, rain gear, bottled water, camp stove, flares, freeze-dried food, energy bars, knife, butane lighter, binoculars and several other items – none of which they'd had to use ... yet.

The farm wasn't like any farm Chase had seen before. The fences were made out of heavy-duty chain link. About every six metres there was a warning: DANGER! ELECTRIFIED!

Electrified against what? Chase thought. *We've gone half a mile and I haven't seen a single animal.*

They came to a second gate. On the other side were four large metal buildings. They pulled the rigs through the gate, parked, and stepped out into the humid air.

A man came out of the building directly in front of them. He was small. Very small. He pulled off his leather gloves as he walked towards them.

"You're Mr Masters?"

"John," his father said, holding out his hand. "This is Tomás. And this is my son, Chase."

Chase shook the man's little hand. The man stared at him with bright blue eyes. "You're probably wondering what to call me."

"What do you mean?"

"Midget, dwarf," the man said. "I don't mind any of them,

but *dwarf* is the appropriate word since I have dwarfism. But the acceptable term if you want to be politically correct is *little person*." He patted his head. "L.P. for short."

He laughed at his own joke. Chase and his father smiled. Tomás smiled too, but Chase doubted he had got the pun.

"My name's Marco Rossi," the man said. "I'm pleased to meet all of you." He looked at Tomás. "I'm afraid your brother, Arturo, isn't here. He and the others took off yesterday with a load of animals, but you're still welcome. In fact, I'm glad to have you. We're a little shorthanded."

"Actually, Tomás and I won't be around much," Chase's father explained. "We need to head to Saint Pete and help prepare for the storm, but Chase will be staying here, and he's pretty handy."

"That'll increase our manpower by a third, so I'm grateful. Do you like animals, Chase?"

"Sure, but I don't know much about cows and horses."

Chase didn't know much about cats and dogs, either. His mother had been allergic to them, so they'd never had any at the house.

Marco laughed. "You don't need to know much about cows and horses on this farm." He looked at the rigs. "What happened to the fifth-wheel?"

"Hailstorm in Oklahoma."

"Hope that doesn't happen here."

"Hurricanes are too warm to produce hail," Chase's father pointed out. "Tornadoes are a different story. Twisters and hail go together. The problems with hurricanes are wind, rain, and storm surge." He looked at Chase. "Ten to three?"

Chase nodded, though his father was three seconds fast.

"We better get moving. I want to be in Saint Pete before it shuts down for the night."

Tomás jogged over to the semi and fired it up.

03:10PM

Within twenty minutes, Tomás and Chase's father had parked the rigs in one of the buildings, loaded their 4x4s with supplies and were on their way to Saint Petersburg.

Chase spent the next hour setting up the Shack & Shop.

The building was perfect. Concrete floor. Steel struts covered by heavy-gauge aluminium panels. Plenty of electrical receptacles to plug in to. Water. Septic system. The only problem was the heat. It was like the inside of a barbecue. Chase turned up the AC in the fifth-wheel and left. It wasn't much better outside, but the light breeze dried the sweat on his face and T-shirt.

After they parked, Marco had needed to hurry off and take care of something. He told Chase to find him somewhere on the grounds when he finished. Chase walked over to the nearest building and opened the door, expecting to see a little person. What he found instead was a girl about his age, his height, feeding a giraffe.

She was wearing shorts and a T-shirt. Her long black hair was wet and combed straight back as if she'd just stepped out of the shower.

"Hi. Dad said you'd be by. I'm Nicole Rossi."

She looked at Chase for a moment, then started laughing.

"What's so funny?"

"The look on your face. Are you surprised to see a giraffe, or are you surprised that I'm Marco Rossi's daughter?"

Chase smiled sheepishly. "Both, I guess."

"Little people can have regular-size children. My older sister is little. My older brother is big. Huge, in fact. He's a defensive tackle for the Georgia Bulldogs. And if you're wondering why my hair is wet, I just finished swimming laps."

"You have a pool?"

"Almost everyone in Florida has a pool, or a neighbour who has a pool you can use. If we didn't have free access to pools, we would melt in the summer."

The giraffe bent its knobby head down and wrapped a purplish tongue around the carrot Nicole was holding.

At that exact same moment, there was a terrifying roar that shook the metal building and reverberated inside Chase's chest and all the way down to his toes. He'd never heard – or *felt* – anything like that in his life.

"Nothing to be afraid of. That's just Simba, one of our lions. He's in a cage."

"You have lions in here?"

"A bunch of them."

"What *is* this place?"

"Winter quarters for the Rossi Brothers' Circus. My dad didn't tell you?"

"Winter quarters?"

"You don't know much about circuses."

"I don't know *anything* about circuses."

"Circuses are seasonal, especially for tent shows like ours. We can't put up the big top or get where we're going if it's snowing. We need a place to keep the animals during the winter. The whole show should be back here by now, but we picked up a couple extra months in Mexico. It's just as well because of the storm. Arturo and our winter quarters crew are hauling animals south of the border."

"Not the giraffe."

"Gertrude," Nicole said. "She'd stand over six metres on a lowboy semi-trailer. Too tall to fit under overpasses. She was only on the show for a couple of years when she was a baby. Now she's a full-time resident here."

"Like you and your dad?"

"That's right. Someone has to be here to take care of the surplus animals and run the farm. And I have school. My mother and sister are on the road with the show, along with my two uncles. Sometimes we catch up with the show for a few days during the summer if I have a swim meet close by."

"So, you compete."

Nicole shrugged. "I can tread water."

Chase was going to ask if her mother was a little person too, but the question was blown out of his thoughts by another chest-rattling roar.

"Come on. I'll take you over to meet the pride."

Ø4:12PM

Simba was as big as his roar. He rubbed his thick black mane back and forth along the chain-link holding area with such force Chase was afraid the wire was going to snap. Nicole didn't seem the least bit concerned. She put her fingers through the links and scratched Simba under the chin.

"Simba's thirteen. He was born the same year I was."

Which means we're the same age, Chase thought. "Why isn't Simba with the show?"

"He mauled our trainer a couple of years ago."

Chase took a small step backwards, which he hoped Nicole hadn't noticed. "How badly?"

"It could have been worse." Nicole continued scratching Simba's chin. "The trainer could have been killed and Simba might have been shot. The trainer was in the hospital for two weeks. We decided it was time for Simba to retire. But I think he misses the road."

"What about the trainer?"

"He's back with the show. Getting mauled is no big deal."

"Unless you're the one getting mauled."

"I suppose that's true," Nicole agreed. "But most cat trainers will tell you that getting mauled is not a matter of *if*. It's a matter of *when* and how bad the mauling is going to be."

Nicole led him outside the building to an attached enclosure with four more lions. "Three lionesses and one lion." She pointed. "You can see the male's just starting to get his mane."

He was about half the size of Simba. "Will he be in the show someday?"

"Maybe. He was someone's idea of a wonderful pet. The state confiscated him. He was starving when they brought him in. We take in a lot of animals like that. I think there are as many exotic animals in private hands in Florida as there are pools. We get the animals back on their feet and give them to rehabilitation facilities or zoos. Sometimes we put them in the show, but not very often. Not all animals are cut out for the circus ... not all people are either."

"How about you?"

Nicole laughed. "Oh, I think it's a foregone conclusion that I'll be in the circus when I grow up. That is, if there are circuses. They aren't as popular as they used to be. A lot of them have folded. One way or the other, I'll be working with animals. If the circus dies, I'm going to be a marine mammal veterinarian. What about you, Chase Masters?" She turned her beautiful brown eyes on him. "What are you going to be when you grow up?"

Chase had spent a lot of time thinking about this. Like his father, he was good with his hands. He enjoyed building and fixing things, but he wasn't sure he wanted to become a contractor or a builder.

"I'm not sure," he said. "Maybe I'll become a lion tamer."

"Funny."

"Why isn't Simba out here with the other lions?"

"He doesn't get along with them. We alternate him outside by himself every other day."

Nicole led Chase over to another building. Inside was a leopard named Hector.

"Odd name," Chase said.

"Odd cat. We didn't name him. He was confiscated from a drug runner."

Hector was a third of Simba's size, but for some reason he looked a lot more lethal. He paced back and forth restlessly.

"You don't want to get too close to Hector," Nicole said. "He's very aggressive and fast as lightning. I'm surprised the drug runner who owned him lived long enough to get arrested."

"What are you going to do with him?"

"He's not going on the show, that's for sure. Dad has a couple of zoos that are interested. He'll be leaving the farm soon, but that won't be soon enough for me. Old Hector is as bright as he is fast. Getting him into the holding area so we can clean his cage is a major ordeal. About half the time, he gets in and out of the holding area with the meat we bait him *in* with before we can even close the door. He figured out that he could get a double portion that way on his first day here."

"He doesn't look fat," Chase said.

"He's not. He burns calories pacing and lunging at us when we get within range of his claws."

In the cage next to Hector's, an ancient brown bear slept curled in a corner. Across from the cages were two large stalls. Three zebras stood together in one, and the other held four ostriches. At the far end of the building was an indoor/outdoor aviary filled with colourful parrots.

As strange and wonderful as the animals were, the thing that was beginning to interest Chase the most was his tour guide. He was looking forward to staying on the farm, learning about circuses ... and Nicole.

"Do you let people come up here to see the animals?" he asked.

"Friends," she said. "We try to keep a low profile. We're not really set up for visitors. But that might change with the baby elephant."

"You have a baby elephant?"

"Almost."

"What do you mean?"

Instead of answering, Nicole led him to the only building they hadn't been in, which was by far the largest. The three other buildings would have all easily fit inside.

"This is where we rehearse the acts and train the animals during the winter. And that's the bunkhouse for the roughnecks." She pointed to a smaller attached building to the right.

"What's a roughneck?"

"They drive the trucks; put up the big top; set up the rings, cages, apparatus; assist the animal trainers and performers. Without them, there wouldn't be a show. Arturo is a roughneck, but he doesn't live in the bunkhouse. He's been with the circus for nearly thirty years and pretty much runs the farm now. He has a house on the property. The bunkhouse is empty at the moment, except for my dad. He's been sleeping down here for a couple of weeks."

"Why?"

"I'll show you."

Nicole opened the door.

The building was lit with bright spotlights hanging from the ceiling, shining down on three large circus rings. The ring closest to them had a steel cage in the centre, which Chase assumed was for the big cats. The middle ring had a huge safety net stretched across it. Hanging above the net was a tightrope and an array of trapeze equipment. Marco Rossi was in the third ring, hosing down an elephant and scrubbing her wrinkled grey skin with a long-handled deck brush.

"How's it going, Dad?" Nicole said.

"I should have gotten AC in here years ago," he said. "It's like a furnace!"

"We could open the doors on either end."

"Right, and Pet will pull her leg off trying to get outside."

Chase noticed the elephant had chains around her left front foot and right rear foot. "Why's she chained?"

"So she doesn't float to the ceiling," Nicole and Marco said in unison, then started laughing.

"Sorry, Chase," Marco said. "Old circus joke. Can't help ourselves. On the show, people ask that question a thousand times a day. Elephants are chained to a picket line so they don't run off – or whack somebody." He handed the hose and brush to Nicole and stepped out of the ring.

"In the case of Pet here, we have her chained up so she

doesn't dismantle the building. We don't have an elephant-proof building on the farm. The elephants we use on our show winter in Texas. Our elephant guy has a good set-up down there. And Pet would be there right now, but she's twenty-two months pregnant and we didn't want to risk trucking her that far so close to term. Elephant births in captivity are rare. We've never had one in the hundred years our circus has been on the road. So, as you might imagine, we're pretty excited..."

"And nervous," Nicole added, shooting a stream of water into Pet's open mouth.

"I'll admit it," Marco said. "I am nervous. What if something goes wrong? Our vet doesn't know anything about elephant births."

"Not many vets do," Nicole said.

"There's a doc on the West Coast who's seen dozens of elephants born. I've been on the phone with him every day, offered him a fortune to fly out here and supervise the birth, but he said it would be a waste of money. He told me that Pet will have her calf when she has it. She'll take care of it or she won't. It'll be healthy or unhealthy. He'll come out after it's born if there's a problem."

"When's the baby due?"

"Anytime now. We're not exactly sure when she was bred. As elephants go, Pet's pretty steady, but the past few days she's been acting up. She can't seem to get comfortable when she lies down, she's off her feed, and yesterday she took a poke at me with her trunk for no good reason, which is really out of character for her. Normally she's the most easy-going elephant

I've ever been around."

Nicole turned the hose off, wound it up out of Pet's reach, then joined them.

"Your grandmother is looking for you," Marco said. "She said something about you not finishing your laps."

"I finished most of them," Nicole said. "I came down to help. You can't take care of everything here, especially with an elephant calf on its way."

"I managed to take care of the farm long before you were born," Marco reminded her. "Your grandmother also said that she needs help with her boxes, and mentioned something about sweet potato pie."

Nicole smiled. "I'll go."

"Take Chase with you. She's probably already mad at you for not taking him to the house to introduce him."

"You didn't take him up there either," Nicole teased.

"I have pachyderm problems. What's your excuse?"

"We better go," Nicole said.

They left Marco and Pet, and started up a long, twisting driveway to a farmhouse overlooking the enclosures and buildings.

"Are there any other animals on the farm?" Chase asked.

"Aside from Momma Rossi's squirrel monkey, Poco, no."

"Who's Momma Rossi?"

"My grandmother. She's up at the house, packing."

"Where's she going?"

"She thinks the hurricane is going to hit the house."

"My dad's pretty good at predicting the weather. He says

it's going to make landfall south of here. Probably around Saint Pete."

"Momma Rossi is rarely wrong," Nicole said. "She can see the future ... and sometimes even the past."

05:02 PM

Chase followed Nicole on to the screened porch of the Rossis' old farmhouse. He looked at the sofas and chairs scattered about and wondered what it would be like to sit there in the evening, listening to lion tamers, clowns, acrobats and little people talking about their day.

To get through the front door, they had to move several boxes of framed newspaper articles, photos and other circus memorabilia to the side.

"Where's she moving this stuff?"

"We have a waterproof storage container out back by the pool."

Nicole led the way into a large kitchen, where the counters, cupboards and appliances were at least half a metre lower than they'd normally be. Momma Rossi, grey-haired and a bit shorter than her son, stood at the sink peeling sweet potatoes. Sitting next to the sink was a small green monkey wearing a diaper. He was holding a potato peel in one hand and scratching his leg with the other. Momma Rossi turned around and gave them a bright smile.

She put her hand out. "You must be Chase Masters. Welcome to our home."

"Thank you." Chase took her hand.

Momma Rossi stared at him with dark eyes and her smile faded.

"I'm so sorry about your mother and sister."

Chase froze.

"What are you talking about?" Nicole asked.

Momma Rossi gripped Chase's hand more tightly. "A car accident on a mountain. I'm sure it hasn't been easy for you or your father."

Tomás must have told Arturo, Chase thought. But looking into Momma Rossi's dark eyes, he had an eerie feeling that wasn't how she knew. . .

TWO YEARS EARLIER . . .

It had rained every day Chase had been at Boy Scout camp, and it was still raining. He was standing in the car park with his troop leader, Mr Murphy. All morning, one by one, parents had been picking up their drenched Scouts. Now it was just Chase and Mr Murphy.

Mr Murphy looked at his watch for the hundredth time. "Are you sure your parents were clear on when and where to pick you up?"

"Yes, sir. Like I told you, I talked to them last night. Mom said that they were driving up with my little sister. On the way home we're going to stop at our cabin and pick up a load of firewood for the house."

"Maybe they stopped at the cabin first."

"I don't think so. Dad wouldn't haul a truckload of wood all the way up here, then drive it back down the mountain."

"You're probably right. Do you have a phone at your cabin?"

"No."

Mr Murphy pulled his phone out and called Chase's house and his parents' phones again. All three calls went to voice mail.

Chase was starting to feel sick. His parents were never late for anything.

"We can't stand here all day waiting," Mr Murphy said. "How about if I leave a note for them here and voice mails on their phones saying I've taken you to my house?"

"OK."

Chase tossed his soggy gear into the back of Mr Murphy's SUV.

About halfway down the mountain, they ran into a terrible traffic jam. Chase was so worried about his parents not showing up that he barely noticed the line of cars stretching ahead of them ... until they reached the end of it. On the opposite side of the highway, at least a half dozen police cars with flashing lights clustered on the shoulder. A tow truck was winching a blue SUV out of the ditch.

"That's my parents' car!" Chase shouted.

"Are you still a Boy Scout?" Momma Rossi asked.

"What?" Chase pulled his hand away from Momma Rossi quickly.

"Are you OK?" Nicole asked.

"Yeah, I just ... uh..."

"I asked if you were still a Boy Scout," Momma Rossi repeated.

"No, we've been travelling," he said.

"Helping people," Momma Rossi said.

Chase nodded, but he knew it wasn't exactly true...

At that moment, John Masters and Tomás were trolling separate parts of Saint Petersburg. John was driving through the business district. Tomás was driving through the wealthier residential areas.

If a business or home owner – never a contractor – was out making preparations for the storm, they'd stop, introduce themselves, then offer to give them a hand ... for free. Tomás's poor English was not a hindrance. His skilled hands transcended all language barriers.

Both men knew precisely how to prepare a home or business for disaster. They were fast and efficient. They also knew that if the wind was strong enough, no preparation was going to save an expensive building or home from damage.

The grateful owner usually tried to pay them for their time, but they refused. Instead they handed over a couple of M.D. Emergency Services business cards and told the owners to call if they had any problems.

If the winds were strong enough, and the water high enough, they would all have problems, and they would call. But the second round of repairs wouldn't be free.

05:07 PM

Nicole picked up a paring knife from the counter. "I suppose you want some help peeling sweet potatoes."

"Since they're your sweet potatoes," Momma Rossi said, "you're darned right I want help. And what about your laps?" She put her hands on her hips and tried to look mad, but there was a sparkle in her eyes. "You did about half of what you were supposed to do."

"I did enough. The meet is in three days. I don't want to wear myself out before the competition. I was feeding Gertrude and the cats so Dad didn't have to."

"All right," Momma Rossi said. "Because we have a guest, and because we have a lot to do, I'll let it go this time."

"Scoot, peel thief!" Nicole said. Poco grabbed another potato peel, climbed to the top of the refrigerator and glared down at her.

"Make yourself at home," Momma Rossi said to Chase. "This could take a while. Nicole is a very fast swimmer but a very slow potato peeler."

"Very funny, Momma."

"I can move those boxes if you want," Chase offered.

"That would be nice," Momma Rossi said. "But it might not be as easy as you think. For one thing, I'm not certain there's room in the container. Marco and Nicole haven't done a very good job of packing. The boxes need to be reorganized and restacked."

"No problem." After a year of Shack & Shop duty, Chase was an expert organizer.

Nicole put the knife down. "Since you're blaming me for the mess, maybe I better give him a hand."

"I think Chase is more than capable of hauling and organizing boxes on his own. And I need you to make the sweet potato pie ... unless you'd prefer for Chase to eat my version."

Nicole laughed. "I guess that wouldn't be polite to our guest."

Momma Rossi snapped a towel at her playfully.

"I'm not exactly your guest," Chase said. It wasn't a rule, but they didn't usually hang out with the people who owned the property they parked on. "We have everything we need in the fifth-wheel. You don't need to feed me."

"Nonsense," Momma Rossi said. "I don't know how to cook for less than a dozen people, and with you, there are only four of us tonight."

"I wouldn't argue with Momma Rossi," Nicole said. "Dad tried to talk her out of getting the container. Guess who won?"

"He'll be happy our things are safe. Do you like sweet potato pie, Chase?"

"I like pie and I like sweet potatoes, but I've never had them together."

"You haven't lived until you've eaten Nicole's sweet potato pie."

*

Chase carried two boxes past a large modern pool, which did not fit with the old two-storey farmhouse. The Rossis must have put it in long after the house was built, for Nicole to swim laps. The container, which was nothing more than a steel box welded to a trailer, was on the opposite side of the pool. He opened the door and a storage box fell out. There was plenty of room inside the container, but it looked like it had been organized by Poco. The only way to fix it was to take everything out and start all over again.

Chase looked up at the sky. Clouds were moving in from the gulf. He jogged down to the Shop, imitating Tomás's perpetual state of emergency, which is exactly what Chase would be in if it started to rain after he pulled everything out. He grabbed a couple of tarps, a hammer and a handful of metal stakes.

Since they'd been on the road, his father had taken the Boy Scouts' motto, "Be Prepared", to a new level. Every job, no matter how small, needed to be thought through before it was started, from beginning to end, with particular attention paid to what might go wrong *in between*.

Chase staked out a ground tarp so it wouldn't blow away, then staged a second tarp to pull over the boxes in case it started to rain. What he neglected to anticipate in between was his curiosity about the Rossi family and their circus. In almost every box, he found something he had to look at or read.

There were stacks of photo albums filled with pictures of the big top, circus acts, animals and people. Nicole's mom was a little person, like Momma Rossi and Marco. Others in the family were regular size, like Nicole. But in every photo, they were smiling and laughing as if there wasn't an inch of difference between them.

Marco walked up as Chase was staring at a painting of a man holding a whip, dressed in a red coat, white trousers, knee-high black boots and a black top hat.

"That's my great-grandfather, Ricardo Rossi. He was a famous ringmaster in Europe before he came over here to start his own circus. The picture doesn't show his stature in perspective very well. He was four inches shorter than I am. He died when I was five years old. He was ninety-six. The day before he died he was in the ring, training a stallion."

"Wow."

"Yep, he was quite a guy." Marco looked at the tarp and boxes. "Did Momma Rossi give you this chore?"

"No," Chase answered. "I offered to help. I'm supposed to be organizing and repacking everything, but I guess what I'm doing mostly is snooping."

Marco laughed. "Hard not to. A lot of interesting history here." He reached into one of the boxes and pulled out a photograph of a man sitting on top of an elephant. "This is my dad. He was killed by an elephant when I was thirteen. He was quite a guy too."

"I'm sorry."

"Thanks. It was a long time ago, but I still miss him. Some things you just don't get over, I guess."

Chase understood this all too well. He'd wondered if he was ever going to get over the deaths of his mom and Monica. "But you still like elephants?"

"They're my favourite animal. They were my dad's

favourite too." Marco looked at the container. "Think this will do the trick?"

"It's not really waterproof, Mr Rossi," Chase answered.

"First, it's Marco, not Mr Rossi. Second, can you waterproof it? Your dad said you were pretty handy."

"I can caulk it, and tarp it, which should keep the water out, but I think the boxes would be a lot safer back in the house."

"Not according to my mother," Marco said. "She's convinced the house is coming down."

"What do you think?"

"I don't agree with her on this, but she's my mother, and she's usually right."

Chase nodded. She was certainly right about the accident and his being a Boy Scout.

"Did Arturo tell you anything about us?"

"Like what?"

"Our past. Where we're from."

"All he said was that you helped people during storms and that you needed a place to hook up your rigs. Is there something else I should know?"

Chase shook his head. "I guess not."

"I better get back down to Pet and see what she's up to. Thanks for taking care of the container. I'll see you at dinner."

It took Chase nearly two hours to reload the container. When he finally got the last box inside, he caulked all the seams, threw the tarps over the top and began securing them with bungee cords.

Nicole came out of the back door of the house as he was stretching the last cord. "Why so many bungees?" she asked.

"So it doesn't float to the sun."

"Funny. It looks like a giant Christmas present wrapped in blue paper."

"It won't leak."

"I'll say."

"How's the sweet potato pie?"

"It's perfect."

Chase smiled. "I suppose anyone who scratches lions under the chin is entitled to a certain amount of confidence. I better go down to the Shack and get cleaned up before dinner."

"Hurry," Nicole said. "Sweet potato pie is terrible when it's cold."

As Chase was drying his hair in the Shack's kitchen, he realized that they didn't have a single photograph hanging up, from either their former or current life.

How can that be? Where are the photos of Mom and Monica? The notebooks with Monica's stories and drawings?

They weren't in the fifth-wheel or the semi-trailer. Chase knew exactly what they had, and where all of it was stored.

What's Dad done with our past?

07:42PM

Chase sat with the Rossis in their kitchen in front of enough food to feed a bunkhouse of roughnecks for a week. Pork chops, fried chicken, garlic mashed potatoes, a trough of Caesar salad, steamed beans, fresh baked rolls, and of course sweet potato pie – all delicious, especially the pie. It might have been the best meal he'd ever eaten. It was certainly the most entertaining, with the Rossis telling him story after story of their life in the circus, pausing once in a while to glance over at Emily on the television...

"Emily has all the makings of a Category Five hurricane. The question is, Where is she going to make landfall and when? For the very latest information let's go to our meteorologist, Cindy Stewart. Cindy?"

"Well, Richard, it's a little premature to say Emily's going to be a Category Five hurricane, but she is gathering strength. Right now Emily is stalled about one hundred fifty miles south-west of here with sustained winds in excess of one hundred thirty-one miles per hour, making her a Category Four at the moment, which is still a potentially devastating storm. Anything in her path is going to be in for a severe pounding."

"Any idea what her path is going to be?"

"No. We'll have a better idea when Emily starts to

move, but even then, she could switch directions. At this point it's up to fate..."

That word again, Chase thought.

Marco took another scoop of sweet potato pie. His appetite was anything but small.

"Looks like you'll have school tomorrow," he said.

"Are you kidding?" Nicole said. "You can't do everything here by yourself."

"Chase will be here."

"Actually, I won't be here," Chase said. "If Nicole has school, I have school."

"And there's that little problem called a Category Five hurricane coming our way," Nicole added. "Besides, what about Pet? If you think I'm going to miss an elephant birth, you're crazy."

Marco held up a thumb. "I'm not completely crazy." Index finger. "Emily's not a Category Five ... yet." Middle finger. "We don't know Emily's coming this way." Ring finger. "Pet might not calve for weeks." Little finger. Marco looked at Momma Rossi as if he couldn't think of a fifth reason. "What do you think?"

"I think if there is school, you both need to go. School is important." She glanced at the TV, then added with an eerie certainty, "After the hurricane, there won't be school for a long time."

Nicole walked Chase back to the Shack & Shop. He gave her a tour, which didn't take long. As she was leaving, she paused and asked, "Why do you always carry your backpack with you? This seems like a safe enough place to leave it, but when we were having dinner, you had it right at your feet."

"Emergencies. If I get separated or stuck someplace, it has everything I need to keep me going for a few days. My dad calls it a go bag. We all carry one."

"It must be strange to travel around from one disaster to another."

"It's probably not that different from being in a circus."

"You might be right," Nicole agreed.

"What time does the bus come?"

"Seven ten."

"Early."

"We're almost the furthest from town."

"I can drive us down to the road on the quad," Chase offered.

"Great." Nicole gave him a smile. "I'll see you tomorrow morning."

Chase watched Nicole walk away and wondered what his father would say if he told him he wanted to become a lion tamer.

05:46 AM

Chase pulled on a pair of combat trousers, T-shirt and trainers, then listened to the weather on the radio as he ate breakfast. Emily was stalled in the Gulf of Mexico, gathering strength, making up her mind which way to go.

His mobile phone rang.

"What time is it?" his father asked.

"Six o'clock ... exactly."

"That's what I thought."

"How do I know you're not looking at the time on your phone?"

"Because your old man wouldn't lie to you. How are things there?"

"I'm getting ready for school."

"Good."

"Uh ... I'm kind of curious about something."

"What's that?"

"I was wondering where all our old photos are ... you know, of the family."

"I gave them to your uncle Bob for safekeeping. We don't have a lot of room in the Shack, and storing them in the places we go is a good way to lose them. What made you think about that?"

"I don't know. Maybe hearing the name Emily over and over again."

His father was silent for several seconds, then said, "I can see that. But the name's just a coincidence. They alternate female and male names every hurricane season, starting with the letter *A*. This year it's been Arlene, Bret, Cindy, Don, and now Emily. I better get going. Tomás is over at the restaurant. Everything OK?"

"Yeah."

"Stay alert, Chase."

"I will."

"Talk to you later."

His father ended the call.

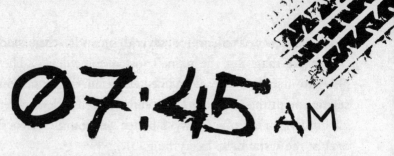

07:45 AM

The school bus slowed down several times along the route but didn't stop because there was no one waiting to be picked up. When they finally arrived at Palm Breeze Middle School the bus was only half full.

The first time Chase had enrolled himself in a new school he'd been nervous. By the third school it had got a lot easier. This time, with Nicole leading him into the office, it was no big deal at all.

She introduced him to the receptionist, Mrs O'Leary.

"Chase is staying with us," she said. "His dad is helping people get ready for the hurricane."

This was not exactly what Chase's father was doing, but he didn't correct her.

Mrs O'Leary peered at Chase above her reading glasses. "Your dad knows where the hurricane is going to hit?"

"Not really. He's just guessing like everyone else."

"What's his guess for Emily?"

"Forty or fifty miles south of here in Saint Petersburg – Saint Pete."

"I hope he's right. Though if the absentee rate is any indication, a lot of parents are guessing differently. Do you have your academic transcripts from your previous school?"

Chase pulled a folder out of his go bag. Attached to the folder was a note from his father with his mobile number in case they needed to get in touch with him. No school had ever called him.

"Take a seat, Chase. Our headteacher, Dr Krupp, will talk to you after she gets off the phone."

"I'll see you later," Nicole said with a smile, then joined friends out in the hallway.

After about ten minutes, Dr Krupp stepped out of her office and invited Chase in.

He sat down on the opposite side of her huge desk. As she skimmed his paperwork he looked around her office.

"Did Nicole's brother go to school here?" Chase asked.

Dr Krupp looked up from the folder. "Tony? Yes, he was an outstanding student and a wonderful athlete. Nicole is following in his footsteps, but the pool is her football field. Is Tony in town?"

"No. I was just looking at your diplomas and noticed that you went to the University of Georgia, where he plays."

Dr Krupp smiled for the first time. "Yes, Tony's a Bulldog. I like to think that I had something to do with that, but he made up his own mind. The Rossis are an independent bunch, but you probably already know that."

Normally, Chase would have let her hold on to her assumption that he knew the Rossis well, but he was getting tired of *tries*. That's what his mother had called a statement or even a silence that was not quite the truth and not exactly a lie. When Chase, or anyone in the family, pulled one on her, she'd say, "Nice *trie*, now try again."

"I just met the Rossis yesterday," Chase said.

"Really?" Dr Krupp said. "Mrs O'Leary led me to believe that you were old family friends."

"We are friends," Chase said. "But we're new friends."

"Are you in the animal or circus business?"

Chase shook his head. "We're in the storm business. My father's a contractor."

"For the government?"

"No, for himself."

"M.D. Emergency Services." Dr Krupp glanced at the file, then back at Chase. "Is he a doctor and a contractor?"

"No," Chase said. "Just a contractor."

"We usually have one or both parents bring their kids in when they enroll them," Dr Krupp said.

"My father's working in Saint Pete," Chase said. "My mom died a couple of years ago. It's just me and him now."

"I'm sorry about your mom, Chase."

"Thanks."

Dr Krupp's phone rang and she picked it up. While she talked, Chase looked at the photos of Dr Krupp's family. Three kids and a husband who looked like a movie star, which surprised him. Dr Krupp was OK-looking, but far from glamorous. And for some reason, her husband looked familiar, but Chase couldn't remember where he had seen the man before.

Dr Krupp hung up the phone. "Now, where were we?"

"You can call my dad if you want," Chase said. "He always answers his phone."

His dad carried a beat-up mobile phone on a lanyard around his neck so he could get to it without having to reach into his pocket. It looked geeky to Chase, and his mom had hated "the phone necklace", as she'd called it, but it was practical. His dad usually answered the phone on the first or second ring.

"That won't be necessary," Dr Krupp said. "I'm sure he's busy or he'd be here with you."

Not necessarily, Chase thought.

Dr Krupp handed him his class schedule and his locker combination. "This is a good school, Chase. You'll like it here."

08:20 AM

Dr Krupp had put Chase in all of Nicole's classes, except PE, starting with Mrs Sprague's homeroom.

For as much work as they were doing in homeroom, Chase thought they might as well have cancelled school. A third of the desks were empty. The television mounted to the ceiling was tuned to the Weather Channel.

At 8:45 a.m. Emily started to move.

While everyone stared up at the screen to watch the white whirl of destruction headed their way, Chase looked out of the window. This is what people did in the old days before satellite imagery and Doppler radar.

When they'd arrived at Palm Breeze Middle School an hour earlier, the sky had been clear, with no wind. Now it was flat grey. Dead palm fronds were tumbling across the soccer field out back. Chase began to get a strange feeling about Emily and wondered if this was what his dad experienced when he made his predictions, or what a lightning rod felt just before a strike. A tingling sensation. A spark of premonition...

"Last night Emily was upgraded to a Category Four hurricane with sustained winds of up to one hundred fifty-five miles per hour. There is a chance she'll become a Category Five, but what's even more disturbing is the speed at which she's travelling.

"Although hurricane winds can exceed one hundred miles an hour, the storm itself usually travels about fifteen miles an hour. This is one of the reasons hurricanes cause so much damage when they hit land. Instead of moving through quickly, they linger, giving the high winds time to cause severe damage.

"Emily is currently barrelling towards the west coast of Florida at thirty-five miles per hour. We have accurate tracking records going back decades, and this speed is simply unheard of.

"On her current track and speed she will be making landfall near the Tampa-Saint Pete area around eleven this evening..."

About forty miles south of Palm Breeze Middle School, just like Dad predicted. Chase continued to stare out of the window. He still had that tingling feeling, and it contradicted what he was hearing from the television and what he was seeing out of the window. Although the wind wasn't even close to hurricane strength, he had a weird feeling that Momma Rossi was closer to the mark than his dad or any of the experts.

Mrs Sprague switched the TV to a local station, and a familiar face appeared on the screen. It was the anchor they had watched during dinner the night before. Chase realized why the photos of Dr Krupp's husband looked familiar.

He turned to Nicole and whispered, "Is that—"

"Yeah, that's Dr Krupp's husband. All the teachers really like him. He comes to talk to us every year." She leaned closer. "I think he's a little strange. He wears more make-up than Dr Krupp even when he's talking to us."

Chase doubted that the morning news was Richard Krupp's regular beat. He was the prime-time anchor.

Chase and his father always got a big kick out of watching television reporters during disasters. They'd say they hoped the storm would pass them, but the truth was that they wanted to be right in the middle of it with their Gore-Tex gear, leaning into the wind, dodging debris, telling everyone how dangerous it was. If the reporters were unlucky and the storm hit elsewhere, they'd insert themselves into the story by jumping into their satellite vans and driving there, as if the town where the disaster struck actually needed more reporters.

Richard Krupp wasn't in his Gore-Tex yet, but Chase was certain he would be before long. His hair was a little dishevelled, and it looked as if he hadn't shaved since the night before. He was wearing jeans and hiking boots, the sleeves to his sky blue dress shirt rolled up to just below the elbow. Emily loomed behind him in high definition like a circular saw looking for something to cut in two.

Richard Krupp was unafraid. He stared into the camera, trying to look concerned, but his shining blue eyes gave him away. He was excited.

"...looks like we're in for a rough night, but the important thing to remember is not to panic. At this point, state police and local law enforcement are not calling for mandatory evacuation, but they are suggesting that if you have somewhere to stay outside of Emily's projected

track, you should proceed there after securing your property.

"The news team and I will of course be here for the duration..."

Of course. Chase looked at his new classmates. They were all glued to the screen, hanging on Richard Krupp's every word.

"Let's go to our meteorologist, Cindy Stewart, in downtown Saint Pete and see what the mood is there. Cindy?"

"As you can see, Richard, a few clouds have moved in and the wind has picked up slightly, but honestly, if we weren't looking at the satellite images behind you, we wouldn't know that a hurricane was headed this way..."

Richard Krupp looked irritated.

"But there is a hurricane coming, Cindy. A big one."

"There's no doubt about that, Richard, but due to Emily's erratic behaviour, we're still unclear about where she'll make landfall. Because of the speed she's travelling, even a slight deviation from the path she's on could put her hundreds of miles away from Saint Pete."

"But not away from Florida."

"That's right, Richard. She's going to hit Florida."

Richard gave her a triumphant look. Cindy rolled her eyes slightly, but continued to smile. Chase was beginning to really like her. He would love to see these two in the news station canteen. He suspected their relationship was a lot worse off camera.

"So, is there anyone downtown making preparations for the storm, Cindy?"

"Yes, there's a lot of activity down here. As you attempted to say earlier, it doesn't hurt to be cautious."

The camera zoomed out and Chase's jaw dropped open at what he saw on the television screen.

M.D. Emergency Services

The camera zoomed back a little more, revealing John Masters leaning against his 4x4.

Nicole turned to Chase and said loudly, "Isn't that your father's truck?"

"Yeah," Chase said. "And that's him leaning against it."

The whole class stared at him.

"Your dad's hot," a girl said.

"What's that hanging around his neck?" someone else asked.

If Chase could have climbed out of the window without anyone noticing, he would have.

"It's a phone," Chase answered.

"That's kind of geeky."

"He's still hot."

Chase had never thought of his dad as hot, but he had to admit that, except for the mobile phone around his neck, his dad did look pretty good. He was wearing faded jeans, scuffed work boots and a sleeveless T-shirt that showed off his tan and well-defined biceps and forearms. Strapped around his narrow waist was his favourite tool belt.

Mrs Sprague turned up the volume. "Settle down, everyone. Let's hear what Chase's father has to say."

Chase wasn't sure what to expect, but his father looked perfectly at ease in front of the camera, as if he'd been on TV every day of his life. He hadn't even been on the local news after the lightning strike. Dozens of shows had called asking him to appear, but he had turned them all down. Chase had thought at the time that his father was camera shy. He was obviously wrong.

"I'm standing next to John Masters, owner of M.D. Emergency Services. What are you doing down here, John?"

"Helping out ... making sure the damage will be minimal if Emily hits here."

"And what makes you think Emily is going to hit Saint Pete?"

"She may not, but she is headed this direction and this is where I happen to be."

"And why do you happen to be in Saint Pete?"

"I've never been here before. Always wanted to come. Bad timing, I guess."

Bad trie, *Dad*, Chase thought.

"Show us what you've been doing."

53

Chase's father walked Cindy through taping and boarding up windows, securing or removing anything that might get caught by the wind, moving valuables to the upper floors...

"In case of storm surge?"

"That's right, Cindy. Just like we saw in Hurricane Katrina. If your house or building is standing after the wind, flooding is the next problem. Water damage can be worse than wind damage ... much worse ... and with all the oil floating around the gulf from the BP spill, there could be a real mess here on shore."

The interview was interrupted by the voice of Mrs O'Leary over the intercom. She called about twenty students down to the office, saying their parents were waiting to pick them up. Four kids from Mrs Sprague's class. By the time they gathered their things and left, Richard Krupp was back on the screen, trying to look worried but brave.

12:15 PM

Chase called his father during lunch. He answered on the first ring.

"Twelve fifteen. How's it going?"

"You're right about the time, and I'm fine," Chase said. "I saw you on TV."

"At school?"

"Yeah. In a classroom."

"That must have been a surprise."

"It was." Chase wondered if his father would have even told him if Chase hadn't mentioned it first. "Cindy Stewart seems cool."

"She is."

"It doesn't sound like she thinks Emily is going to hit down there."

"She might be right. And if she is, we may have to move the Shack and Shop closer to Emily's track. Tomás and I will stay here tonight, but if Emily misses us we'll be heading up your way first thing in the morning to get you and pick up the rigs."

Great, Chase thought. *A new record. One day in school.*

"That might not be as easy as you think," Chase said.

"What do you mean?"

"The clouds have moved in and the wind's been picking

55

up all morning." Chase hesitated. "I think Emily is going to hit up here." This was followed by a long pause on his father's end of the line. It went on so long that Chase thought the call had been dropped. "Are you there?"

"Yep, I'm here. What other evidence do you have?"

"Nothing scientific, if that's what you mean." Chase didn't want to get into Momma Rossi's soothsaying. "It's just a feeling I have."

"Have they cancelled school?"

"No, but a lot of parents have picked their kids up. The headteacher is married to that Richard guy on TV."

His father laughed. "Cindy's not too fond of him. You should have heard what she had to say off camera about Saint Pete's Number One News Anchor."

"What about Emily?" Chase asked.

"I don't know. They're still predicting that it's going to hit down here, but at this point, your guess is as good as anyone else's. You want us to head up tonight?"

"I guess not," Chase said. "You're already set up down there. If you come up here and I'm wrong, you might not be able to get back in."

Roads were often closed during a disaster, which was why his father liked to be at ground zero beforehand.

"You know the drill. If you think someone's making a bonehead decision, don't go along with them. Remember that you've had more experience with storms than they have. Stick with what I've taught you. Do what you think is right. If the storm hits up there, save yourself. You're no good to anybody if you're dead ... including yourself."

Chase could not remember how many times his father had said these exact words to him.

"I will."

His father continued in a lighter tone. "I didn't get to ask you this morning, but what's the farm like?"

"It's a circus."

"Wild, huh?"

"Literally." It was obvious his father had no idea what Chase meant.

"That's great. Well, I better get back to work. Keep an eye on that weather. Call me this evening." He ended the call.

Nicole walked up. "Who were you talking to?"

"My father."

"What did he say about his television appearance?"

"Not much."

"He's probably used to it by now."

"As far as I know, that's the first time he's been on TV."

"Really? I would think he'd be on all the time, considering what he does for a living."

It's now or never, Chase thought. No more *tries*. Especially with Nicole. "How long before we have to be back to class?"

"About twenty minutes. Why?"

Chase started with his mother's and sister's deaths, then moved on to the lightning strike and M.D. Emergency Services, and ended with their arrival at the Rossi Brothers' winter quarters. He skipped a few things, like his father storing away all the evidence of their former life.

Nicole listened without saying a word until he finished.

"I've never met anyone struck by lightning."

"That's not surprising. Most people don't survive lightning strikes. Believe me, it's no fun to see someone struck by lightning."

"Especially your own father," Nicole said. "Does he have any other ... uh ... ill effects from the strike?"

"You mean besides selling everything we own, becoming a nomad, and charging desperate people a ton of cash to help them?"

Nicole grinned. "Yes, besides that."

"When he got out of the hospital, he got his ear pierced."

Nicole laughed. "That sounds more like a midlife crisis."

"Except for the fact that he had a jeweller melt down his gold wedding band and turn it into a lightning bolt earring."

"That's a little strange," Nicole admitted.

Ø3:33PM

Throughout the afternoon, parents arrived to pick up their kids. Several came with their SUVs packed, ready to head out of the storm area. The teachers seemed eager to leave too, especially the ones with children.

By the time the final bell rang, there were only a hundred students left in the building. More than half of them had parents waiting for them at the kerb, leaving only forty-two bus riders to put on nine buses.

Dr Krupp thought it was ridiculous to send out that many buses with so few students – an opinion all the bus drivers agreed with.

"The traffic's terrible."

"It's the worst jam I've ever seen."

"The highways are like car parks."

Dr Krupp drafted the two most experienced drivers to take the remaining forty-two students home in two buses.

While they were figuring out who to put on which bus, Chase stared up at the sky. He didn't like what he saw. The clouds were an angry swollen grey and looked like they were about to burst.

"What time does it usually get dark around here?" he asked Nicole.

"Seven thirty or eight," she answered. "Why?"

He looked at his watch. "It's three forty and look how dark it is."

"You're right. It looks like it's going to rain."

"It's going to do a lot worse than that." He looked back up at the sky and was tempted to call his father again.

Instead he said loudly, "What's the latest on Emily?"

He hadn't seen a weather report for a couple of hours, but he estimated that the wind was blowing at least fifteen miles an hour where they were standing, and gusting to twenty-five or thirty. The thick, bruised clouds above were moving fast.

No one answered him. He asked again. Louder.

This time everyone turned his way.

Dr Krupp looked annoyed. "I talked to my husband fifteen minutes ago. He said that Emily is going to hit south of here around midnight."

"How far south?"

"No one knows."

"What category?"

"Right now it's a Category Five. But they're predicting Emily will be downgraded back to a Category Four by the time she makes landfall."

"I heard it's gonna be a Category Three," one of the bus drivers added.

"That's still winds in excess of one hundred miles an hour," Chase said. "I don't think the buses are a good idea."

Dr Krupp put her hands on her hips. "Really? And how do you suggest we get you and the other students home?"

"I don't think we should go home. We should stay

right here. The school has a low profile. The buildings are constructed out of reinforced concrete. The safest thing for us to do is to ride out the storm in the cafetorium. It's right in the middle of the campus, no windows, protected on all four sides by other buildings."

"How long have you been in Florida, Chase?" Dr Krupp asked.

Here we go, Chase thought. He took a deep breath. "Two days."

"And how many hurricanes have you been in?"

"None, but I know enough to stay exactly where I am when I have everything I need to survive."

"You're getting on the bus, Chase. We are not spending the night at the school. We don't have authorization from the district, or your parents. Getting permission would take several hours." She looked at her watch. "You'll all be home in less than two hours."

Nicole stepped forward. Chase didn't want her to get involved. This was his argument.

"Let me talk to him, Dr Krupp."

"Make it quick. You're leaving in two minutes."

Dr Krupp walked back to the drivers. The kids stared at Chase like he had lost his mind. One of them made clucking noises like a chicken. Chase took a step towards the boy, but Nicole grabbed his arm and pulled him down a breezeway where no one could hear them.

"What do you think you're doing, Chase?"

"You're mad at *me*?" He couldn't believe it. He'd expected Nicole to be on his side, but she looked more upset than Dr Krupp.

"Dr Krupp is trying to get everyone home safely and you're—"

"Dr Krupp is trying to get us out of her hair so *she* can go home. She doesn't want to spend the night with forty-two kids in the cafetorium."

"That's right! She wants to spend the night with her own family just like I do. Just like everyone here does. Just because you don't have—" Nicole stopped herself.

"You think this is about me?" Chase asked.

"Who else would it be about?"

"It's about all of us. We are leaving a perfect place to ride out a hurricane. The two buses are going to take us to homes that are not nearly as safe as Palm Breeze Middle School. That is, if we even make it home. Everyone is talking about where the hurricane is going to make landfall." Chase pointed at the ground. "I've got news for you. It's going to be here. Right where we're standing. And it will be here a long time before midnight. Dr Krupp cannot make anyone get on a bus. If we stick together we can stay at the school, where we'll be safe."

"You can spend the night here if you want," Nicole said. "But I'm getting on the bus and going home. You are being paranoid!"

Chase watched her stamp back to the kerb and the waiting buses. He thought about the farmer in Oklahoma who left his combine in the middle of the hailstorm. He'd been going home too. He'd made it about a hundred metres before being stoned to death. He'd got hit in the head twice. The first stone knocked him out. The second killed him, according to the newspaper.

Dr Krupp started dividing the forty-two students into two groups. Chase thought about holding his ground and refusing to go, but it wouldn't accomplish anything. She would still put the other kids on the buses and send them on their way, including Nicole. Dr Krupp would stay behind with him and either call his father and tell him to pick Chase up, or call the police and have them deal with him.

Going against everything he knew, everything his father had taught him, he joined the others at the kerb, ignoring the smirks and clucking sounds. He wasn't about to let Nicole ride on the bus without him.

"Mrs O'Leary is calling your parents to tell them you might be a little late because of the alternate route, the traffic, and the weather so they don't worry."

Chase was the last to board his bus. As he stepped through the door, Dr Krupp put her hand on his shoulder.

"There's nothing to worry or be nervous about, Chase. Don't be afraid. You'll be at the Rossis' farm in no time at all."

"There is everything to be worried about, Dr Krupp." He pointed at the sky. "Emily is here. You'd better drive straight home and stay away from windows."

Chase realized that Dr Krupp was trying to be kind, but being kind didn't make someone right. He was not afraid to ride on a bus. But there wasn't time to explain to her what his father called The Gut Barometer, or TGB. "Everyone has one," his father had told him. "It works just like a real barometer: when the pressure drops, the weather is going to change. The TGB is in your solar plexus. You feel the pressure drop in your gut." Most of the time people ignored their gut gauge, and most of the time it was OK to ignore it, until the one time it wasn't OK.

Chase knew this was one of those times.

He got on the bus, and the driver pulled the door closed behind him. The kids had all paired off and were grinning at him as he made his way past them. Nicole had taken an aisle seat next to some guy and didn't even glance at him as he walked by.

"Cluck … cluck … cluck…" someone said from the front of the bus.

A few kids laughed.

Chase took the bench seat at the back of the bus. Right next to the emergency exit.

05:15 PM

"Does anyone have a phone signal?"

Three hours before nightfall, it was almost completely dark outside.

Chase sat in the back and watched the lights as sixteen mobile phones flicked on. They had been on the bus an hour and a half and had dropped off four people. He knew there wasn't a signal because he'd been checking his phone since they'd left the school. He wanted to talk to his father, and thought about breaking out the satellite phone, but it was only to be used in case of emergency. And in order for it to work, his father would have to have his satellite phone on, which was unlikely at this point in the storm.

"No signal."

"No bars."

"Dead as a doornail."

Gusts of wind crashed into the bus like ocean waves as they inched along in bumper-to-bumper traffic. The rain poured down so hard it was pointless to look out of the window. All they could see were headlights and glimpses of angry motorists.

The bus stopped again. The kid next to Nicole got up, along with four others, and they made their way to the front.

"OK!" the driver shouted. "Do you see your parents' cars out there?"

The kids peered through the steamed windows. They said they did.

"Are you sure? 'Cause I'm not letting you off this bus unless you do. I don't care how close your house is to this stop. You can't walk in this stuff. If your folks aren't there, I'll drive you to your doorstep."

They all swore their parents were waiting.

"OK. On the count of three I'll pull the door open and you all bail out quickly so I don't get too drenched. One ... two ... three..." The doors shuddered open and the kids jumped out into the wind and rain like paratroopers.

The driver got soaked anyway to everyone's amusement, except Chase's.

Chase noticed Nicole move over into the window seat vacated by the boy. Why? She wouldn't be able to see out, and it was more dangerous to sit near the window than the aisle. He knew he should make his way up to her and say something, but the only things he had to say would sound wimpy, so he stayed where he was, thinking about how dangerous school buses were. At his last school he'd done a report on them and got an A, but the teacher had said it would be best not to put it up on the notice board with the other reports because it might scare people.

School buses are not designed to operate in winds exceeding fifty miles an hour. Even on a calm day, school buses aren't safe. In every state, it's against the law to drive in a car without a seat belt. By law, children under a certain weight have to ride in the back, strapped into an appropriate car seat or booster. Parents wait with their kids at the bus stop so nothing bad happens to them, then they watch them climb into the yellow death trap and blow them kisses goodbye.

Florida is one of the few states that require seat belts in school buses, but only in newer school buses. The Palm Breeze bus was not new. The driver was the only one belted in.

Wimp, Chase thought. But he couldn't help himself. Over the past year he'd seen too many disasters and what happened when people didn't recognize them for what they were. The kids on the bus thought this was an adventure. But Chase knew it was just the beginning of what, for some of them, would be the worst night of their lives.

07:10PM

The wind got stronger and the rain fell harder. When there were just five of them left on the bus, Nicole finally joined Chase on the back bench.

"This is pretty scary. You might have been right about staying at school."

"We're almost at the farm, aren't we?"

Nicole started talking very quickly. "I can't tell. The driver's been following a crazy route to get around traffic. The girl sitting right behind the driver lives the closest to us. I think her name's Rashawn. She's a new girl. Someone told me her father's the caretaker of the wildlife refuge next to our farm. The caretaker's house is five miles further out. She's usually already on the bus when I get on in the morning. I guess her parents took her to school today. She's probably wishing they had picked her up too... I'm sorry I called you paranoid."

Chase smiled. Not at Nicole's nervousness but at something his father had said to his uncle Bob when Uncle Bob accused him of being paranoid.

"I wasn't insulted," Chase said. "Paranoia is just another word for heightened awareness."

"Funny," Nicole said, relaxing ... a little. "Why are you sitting way back here?"

Chase pointed at the emergency door. "Safer."

The bus stopped. Two more people jumped off, leaving Chase, Nicole, and the girl sitting up front.

"Tell me about the refuge," Chase said, as the bus lurched forward. He didn't really care about the refuge, but he felt that if he could keep her talking, it might calm her down.

"It borders one end of our farm. We actually used to own a good piece of the refuge land, but my grandfather donated it to the state."

"How big is it?"

"It's huge, and getting bigger. The state bought a large parcel of land down the road from us with a levee on it. Eventually they'll buy our place, which will connect the levee property to the refuge."

"Your dad's going to sell the farm?"

"Not any time soon, but yeah, he'll sell it. If the circus goes under, we won't need the land."

"What's on the refuge?"

"I haven't really spent any time there. If I'm not swimming, I'm taking care of the animals. There isn't much time for exploring. I suppose the refuge has birds, gators, deer, snakes ... Florida things."

Chase scooted over to the window. All he could see was pitch-black through sheets of rain, no car lights, no streetlights, no house lights. He scooted back to Nicole.

"Maybe we should invite Rashawn to come back here with us. She's probably just as scared as we are."

"You're scared?"

"Yeah, aren't you?"

"I'll get her."

Chase pulled the handheld GPS out of his go bag and fired it up.

Nicole returned with Rashawn. She was big, almost as tall as he was. She was sopping wet from sitting close to the door, and she was shivering. He hoped she was shivering because she was cold, not frightened. None of them was dressed for a hurricane. Rashawn sat down on the bench across the aisle from them. Chase took a Mylar first aid blanket out of his bag and handed it to her.

"Why're you sitting all the way back here?" Rashawn asked through chattering teeth.

"Chase thinks it's safe—"

"Warmer," Chase interrupted. No use scaring Rashawn any more than she was. "And drier."

"You're the boy who was afraid to get on the bus."

"Yeah."

Rashawn shook the blanket out and put it around her broad shoulders. "What kind of kid carries a blanket in his backpack?"

"A Boy Scout," Nicole answered.

"Former Boy Scout," Chase clarified.

"That bus driver's lost," Rashawn said.

"What makes you think that?" Chase asked.

"Been sitting behind him since we left school. He talks to himself. He also curses ... a lot. Everything was fine until he dumped off those last two kids. He took what he thought was a short cut."

"Do you know where we are?"

Rashawn shook her head, splashing water from her wet hair on both of them. "I've only been here a month. I couldn't find my way home from school on a bet. Guess I should have been paying better attention."

Chase slid over to the window to get a better angle on the satellites for his GPS. Once the satellite located them he could he could punch in where they needed to go and tell the driver.

"Maybe we can help him."

07:20 PM

Their location popped up on the little screen, but it meant nothing to Chase. As he turned to ask Nicole for her address, a gust of wind lifted the bus completely off its tyres. Just as suddenly, the bus slammed back on the road and started to tip.

"On the floor!" Chase shouted above Rashawn's and Nicole's screams. He reached out and grabbed an arm – he couldn't tell who it belonged to – and pulled one of the girls to the floor. "Brace yourselves!" He wrapped his legs and arms around the steel seat rods, hoping Nicole and Rashawn had done the same. If they were lucky, the bus would simply land on its side.

They weren't lucky.

The bus rolled three times, maybe four… It was impossible to tell in the dark with the deafening sound of screeching metal, shattering windows and terrified screams – including Chase's own.

The bus came to a stop, but only long enough for Chase to reach out and grab his GPS. He glanced at the screen and saw a single black line surrounded by blue.

The bus started to slide. Front end first.

"We're going into the water!" he shouted, hoping someone was alive to hear him. "Stay on this end of the bus! We'll use the emergency exit!"

No one responded. They were either too frightened to speak, unconscious, dead, or had tumbled to the front of the bus.

The bus hit the water like a torpedo, pushing Chase's face into the seat frame. He felt a front tooth snap, followed by the coppery taste of blood. Frantically he felt around for his go bag. He'd need the first aid kit and everything else in the bag if they survived the crash.

He grabbed a handful of hair.

"Ouch!"

Chase spat out a mouthful of blood. "Nicole?"

"Yeah."

"Anything broken?"

"I don't think so. You?"

"Front tooth. Where's Rashawn?"

"I'm next to Nicole," Rashawn said.

"My go bag," Chase said.

"I have it," Nicole said. "We're sinking."

"Give me the bag."

Chase pulled a headlamp out of the side pocket, turned it on and slipped it over his forehead. Nicole looked pale in the bright light.

"You and Rashawn go through the emergency door and get to shore. It can't be too far."

He pulled a second headlamp out and handed it to her.

"What are you going to do?" Nicole asked, putting the headlamp on.

"I'm going to check on the driver."

They looked down the length the bus. Water was gushing through the cracked windscreen.

73

"I'm a better swimmer," Nicole said.

"I'm sure you are," Chase said. "But I'm stronger."

"I'll go with you."

"No, get Rashawn to shore. I'll be right behind you. Go!"

The water was rising fast. The bus would be completely submerged within minutes. He made his way down the steep, slippery aisle, wondering how he was going to get the driver back up the aisle if the guy was unconscious.

The driver *was* unconscious, slumped over the steering wheel. Chase pulled him up. There was a deep, ugly gash on the man's forehead oozing blood.

Chase shouted at him, then tried to shake him awake.

No response.

After the lightning strike, he and his father had taken first aid classes three nights a week for months. By the time they'd finished they could have become paramedics.

He felt the man's neck for a pulse. He didn't feel one, but that didn't mean the driver was dead. Chase's hands were numb with cold. He felt his jagged tooth with his tongue and glanced up the aisle to the rear of the bus. Nicole had the emergency door open and was helping Rashawn through.

The water was up to the driver's chest now and rising fast. Chase shouted and gave him another shake. The driver let out a weak moan just as the front end of the bus plunged completely underwater.

Chase was washed backwards in a rush of water. He managed to get a gulp of air just before he was slammed into one of the seats as the bus slipped sideways, then rolled. As the bus slid further he pulled his way up to the driver again and grabbed the man's arm. He tried to yank the driver free of the seat, but he wouldn't budge.

Seat belt!

Chase wasted several precious seconds trying to find the release. If he didn't get the driver to the surface on his first try, the driver would drown. If he didn't get to the surface himself in about thirty seconds, *he* would drown. Chase shrugged the pack off his back and unzipped one of the pockets. The bus settled to the bottom with a dull *thump*.

Chase tried to keep the panic down. He couldn't afford to make a mistake. He pulled his knife out of the pocket and sliced the seat belt in two places. The driver rose from the seat like a balloon and came to a stop against the door, blocking the exit.

Chase knew he wouldn't make it to the emergency exit in the back of the bus with the driver in tow. That left the windscreen. It was cracked in several places. He braced his back against a pole and was about to try to kick the windscreen out, when something dark and very big swam past outside. Chase couldn't tell what it was, but it frightened him so badly that he nearly sucked in a lungful of water.

Get ahold of yourself! Oxygen deprivation is making you see things.

The windscreen popped loose on the third kick. On the fourth it came out of the frame and dropped into the dark water. With his lungs screaming for air, Chase grabbed the driver by his shirt collar and pulled him through the opening.

Nicole was waiting for him.

As soon as she'd seen the bus sink, she'd dived back into the water, leaving Rashawn to make it to shore on her own. She'd got to the bus just as Chase was pulling the driver through the windscreen. She grabbed Chase's free arm, wrapped it around her neck and kicked towards the surface.

The second they broke the surface, Chase took a deep breath of air and started choking. Nicole helped him pull the driver's head above water.

"Can you swim on your own?" Nicole shouted.

Chase could barely hear her above the howling wind. He nodded.

Nicole wrapped her arm around the driver.

"Follow me. The shore's close."

They dragged the driver up on the bank where Rashawn was sitting huddled under the first aid blanket.

"We might need that blanket," Chase said.

Rashawn took the blanket off and gave it to Nicole. "Is he alive?"

"Not at the moment," Chase said, pushing the driver on to his stomach.

"What does that mean?"

Chase glimpsed his watch as he began pushing on the driver's back.

It was 7:32.

07:56 PM

"Are you sure he's dead?" Rashawn asked.

Chase nodded.

No pulse. Dilated pupils. Instead of water, blood had come out of his mouth when Chase tried to resuscitate him, which meant he was probably dead before Chase cut the seat belt.

"I've never seen a dead person," Rashawn said.

Chase had seen more dead people than he cared to remember and wished he could have done more for the driver. But there were other priorities now. He didn't have time to think about what he might have been able to do, not now ... except for one small detail, which he hated to bring up in front of Rashawn because she was already pretty freaked out.

"Are there alligators here?" he asked.

"That depends where here is," Nicole said.

"We're on the levee you were telling me about. Part of the refuge."

"Then there's gators," Rashawn said. "Thousands of them, according to my daddy, although I haven't been down on this part of the refuge."

Chase looked at Nicole. "Did you see one underwater?"

"No. Did you?"

"I think so. Just before I kicked the windscreen out. I

almost died right there. Thanks for coming back for me. I don't think I would have made it to the top on my own."

"Gators aren't nearly as aggressive as people think," Rashawn said.

"She's right," Nicole agreed. "You shouldn't mess with them, but they aren't usually a threat."

"Unless you stumble across a nest of gator eggs," Rashawn added. "Then you might have a big problem from the momma."

"I only saw it for a second, but something told me it was aggressive ... very aggressive."

"Daddy's been dealing with gators for ever," Rashawn said. "I suspect the gators are all riding out the storm on the bottom. The bus probably jarred one loose and it was popping up to get some air."

Chase was happy to hear Rashawn's little gator lecture. It meant she wasn't nearly as frightened as he'd thought she was. If they wanted to survive the storm, they could not panic. They had to keep their senses about them.

"It scared me," Chase said.

"Heightened awareness?" Nicole asked.

They would also have to keep their sense of humour.

"No," Chase said. "This time it was real paranoia. So, neither of you has been on this road?"

The road was about six metres above them, up a steep bank. The girls shook their heads.

"We have to find some shelter to ride out the storm," Chase said.

"It's not too bad right here," Rashawn said. "We're protected from the worst of the wind on this side of the levee."

"For now," Chase said. "But Emily's just getting started. The water's rising. It's gone up a foot since we've been sitting here."

He pulled the GPS out and turned it on. It was supposed to be waterproof, but the way their luck was going... The screen lit up and immediately picked up a satellite. Chase breathed a sigh of relief.

"What about your satellite phone?" Nicole asked.

His dad would certainly have his sat phone on now. "It's—" Chase felt his shoulder for the familiar strap. The go bag wasn't there. "I left it on the bus," he said. "The phone wasn't waterproof anyway and the bag was drenched. I guess I should dive back down and look for it. We could use some of the other stuff, like the first aid kit."

"I don't think that's a good idea," Rashawn said. "Gators aren't usually aggressive, but who knows what they're like in a hurricane."

Chase was beginning to really like Rashawn.

"You probably wouldn't find it anyway," Nicole said. "We have the headlamps and the GPS. The first aid kit would be nice, but..." She looked at his face. "Your lip is swollen and split. Are you OK?"

"I'm fine."

"Did you say something before we went down about your front tooth?"

"Yeah, but there's nothing in the first aid kit that's going to fix a tooth. I could use a painkiller, but that's the least of our worries."

He handed Nicole the GPS.

"This is the zoom button. Zoom out and find the nearest house. I'm going to check out the road."

Chase climbed up the bank, trying not to berate himself for failing to save the driver and forgetting the go bag. If he had the sat phone, and it worked, he'd be calling 9-1-1 right now and telling them where they were. Ninety per cent of their problem would be over ... maybe seventy-five per cent. It would take a rescue team a while to get to them.

The wind was fiercer up on the road. He had to spread his legs as far as they would go and hunch over to keep from being blown back down the bank. He recalculated their chances of getting rescued even if they had the sat phone.

Ten per cent, he thought.

He lumbered back to where the bus had gone into the water and discovered the wind had not blown it off the road. A large section of road was gone and water was rushing through the gap from the lake on the other side. It could have been the weight of the bus that caused the collapse, but he didn't think so. He walked forward a hundred metres and found another section of collapsed road.

Not good. *We need to get down this road while there's still a road to get down.*

He hurried to the spot he'd climbed up, and slid back down the bank.

Nicole and Rashawn were smiling.

"Did you find out where we are?"

"Right in the middle of the levee road," Nicole said. "A little less than five miles from the farm gate and ten miles from Rashawn's." She looked down at the driver, her smile fading. "He almost got us home."

"Are there any houses closer?" Chase asked.

Nicole shook her head. "Mine's the closest."

"Five miles isn't too bad," Chase said, not mentioning that walking five miles in a hurricane was probably like walking fifty miles.

"I bet my daddy's driving around, looking for me right now," Rashawn said.

"He's not driving this way," Chase said. "The road's collapsing. The only way to the farm is on foot. The good news is that there aren't any trees on the lake to fall on us, and there isn't much debris flying around. I had a couple of rain ponchos in the go bag, but—"

Nicole held up his go bag.

"Where—"

The girls' grins reappeared.

"I told her not to go," Rashawn said. "But she was in the water like a cormorant before I could stop her."

"What's a cormorant?"

"You don't know much about animals, do you?" Rashawn said. "It's a bird."

"It only took one dive," Nicole said. "It was right by the driver's seat."

"What about the gator?"

"Didn't see it. You must have scared it off."

Chase took the sat phone out and turned it on. Not surprisingly, it didn't work. Next he took out some energy bars and handed them out.

"I'm not hungry," Rashawn said. "We can eat when we get to Nicole's."

"Stick them in your pocket anyway," Chase said. "It will

be a long time before we get to the farm." *If we get to the farm,* he thought. "They actually taste terrible, but they'll keep you going. We're going to burn a lot of energy in the next several hours."

Next he took out a bottle of water for each of them.

"I don't think water's going to be a problem," Nicole said, pointing to the sky.

"The water's falling on the outside of your body, not inside. We need to keep ourselves hydrated."

He took out a waterproof plastic bag with paper towels in it, wiped the sat phone down as best as he could, then put it in the plastic bag.

Finally he pulled out the two rain ponchos and handed one to each of the girls.

"What are you going to wear?" Rashawn asked. "Not that these are going to do us much good now. I'm soaked through."

"I'll use your blanket," Chase said. "It won't be as stylish as your ponchos, but it will work fine after I cut a hole for my head to fit through. I know you're wet, but the ponchos will help keep the wind out and your body heat in."

"You must be some kind of super Boy Scout," Rashawn said. "I've never seen a bag of tricks like that."

"It's a long story," Chase said.

"What about him?" Nicole asked, pointing to the driver.

Chase was sorry the man had died, very sorry, but he wanted to leave the driver exactly where he was. It would take a lot of energy they would need later to move him. "We can't take him with us," he said.

"We can't leave him here," Rashawn said. "Tomorrow

morning after this storm passes, some ol' gator's going to come along and make a meal out of him."

"She's right," Nicole said.

"We'll drag him up to the road. High ground. That's the best we can do." Chase didn't want to see him get eaten by a gator either, but the result would probably be the same whether they moved him or not. He didn't think the levee road was going to be there tomorrow morning.

He took everything he thought he needed out of the pack, along with the satellite phone, and stuffed it all into his pockets, glad he had chosen to wear combat trousers that morning. He took a couple of pain pills and washed them down with water, which sent fire through his broken tooth. He cut a hole in the blanket for his head. Then he hung the GPS around his neck by its lanyard.

"Did you learn that from your dad?" Nicole asked.

"Funny," Chase said.

10:32PM

Chase began to think they were walking backwards instead of forward, or else that the GPS was wrong. How could it take over two hours to walk less than half a mile?

At this rate we won't get to the farm until sunrise, if at all!

The wind and rain were dissolving the road as if it were a sand castle. Twice they'd had to wade around a gap in waist-deep water. The last time, all three of them had nearly been swept out into the lake by the current rushing through the opening.

The ponchos, and the blanket he was wearing, were little help in this weather. Wet suits would have been better.

I'll have to suggest that to Dad, if I ever see him again, he thought. *And we need more batteries in the go bag too.*

He stopped to let everyone catch their breath and change the batteries in the headlamps, which were getting too dim to see.

"This is the last of the batteries. We're dead without light. We'll have to use one headlamp at a time. Whoever's wearing it will have to take the lead and call out problems to the two in back."

Whoever meant Chase or Nicole. Rashawn was doing a lot better than he expected, but every thirty minutes, like clockwork, she froze and burst into tears. The fits didn't last long, and she was perfectly fine when they were over, but he couldn't risk having her lead them up the dark road.

Nicole took the first lead, and it went smoothly for the first ten minutes, discounting the wind, the stinging rain, and Chase's throbbing front tooth, which the pain pills had done nothing to help.

Chase was a step behind Rashawn, holding on to her arm. Rashawn was a step behind Nicole, holding on to her arm. They'd tried hooking arms and walking three abreast, but when the crosswind gusted, it blew them into one another and their legs got tangled. The chain formation seemed to be working. When the wind picked one of them up off the road, which happened every few minutes, they would drop to their knees and huddle until it was safe to move again.

Huddle ... hold ... walk... Huddle ... hold ... walk...

"Stop!" Nicole shouted.

They huddled. Chase switched on his headlamp, expecting to see another breach in the road. But the road looked fine except for the large log up ahead. "We'll have to be careful," he said. "But we can get across that log."

Rashawn and Nicole laughed.

"What's so funny?"

"That ain't no log," Rashawn said. "That's a gator."

Chase stared ahead in horror. "That's not a gator, it's a *Tyrannosaurus rex*!"

"I thought you said the gators were riding out the storm underwater," Nicole said.

"Not this one. I bet he's thirteen feet if he's an inch. Probably fifty or sixty years old. My daddy would flip if he was here."

Chase wished her daddy was there to tell them what to do. The only way they could move forward was to scare it off the road or step over it.

"I'm surprised he hasn't moved, with the headlamp on him," Nicole said. "We must look like aliens to him."

"More like poachers," Rashawn said. "Which makes it even stranger he didn't bolt into the water as soon as he saw your light. They hunt them at night with spotlights. At his age and size I bet he has a bullet hole or two in him from poachers."

Chase looked at Nicole. "Any ideas?"

"I guess we move closer and see what the gator does."

11:02PM

"...as you can see, Richard ... Emily has bypassed Saint Pete. All we have here is a bit of rain and some wind as the outer edge is skirting past us, heading north. It made landfall at 7:00 p.m. in Palm Breeze."

"Where I live," Richard said.

"I hope your family is safe, Richard."

"I hope so too. The last time I spoke to them, which was just after my wife got home from school – she's a headteacher, you know – everything was fine. An hour later I called back and the mobile and landlines were completely dead.

"I guess what I don't understand – and I'm sure our viewers are wondering the same thing – is how could the forecasters be so wrong? Emily's landed fifty miles north of here. But what's even more surprising is that she made landfall four hours early, stranding tens of thousands of people trying to get home or leave the area."

"Those are some pretty big questions, Richard. I hardly to know where to begin...

"Everything we know about hurricanes is based on previous data. Emily is an anomaly. This afternoon she was moving faster than any other hurricane on record. No one could have predicted that she would actually pick up speed as the afternoon progressed. Because of

her speed and her direction changes, forecasters were simply unable to predict where she would make landfall.

"As to the tens of thousands of stranded people, I don't think it's that many, but there are certainly people who have gotten caught by this storm. As you mentioned, Richard, we have a complete communications blackout with the exception of satellite phones. Here's what we think is going on, and please remember that none of this information can be verified until communications have been restored.

"All roads in and out of Palm Breeze have been closed due to flooding, wind damage or car accidents. Because of the severe weather, all nonessential emergency personnel have been sent home until such time that the weather allows them to return.

"There have been seventeen reported fatalities, and I want to emphasize that these are reported, not verified. Five people have died in automobile accidents, two people had heart attacks, and three people have drowned. The rest were reported killed by flying debris and in building collapses.

"Law enforcement and emergency workers have set up dozens of temporary shelters in schools and other government buildings. Those stranded in their cars have been moved into the shelters to wait out the storm.

"There is no doubt that the area has received a great deal of damage and there will be more to come. I don't want to speculate any further."

"Do we have news crews headed up there?"

"No, Richard. As I said, no one is being allowed in

*or out, including local and national news media. We've
tried, but we were turned back. Officials will reevaluate
the situation in the morning and let us know when we'll
be allowed in."*

*"As a resident with a family there, they would certainly
allow me through."*

*"They are turning all residents away, Richard. The
problem is the roads. They aren't passable. And with
Emily in full swing, it's simply too dangerous."*

*"Thank you, Cindy. Right now we need to take a short
commercial break. We'll be back with more about the
storm of the century."*

As soon as the camera stopped, Cindy shook her head in
disgust and handed the mic to her young cameraman, Mark.

"Richard's a piece of work," Mark said.

"You got that right."

Cindy walked over to a 4x4 truck. John Masters was
sitting in the cab with the door open, looking at a map on
his laptop.

"Any luck?"

"Reaching Chase on the sat phone? No."

"Maybe his battery's dead."

"Chase makes sure all of our phones are charged. The
sat phone is either broken or he's in trouble. He'd have the
phone on by now if it worked. The school secretary called
and said he'd been put on a bus. Hard to break a phone on
a bus."

"Maybe they stopped the bus and moved him into a
shelter."

"He'd still be able to call from the sat phone if it worked."

"From what you've told me, he knows how to take care of himself."

"He does. But I've got to make sure he's OK." John pointed to the map on the computer screen.

"You're going up there."

John nodded. He had been with Cindy on and off throughout the day. They'd had lunch and dinner together. They'd also been together when Chase called from school that afternoon.

"I have pretty good sources," Cindy said. "There is no way in or out of Palm Breeze, and it's going to stay that way until at least tomorrow, maybe longer."

"There is always a way in," John said.

"Devil's advocate," Cindy said. "Let's say you manage to get past all the roadblocks. Chase may not be at the farm."

"Wherever he is, we'll be closer," John said. "And I'll be where the damage is. There's not much to fix around here."

"What do you mean by *we'll*?"

"Tomás and I. We'll take different routes and keep in touch on the sat phones and CB. We'll get in. We've done it before." He looked at Cindy for a moment, considering…

"What?" Cindy asked.

"Do you want to come with us?"

Cindy smiled and looked at her watch. "I'm off the clock until tomorrow morning. What are the chances of getting me back in time for work?"

"I would say the chances are absolutely zero."

"Fine, then I'm taking my work with me."

She looked over at Mark, who was packing his camera up. Cindy called him over.

"What's happening?"

"Do you want to head up north to the hurricane of the century with two complete strangers, without pay, without telling the station ... oh, and you'll probably get fired if the hurricane doesn't kill you first?"

"Sounds good," Mark answered. "Let me get my camera."

11:09PM

Chase, Nicole and Rashawn were standing – crouching, actually, so they wouldn't get blown off the road – about ten metres from the largest gator any of them had ever seen.

It looked a lot bigger than four metres to Chase, and it hadn't moved an inch during their noisy approach. They had yelled, jumped up and down, and even thrown rocks at it. Chase was certain he'd hit the gator at least twice.

"You're the lion tamer," Chase said to Nicole. "What do we do?"

"I'm not a lion tamer," Nicole said. "And even if I was, there's a big difference between a lion and a gator."

"Yeah," Chase said. "About eight feet of difference." He looked at Rashawn. "What do you think?"

"I've seen a lot of gators, but I've never seen one act like this. Maybe he's dead. I'll tell you one thing: it wasn't easy for him to get up that slippery bank. Gators don't move so good uphill. Especially ones this size."

"Fate," Chase said.

"What?" Nicole and Rashawn said at the same time.

"Fate," Chase repeated. "I mean, what are the chances of a thirteen-foot gator hauling out on to this levee during a hurricane and dying lengthwise across the road at the very moment we need to walk past?"

"So, you're saying you don't think it's dead," Nicole said.

"I'm saying it doesn't make any difference. Dead or alive, we have to get by this prehistoric speed bump or we're going to die on this road. One way or the other we're dead."

He took the GPS from around his neck and slipped it over Nicole's head. Before they could say anything he half walked, half crawled towards the behemoth, angling towards its tail, thinking it would be easier to step over the tail than the body or snout. And the tail couldn't bite him.

But gator tails do move, Chase discovered, like armoured whips. Just as he was stepping over, the tail came to life, flicking his feet out from under him. The gator's head whipped around and its jaws snapped closed loudly enough to be heard above the howling wind.

Chase dived head first over the bank and rolled, stopping just before he hit the water. He heard the gator following him over and began scrambling as fast as he could on his hands and knees along the water. He heard a splash behind him and immediately started crawling up the bank, hoping Rashawn was right about how difficult it was for a large gator to get up a slippery hill.

When he reached the road, he lay on his back, gasping. Nicole's and Rashawn's worried faces appeared above him. They pulled him to his feet and half dragged him fifteen metres down the road before they had to stop to catch their breath.

"That might have been the stupidest thing I've ever seen a human do with a wild animal," Nicole said.

"It worked," Chase said, but he knew she was right. He'd have to rank it right up there with leaving the tools in the back yard so his father could get struck by lightning.

"We thought the gator ate you!" Nicole said.

"He wouldn't have eaten him," Rashawn said matter-of-factly. "At least not right away. He would have killed him and buried his body underwater in the mud, then waited for it to rot so he could tear off the soft flesh and gulp it down."

"Well, that's a relief," Nicole said.

She and Chase started laughing.

Rashawn smiled. "I'm not so sure what you two find so funny about alligator eating habits. Lying across the road playing possum is how that gator hunts." She pointed to the spot where the gator had been parked. "There's only one way across this water without swimming. When a deer, or some other kind of animal, comes along down the road, he just waits and snaps it up when it gets close enough. I bet that's how he got so big and old."

"And fast," Chase added. "I've never seen anything move like that."

"Speaking of which," Nicole interrupted, "we need to get moving."

Chase retrieved his GPS from Nicole's neck and turned it back on.

"A little over a mile and we're off the levee. Two miles after that, we're at your front gate."

Ø1:15 AM

Every hundred metres the levee was breached.

They made it across the first four gaps by climbing down in the gap and forming a human chain, linking hands so they weren't swept out into the lake by the water gushing through.

The fifth breach was three times wider than the others, and only eight metres beyond the last one.

"We're on an island," Nicole said.

"A very tiny island," Rashawn confirmed.

Chase glanced back at the previous breach just in time to see a large piece of asphalt slough off. "And it just got smaller. The chain idea is not going to work here. It's too wide. We have to figure out an alternative."

If he ever saw his father again, he was going to suggest several new items for the go bag. Right now a length of rope would be pretty handy.

"I think I can jump it," Rashawn said.

Chase and Nicole stared at her. She was big and strong, but she didn't look like she could jump a five-metre gap and land on a jagged piece of asphalt.

"What are you looking at?" Rashawn said. "You're not the only athlete here. I'm a good long jumper. The best at my old school. I got a case of medals and trophies to prove it."

"If you made it across," Nicole said, "how would that help *us*?"

"I'll scramble down, anchor myself on the other side, and hold out my free arm. I got a very long reach. We'll build a chain from the other side. Chase can grab my hand, you grab his, and I'll pull you both across."

"A running start is going to be nearly impossible with this crosswind," Chase pointed out.

"We have to do something," Rashawn said. "What have we got to lose?"

"You," Nicole said.

Chase glanced back again at the breach behind them. "Rashawn's right. If we don't do something right now, we'll end up in the lake."

Rashawn pulled her poncho off and handed it to Chase. "Stuff that into one of your Boy Scout pockets. It'll just get in my way. I'll need to have you stand on both sides of the road, shining both headlamps on my landing spot on the other side. I'll jump right between you."

Chase switched his headlamp on and took the right side. Nicole took the left, about five metres away.

Rashawn walked back to the previous breach, checking for anything on the road that might trip her. She took a couple of deep breaths, stared at her landing spot on the other side, then took off.

Chase was right about the crosswind. He noticed Rashawn angling to his side, and he hoped it would be enough to compensate for the drift when she was in the air. He and Nicole stared in horror as Rashawn sailed off the edge, then stalled midway across as if she'd smashed into an invisible wall. She seemed to hover for a moment, her arms and legs flailing away as if she were trying to fly. Then she dropped like a stone into the black rushing water.

01:19 AM

"So, John Masters," Cindy said. "What do you really do for a living?"

"I'm just a working guy, travelling around helping people."

"I didn't ask what you did. I asked how you make a living."

"What's the difference?"

"Money, for one thing. It must cost a lot to travel around helping people. How do you pay for it?"

"Are you a meteorologist or a reporter?"

"Right now I'm a weather woman. In my previous life, which was about a year ago, I was an investigative journalist. A good one . . . too good, as it turned out. I was investigating a case of political corruption in San Francisco. Turns out that the man who owned the television station I worked for was up to his eyeballs in the scandal. And so was our lead news anchor, who also happened to be my now ex-husband, who happened to know a lot more about me than I wanted the public to know. Long story short. They won. I lost. And I got a job as far away as I could, hoping to get promoted to investigative journalist again."

"Is that why you don't like news anchors?"

"You mean Richard Krupp? I don't like Richard because

he's an arrogant jerk. But he is the top-rated anchor in Saint Pete. The viewers adore him. And he hates me."

John laughed. "I can see why. I saw you throw him under the bus several times, and that's just when I was watching."

"Bad move on my part. By contract, Richard has final say on all on-camera promotions. I'm pretty certain I'll be looking for another job as soon as Emily blows herself out."

"Even though you were right about where Emily would make landfall," John said.

"I didn't know where she would land. I just reported that we didn't know. I'm kind of old-fashioned in that regard. Reporters should report what they know, not what they think or want to have happen. Just once in my life I'd like to see a reporter, or a talking head with a half-hour time slot to fill, say, 'Sorry, folks, we don't have any news worth reporting tonight. Instead we're going to run an episode of *SpongeBob SquarePants*. Check back with us tomorrow and we'll let you know if anything has changed.'"

John laughed. "That's never going to happen."

"You're right, and it's a shame."

"Why'd you hitch a ride with me?"

"If I recall – and I am a trained reporter – you asked if I wanted to go with *you*."

"I stand corrected," John said.

Cindy nodded. "I'll tell you why I accepted your offer. If you can get us through, I'll be able to get footage. That might save my job. It would also show up Richard Krupp. Like all good journalists, I'm very competitive. You can bet that Richard is in a news van right now with a producer, a cameraman, a sound person and his make-up artist."

"I'm not here to get footage," John said. "I'm here to find Chase. Something's happened. I think he's in trouble."

"I understand. We won't get in your way, and I'll help any way I can, but I want to be honest. A father trying to save his son in a hurricane is a good story." John looked through the windscreen at the rain. "Can we get back to the original subject?" Cindy asked.

"What's that?"

"You."

John pointed at the flashing red and blue lights beyond the windscreen. "Let's wait and see if we can talk our way through this roadblock first. If you get past the first roadblock, the others are usually a breeze. And don't pull the TV card on them. They don't want you here. That's the best way to get turned around."

"Where's Tomás?"

"He's taking a road less travelled."

Cindy smiled, then recited:

> "'I shall be telling this with a sigh
> Somewhere ages and ages hence:
> Two roads diverged in a wood, and I –
> I took the one less travelled by,
> And that has made all the difference.'"

"'The Road Not Taken' by Robert Frost," John said. "Tomás is a genius at finding back roads into towns. And perhaps more important, roads out of towns if we need to leave quickly because of a storm. But his routes are less direct and more dangerous."

"So, are you a man who takes the road less travelled?" Cindy asked.

"I'm just a working guy who travels roads."

"I don't believe you, John."

John looked through the wet windscreen at the flashing police lights, then glanced back into the crew cab, where Mark was sound asleep.

"Cover that camera with a coat or something," he said. "If they see it, we're not going anywhere."

01:20 AM

Nicole didn't hesitate. She dived over the edge immediately.

Chase dived in a split second later.

He was surprised by the power of the current. As he tumbled through the breach a large chunk of asphalt from the other side broke off and hit him in the right shoulder, pushing him under for a second or two. He surfaced, sputtering, shoulder aching, his arm going numb. He realized that even if Rashawn had made it across, the asphalt would have broken loose and she would have still ended up in the water.

He let the current carry him into deeper water where it was calmer. He was a good swimmer, but he had no doubt that Nicole was better. He looked around for her light and finally saw it fifty metres further out, bobbing in the windblown whitecaps. That's when he remembered the gators. Thousands of them, Rashawn had said. But he was worried about one in particular. Where was that big boy now?

He swam forward, calling for Rashawn. It was difficult going, with his sore shoulder and the stuff in his pockets weighing him down. He thought about dumping some of it but resisted the urge. Before the night was over they might need everything he was carrying.

He drew close enough to Nicole to hear her shouting for Rashawn.

He had no idea how good a swimmer Rashawn was. After all they'd been through, he did not want to lose her.

"Rashawn!" he shouted. "Rashawn!"

He reached Nicole. They were both exhausted and out of breath.

"No sign of her?"

"None. Rashawn!"

"What do you want to do?" Chase asked.

Nicole didn't answer him. "Rashawn! Swim towards the light. Shout! We'll swim to you!"

They listened. All they heard was the wind. All they saw was a lake that looked like a stormy sea.

"How far are we from the levee?" Nicole asked.

"Further than we should be."

Nicole looked at her watch. "Ten minutes! You swim that way, I'll swim this way."

Chase shook his head. "I'll swim for five minutes, then I'm going to swim towards shore. This will give me time to get in front of the breach. That way you'll know where to swim to. We don't want to go through this a second time. When you come in, swim towards my light. If you find her or you need help, hit the button on the headlamp twice. That will send it into emergency blinking mode with alternating white and red lights. I'll do the same if I find her or need help. Good luck."

"You too," Nicole responded. "We're gonna need it."

01:23 AM

"What are you doing out here?" the sopping-wet policeman shouted through the driver's window of John's truck.

"Emergency services," John answered calmly.

The policeman acted like he hadn't heard him. "Maybe you missed the memo, or maybe you're just insane. Do you realize that you're driving around in a Category Five hurricane?"

The shouting policeman woke Mark. He pushed his long hair behind his ears. "What's happening?"

Cindy turned. "Go back to sleep."

"Fat chance. Where are we?"

The policeman shined his light in Mark's face. "You're smack-dab in the middle of the biggest hurricane ever to hit here. Maybe the biggest to hit the United States."

"I heard that it's been downgraded to a Category Four," John said.

"Three, four, five ... makes no difference to me. It's destroyed every road up ahead. It's an ongoing disaster. A national disaster."

"Which is why we're here," John said. "We're contractors. If the roads are impassable ahead, how did you get here?"

The policeman glared at him for a second, then said, "I just turned back two Federal Emergency Management Agency trucks. The FEMA people weren't too happy with me either, but I have my orders. The only people we're letting through are law enforcement and National Guard. We'll let you know when you can pass."

"It's hard to help people if you aren't there to help them," John said.

"I hear you, but there's nothing I can do. And there's nothing you can do for anybody in a little four-by-four with a winch."

"We have two big rigs stationed ahead with supplies." Cindy raised her eyebrows but didn't contradict him.

"Providing that your rigs are still intact, and there's a good chance they aren't. As bad as it is here, it's worse up ahead. A lot worse. About five miles back down the road is a high school. We've set up a temporary shelter in the gym. You'll find uncomfortable cots, bad coffee, stale doughnuts, and dozens of annoyed people just like you waiting to get through to do their thing. Don't expect to get through until midmorning at the earliest. We'll assess the damage and let you know if and when you can proceed."

John turned the truck around and headed back down the road.

"It's not that long before daylight," Mark said. "Bet that shelter is filled with news people. I'm kind of partial to bad coffee and day-old doughnuts."

John passed his Thermos back to him. "Help yourself. There's half a box of doughnuts under the seat. You'll need the bad coffee to soften them up."

Mark took the Thermos. "I take that to mean that we're not going to the shelter."

"Nope."

"Then where are we going?"

"The road less travelled," Cindy said.

"First I have to talk to Tomás."

John pulled to the side of the road and called his partner on his sat phone. They proceeded to have a short conversation in Spanglish, which Cindy and Mark could barely understand. He ended the call and punched in some coordinates on his in-dash GPS, then studied the map.

"Tomás thinks he's found a way past the roadblock. Do either of you know how to use a chain saw?"

01:28 AM

Chase swam in widening circles for six minutes, shouting Rashawn's name, listening, then shouting again, ignoring the pain in his shoulder. He hated to stop looking, but they had to get back to shore or risk drowning themselves. He treaded water and looked at his GPS. Rather than risk having to cross another breach he decided he'd haul out where the road ended. As he swam towards shore he continued to call out for Rashawn.

Nicole was exhausted and hoarse from shouting.

Rashawn wouldn't be able to hear me from twenty feet away.

She spotted Chase's light, which seemed impossibly far away in the dark rough water.

"Rashawn! Rashawn!"

Chase stumbled up on shore, staying low to the ground to keep from getting knocked over by the wind. He shined his headlamp all around, looking for gators, then sat down on the bank to catch his breath.

Now that he was still he could feel the throbbing pain in his shoulder. If he had jumped a second later, the entire slab of asphalt might have hit him, knocking him out, or worse, pinning him underwater.

He scanned the churning water for Nicole's light and began to panic when he didn't see it. He stood and squinted against the rain, then let out a sigh of relief when he spotted a pinpoint of light much further away than it should have been.

If she's having trouble, the light should be flashing. What is she doing?

"Thank God you're OK!"

Chase nearly pitched forward into the water. "Rashawn? What are you doing here?"

She ran forward and threw her big arms around him, crunching his shoulder, but he was so happy to see her he didn't care. She squeezed him tighter and he grunted in pain.

She let go of him. "You hurt? What's the matter?"

"Some of the road fell on me when we went in after you, but I'm fine. What happened to you?"

"I really thought I could make it across, but you were right about the wind. It picked me up like I was a goose feather, then the current sucked me under. I thought for sure I was going to drown. When I finally came up I had no idea where I was. I just started swimming and climbed out about a hundred yards down from here. I hurried back to the breach, which is huge now. When I didn't see you or Nicole, I freaked. I thought you got washed away. Where were you?"

"We jumped in the water after you. We kept calling, but you couldn't hear us up on the road."

"Where's Nicole?"

Chase pointed to the water.

"You mean that tiny light out there?"

"She should be heading in by now, but it doesn't look like she's getting any closer. I'm worried. She's been out there too long."

"This is all my fault," Rashawn sobbed. "If I hadn't tried to jump, you and—"

Chase cut her off. "If you hadn't tried to jump, one or all of us might have been crushed by the asphalt that got me. We were wasting time talking. You got us moving."

"Thanks, Chase."

"It's the truth."

"Let's get Nicole." She started towards the water.

Chase took her arm and pulled her back. "I'm not going to get far with this bum shoulder. And I'm not about to let you get back in the water. We need to stick together. I'll let her know you're safe. Let's get up on the road."

They scrambled to the top. It was hard to believe, but the wind seemed to be blowing even harder. They had to get on their knees and hang on to each other to keep from being blown back over the edge into the water.

Chase took his headlamp off, switched it to emergency mode, and held it above his head. He hoped Nicole could see the light. He hoped she'd understand that Rashawn was with him. He hoped she had the stamina to make it back to shore against the wind.

01:41 AM

Everything the make-up artist had done to Richard Krupp's face and hair came undone the moment he stepped outside into Emily. The sound and ferocity of the wind and rain scared him and his two-man crew half to death. If the crew hadn't been there, Richard might have run back through the doorway they'd just slipped through. He locked arms with his cameraman, who in turn linked up with the sound guy. The three of them made their way to the filming location they'd picked from the van when they first drove up. When they'd chosen the spot, it had looked easy to get to. Halfway there, they all had serious doubts. Bits of flying debris slammed into their Gore-Tex rain suits like shotgun pellets.

"We should be wearing body armour!" the cameraman shouted.

"I'm getting way too old for this..." The sound guy's last word was carried away by the wind.

Richard was speechless. It was all he could do to move his legs forward and breathe. The wind was blowing so hard it was tough to catch enough to fill his lungs.

He was worried about getting hit by a large chunk of debris. He was also worried about being completely blown away by the wind. But his biggest concern was how he was going to look on camera and what he was going to say.

If they could manage to get the video uploaded, there was a good chance that it would be played all over the world. His producer wanted to run a live feed of the video, but Richard insisted on a review before it hit the airwaves. He argued that at this time of morning, viewership would be low, especially locally with the widespread power outages. He wanted a second shot if he didn't like the first one. But now that he was out in the storm, he had absolutely no desire for a second take. Somehow he had to mask his abject terror with a look of calm courage.

The cameraman stopped, and started pushing buttons on the video camera and wiping the lens. "You're going to have to do double duty!" he shouted at the sound guy. "You'll have to keep the lens dry!"

"Can't you just change the angle?" his coworker shouted back. "I'm going to have my hands full with the sound in this wind."

"It doesn't matter what angle the camera is at. The rain's coming from every direction. The lens is going to get drenched."

The sound guy looked at Richard. "You'll have to use the hardwire mic. The wind's too loud for the lapel or boom mic." He handed the mic to Richard. "Hold it right to your lips. Don't shout, but talk loud, or no one's going to hear you. On three."

Richard spread his legs and braced himself as best as he could. He tried to set his expression into "bravery in the grip of terrible adversity" but it was difficult with the wind contorting his face as if he were in a free fall without a parachute.

The cameraman held up his index finger. When his ring finger went up, Richard began.

"If Emily has been downgraded to a Category Four hurricane, I would hate to be standing in a Category Five hurricane to bring you this update.

"As you can see, I'm right in the thick of it. All around me is complete and utter devastation as I try to get home to my loved ones. But they say there is no way home. Every road in is impassable. I've fought my way through the storm all night, and I'll continue to fight regardless of personal risk.

"I realize that it's difficult for you watching in your living rooms to get a true sense of Emily's power, but let me tell you ... it ... is ... immense. I have stood in the face of at least a dozen hurricanes in my life, but never one of this magnitude.

"I'm going to sign off now because I need to push forward. Stay tuned and stay safe. I'll update you when I can."

Richard stared at the camera for a dramatic beat, then gave the crew a nod to shut the equipment down. "Let's get out of here."

Huddled together against the wind and rain, they shuffled five metres to their left, yanked open a door and stumbled into a large gymnasium filled with people, cots, food, water, warmth, light, the smell of coffee and the hum of generators.

His producer met them with an armload of fluffy white towels, hot coffee and a dozen glazed doughnuts.

Richard grabbed a towel and looked down at the box of doughnuts. "No sugar doughnuts?"

"They're out," the producer said. "But the rumour is that more are on the way. How'd the shoot go?"

"We'll have to run tape to be sure, but I think it's good."

"You weren't out there very long."

"And you weren't out there at all," Richard snapped. "I just risked my life." He grabbed two doughnuts. "Let's take a look at the vid and get it on the air. I need to get some sleep."

01:53AM

John, Cindy and Mark had left the main road and managed to circumvent the first roadblock.

John bumped the 4x4 back on to the highway and stepped on the gas. He'd been on the sat phone with Tomás almost constantly.

"Tomás says they aren't letting anyone past the roadblock he's at, but he thinks he's found a way around it. He's waiting for us seven miles up ahead. If we can get around it, we're home free." A large branch hit the windscreen and cracked it. "Well, at least we'll be past the authorities. We'll still have to deal with Emily."

Cindy looked at her watch. "That should just about give you enough time to tell me about your earring."

John stared straight ahead, then told her what it felt like to get struck by lightning.

01:54 AM

"I think her light is definitely getting bigger," Rashawn said.

Chase couldn't tell, but he was certain the wind was blowing harder. He and Rashawn were nearly hugging the road, trying to stay in one place. He hoped that when Nicole made it to shore she had enough strength left in her legs to walk.

"Maybe I should swim out to her," Rashawn suggested again.

"I thought you said she was getting closer."

"I think she is. But she's been in the water a long time. She has to be getting tired."

"Let's wait," Chase said, but he was tempted to let Rashawn go. The problem was that they might have to carry Nicole, and he would need Rashawn to help him. They were fifty metres from the end of the levee road. As soon as Nicole reached shore they'd have to move quickly or they'd be back in the water with the gators. According to the GPS, about a hundred metres past the levee the road took a sharp turn to the left. If the wind held its current direction, it would be at their backs all the way to the road the Rossi farm was on. Two miles up that road was the gate. They were less than three miles from safety.

"Three miles!" he said aloud, but the words were swept away by Emily.

02:08 AM

"I'm so sorry about your wife and little girl. I don't know how I would have—"

Something large and loud slammed into the side of the truck. John yanked the steering wheel towards the impact and stepped on the gas, trying to get the 4x4 under control. The truck slid sideways for six metres, then came to an abrupt stop against something hard.

The airbags deployed.

The engine stopped.

John felt the side of his head where it had bounced off the window. There was a bump the size of an egg, but no blood.

"Everyone OK?" he asked, pushing the airbag away from his face.

"You need side-impact airbags."

"I'll get them when I replace this truck, which I probably just totalled."

"There are *no* airbags back here," Mark said. "But I'm fine even though we just got hit by a flying tree."

"We got hit by a boulder," John said. "Then we hit a tree."

"Whatever," Mark said.

Bright headlights filled the windscreen.

"Tomás," John said. They'd been following him on back roads for nearly fifteen minutes.

John tried to start the engine.

"Dead." He rolled the window down.

A yellow rain slicker appeared at the window. "Hurt?"

"No, but I think we're going to have to buy another truck. Let's get the stuff transferred."

Tomás nodded, then jogged around the back, seemingly oblivious to Emily's fury. A few minutes later they were back on the road, with Tomás behind the wheel and Saint Christopher on the dash.

02:11 AM

Nicole knew she should have headed back to shore sooner, but every time she started in that direction the possibility of missing Rashawn's call for help stopped her. Finally she saw Chase's red and white flashing light. It was above her, which meant it had to be up on the road. Chase was either in trouble, or Rashawn was with him. She prayed it was the latter and started towards the light.

It turned out to be the most difficult thing she'd ever done in her life. She was swimming hard, but Chase's light was not getting closer. In fact, it looked like it was getting further away. And it was. Despite her efforts, the wind was pushing her backwards. She began to think she should turn around and swim to the opposite shore, but she had no idea how far away it was, or how hard it would be to get back around to the levee. The lake was surrounded by thick vegetation. She might have to find a place to shelter and wait out the storm.

She decided to try to reach Chase one more time before giving herself to the wind.

"See?" Rashawn shouted.

Chase squinted against the rain at Nicole's light.

"It's getting bigger!" Rashawn said. "And there's a pattern to it. Her light disappears at regular intervals. The whitecaps could not possibly be causing that."

Nicole's headlamp did seem to be getting bigger, or at least brighter. Chase stared at it until it disappeared. He glanced at his watch, noted the second, then looked back at the water where the light had been. The light reappeared. He looked at his watch. Thirty seconds. The light bobbed crazily for ten seconds, then disappeared again. He timed it two more intervals. They were the same within a couple of seconds. He looked at Rashawn.

"See what I mean?" she said.

What Chase saw was a sixth-grade girl with incredible courage. Instead of succumbing to paralysing fear, like any normal person would in a storm like this, she'd been able to figure out the pattern to Nicole's swimming. This meant that Rashawn was no longer afraid.

Fear extinguishes thought.

In the past year, not a week had gone by without his father reminding him of this.

Rashawn had just reminded him again.

02:15 AM

Tomás slowed the truck and came to a stop a metre in front of a downed tree blocking the road.

"Guess it's time to see how a chain saw works in hundred-and-fifty-mile-an-hour winds," John said.

Tomás was out of the truck before John finished the sentence. John turned to Cindy and Mark.

"Stay put," he said.

"No way," Cindy said. "We need to start getting some footage for *The Man Who Got Struck by Lightning*."

"Huh?"

"The documentary I'm planning to produce about you."

"I'm not sure I like the name, or being filmed," John said.

"We can discuss the title later," Cindy said. "Grab your camera, Mark."

Tomás's yellow form appeared in front of the headlights, holding a chain saw. He fired the saw up, but the sound was overwhelmed by the wind.

John jumped out and joined him. Tomás had brought two chain saws, but they immediately decided it would be safer for one of them to use the saw while the other pulled branches and pieces of trunk out of the way.

"Try not to get blown away," Cindy said to Mark. "And don't think news segment. Think documentary. This is not a whoa-look-at-me-I'm-in-a-hurricane-and-I-can-barely-stand-up thing. This is the real deal."

"*The Man Who Got Struck By Lightning* thing," Mark said.

"That's right." Cindy had trouble opening the crew-cab door because of the wind. She finally resorted to pushing it open with her feet. She had to hold on to the door handles, then the front wheel well, to keep from getting blown away. Mark had reached the front of the truck and was already filming by the time she got there. He was holding on to the winch with one hand and the camera with the other.

John had been in a lot of storms, but nothing like this. The branches lashed their heads, arms, backs and legs like bullwhips. There was hardly any need to haul anything away. As soon as Tomás cut through something, it blew off into the darkness.

All John could really do to help him was to shout out when a piece of flying debris was coming his way.

He glanced behind him and saw the camera light. Cindy started to crawl forward, but he waved her back with both hands. They didn't need her help. Tomás barely needed *his* help.

02:20 AM

When Nicole got about fifteen metres from shore, Chase and Rashawn slid down the muddy embankment. Chase waved his flashing headlamp over his head. Rashawn cheered Nicole on as if she were competing in the Olympics. At six metres they both waded into the water, grabbed Nicole under her arms and dragged her to shore. Chase gently removed her headlamp and handed it to Rashawn. Minutes passed before Nicole was even able to speak.

She looked up at Rashawn. "I'm so happy you're OK. I thought you drowned."

"I thought you were going to drown trying to save me!" Rashawn started crying.

Nicole took her hand and started crying too.

Chase looked at his watch. He gave them about half a minute, then said, "We have to get off the levee before it collapses. Can you walk?"

Nicole sat up slowly. "I'm not sure. My arms and legs feel like noodles."

"Let her rest some more," Rashawn said.

Chase nodded, but he really wanted to get moving. "Rashawn noticed that your light kept disappearing."

Nicole smiled. "I was getting pushed to the other side of the lake by the wind. The only way to get around it was to avoid it. I started to think about what Rashawn had said about the gators sitting on the bottom riding out the storm. I dived and swam underwater and under the wind. I lost ground every time I came up for air, but not as much as I was gaining. I don't think I would have made it if I'd waited five minutes more figuring this out."

Nicole turned her head and looked at the steep bank. "I'm not sure I can make it up to the road."

"We'll help you," Chase said. He and Rashawn got on either side and pulled her on to her feet.

Nicole tried to stand on her own and would have fallen over if they hadn't caught her.

"We can carry you," Rashawn said.

"Not up that, you can't."

"We'll get you up there even if we have to drag you," Chase said. "But the wind's a lot stronger up on the road."

"My legs will come back," Nicole said. "They always have before. How far is it to the farm?"

"After we get off the levee, a couple of miles."

"My legs feel better already," Nicole said.

Chase draped Nicole's arm around his neck. Rashawn did the same with Nicole's other arm.

On the first attempt they made it halfway up the bank, then stumbled, and all three of them slid back down to the water. The second try wasn't much better. On the third they were within inches of the top when Nicole's legs went completely dead. She reeled over backwards, taking Chase and Rashawn with her.

"Just leave me here!" Nicole said. "You and Rashawn go to the farm and get my dad!"

"Forget it," Chase said. "We're sticking together."

Rashawn started massaging Nicole's legs.

"That hurts!"

"Good," Rashawn said. "It's supposed to hurt. Some athlete you are. I gotta get the circulation going in your limbs. Push out all that nasty lactic acid poisoning your muscles."

Nicole knew all about lactic acid buildup, but she was surprised Rashawn knew about it, and what to do to get rid of it. After a long or fast swim the team's physical therapist always gave her a rubdown.

"How do you know about lactic acid?"

"I told you, you aren't the only athlete here."

"We really have to go," Chase said.

"We aren't going anywhere until we get some life back into these legs," Rashawn snapped. "If we'd done this in the first place, we'd be off the levee by now."

"Rashawn's right," Nicole said.

Chase nodded, then looked at Rashawn. "I'll work on one leg, you work on the other."

02:35 AM

Tomás and John climbed back into the truck after cutting through their third tree. Cindy and Mark had stayed in the cab because getting in and out wasted too much time.

"That should be the last one for a while," John said, wiping his head with an already sopping towel. "There's a lake up ahead."

Tomás put the truck into gear and stepped on the accelerator. The wipers could barely keep up with the rain, and the defroster was having a hard time with the damp heat coming off their bodies, making it nearly impossible for them to see through the windscreen.

As soon as they left the tree cover, they were hit by a vicious blast of wind. The truck fishtailed, but Tomás got it under control and pushed ahead. The sheeting rain prevented Cindy from seeing anything out her little side window.

Tomás slammed on the brakes and shouted something in Spanish that Cindy didn't understand. John began swearing. She understood everything he said.

Tomás put the truck into reverse and backed up twice as fast as they had driven forward.

"What's going on?" Mark shouted.

"Road's out," John said.

Tomás drove the truck back into the cover of the trees

and stopped. He and John had another short conversation in Spanglish.

"We're going to walk back up and take a closer look at the levee road," John translated. "If we can't get across, we're going to have to backtrack all the way to where we met up with Tomás and find another way around."

"I'm going with you," Cindy said.

"No," John said. "The little bit of road we're on might collapse."

Cindy zipped her coat and pulled up her hood. Mark did the same.

"Suit yourself," John said.

They got out of the truck. John linked arms with Cindy. Tomás linked arms with Mark. In their free hands they carried heavy-duty flashlights.

They hunched into the powerful wind and shuffled forward. It took them several minutes to reach the break. It was five metres across, if not more.

John and Tomás got down on their stomachs and crawled to the very edge of the break. They shined their lights under the jagged asphalt and stuck their heads over the edge.

Cindy could not even imagine what they were looking for. It was a dead end. Getting across was impossible.

She looked down the long road and thought she saw something. She wiped the rain from her eyes and looked again.

"John!"

John got up.

"I saw a light. Maybe two lights."

"The power's out and we're in the middle of a refuge.

No one lives here, which is one of the reasons we came this way. The road to the farm is on the other side of this lake."

"I saw it too," Mark said. "The light was a long way off, but I might have caught it on video."

"Where?" John asked.

Cindy pointed. "Straight down the road."

John held his light above his head and flashed it on and off several times. No lights flashed back at them.

"Let's get back to the truck," John said. "I'm not sure how long it's going to take to get around this lake. Or if there even is a way around it."

Tomás jockeyed the truck around and headed back the way they had come.

Cindy tapped John on the shoulder. "What were you and Tomás looking for over the edge of that road? For a second I thought you were trying to figure out a way of jumping it."

John laughed. "We hate backtracking, but we're not crazy ... well, not that crazy. We were looking at how a levee disintegrates. It's not often that you get to see something like that. It's interesting."

"I've got news for you, John," Cindy said. "You *are* crazy."

"Nah, we're storm runners."

"Got it!" Mark said.

"What?"

"The lights. And Cindy was right, there were two of them."

Mark turned the camera around so they could see the

small screen, and hit play. It wasn't very clear, but two lights definitely appeared at the end of the dark road. They moved from left to right, then disappeared.

"Play it back," John said.

Mark played it back in slow motion.

"That's pretty strange," John said. "I guess I should have been looking down the road instead of under it."

"What do you think they were?" Cindy asked.

John shook his head. "I have no idea, but weird phenomena happen during storms like this. Most of the time nobody sees them because we're inside under shelter."

"Maybe it was a couple of storm runners out for a stroll," Cindy said.

"Back the truck up!" John shouted.

Tomás immediately put it into reverse.

"What are you doing?" Cindy asked.

"I need to check something out. This is far enough."

Tomás slammed on the brakes, and John jumped out of the cab with his flashlight and began searching the road. Five minutes later he climbed back into the cab and grabbed his sat phone from the dash.

"What did you find?" Cindy asked.

"Tyre tracks. School bus tyre tracks. Those lights might have been Chase."

He punched in Chase's number.

03:00 AM

Rashawn's massage coupled with Nicole's determination to get home brought Nicole's legs back to life. They reached the road on the fourth try with relative ease. Once there, they didn't hesitate. They locked arms, with Nicole in the middle, and started walking, which got a lot easier when they turned to the left and had the wind at their backs. The only things they had to contend with were downed trees and flying debris. They stumbled out on to Nicole's road, bruised, cut, scraped and out of breath, but they were alive, for which they were all very grateful.

Chase looked at his GPS while they took a short rest. He wasn't sure which part of his body hurt the most. His shoulder and tooth seemed to be in a sharp competition for the top spot.

"Half a mile to the gate," he said, covering his broken tooth with his upper lip so the wind couldn't get at it.

"There's a lot of water on the road," Nicole said.

Chase had been wet for so long he'd hardly noticed, but she was right. The water was up to their ankles. He tried to picture the long driveway up to the Rossi house and thought it was uphill, but he wasn't sure. He was so exhausted he was having a hard time focusing. The only things keeping him going were Nicole, who had to be more exhausted than he was, and Rashawn, who had turned out to be a bulldozer of will and endurance.

"Ready?" Rashawn said.

Chase nodded and was about to forge ahead when he felt something tickle his leg. He reached down to scratch it and realized what it was.

"Wait!"

He pulled the sat phone out of his pocket and took it out of the plastic bag.

"Hello?"

"Where are you?" His father's voice sounded a million miles away.

"About a half a mile from the farm," Chase shouted above the wind. "The bus sank."

"Are you OK?"

"Yeah."

"Is the bus driver with you?"

"He's dead. I'm with Nicole Rossi and a girl named Rashawn. Where are you?"

"On the other side..."

"What?"

"We're ... lake ... saw ... light..."

"Is that your father?" Nicole asked. "What's he saying?"

"Hang on," Chase said. He squatted down and pulled the blanket over his head to get the phone out of the wind and rain.

"Are... Chase?"

"I'm here, but you're breaking up."

"Get to... We'll be ... as soon as..."

The phone went dead.

Chase put the phone back in the plastic bag and came out from under his makeshift shelter.

"That was my father," he reported to Nicole and Rashawn. "It was a lousy connection, but I think he's on the other side of the lake. He may have seen our headlamps on the other end of the levee. He's going to try to get to the farm. That's all I can tell you."

"So that phone of yours works?" Rashawn said.

Chase shook his head. "It worked for about twenty seconds, then it went out. If I can get it dried out, it might come back on. Let's go."

They locked arms and started up the road, with Nicole back in the middle, but this time they weren't holding Nicole up, they were holding one another up. None of them could have made it without the others.

As he leaned into the final stretch with his friends, Chase couldn't help but think about how the night would have gone if Dr Krupp had listened to him.

They'd be in the cafetorium in the dark with the wind roaring outside, but safe, uninjured, with their bellies full from raiding the coolers and vending machines.

The bus driver would be alive at home with his family, if he had a family. Chase didn't even know the bus driver's name.

And what about his father and Tomás? Chase was certain his father was worried about him, but there was nothing he could do until the storm passed.

Save yourself. You're no good to anybody if you're dead ... including yourself.

Ø3:33AM

At last they were standing at the gate, almost exactly twelve hours after they'd left the school.

"It's locked," Nicole said, obviously upset.

"Don't you have a key?" Chase asked.

"Of course, but that's not the problem. The padlock is hanging on the outside. We only lock the gate when we're not here. That means Dad isn't here. He must have gone out looking for us."

"What about Momma Rossi?" Chase asked.

"She would have stayed behind in case the phones came back on and I called."

"I'm sure your dad's fine. He probably got forced into a shelter."

"I hope so."

"Do you have a backup generator on the farm?"

"A small one, but it only powers one building at a time."

"We have three generators in the rigs. Let's get through and power the farm up."

Nicole unlocked the gate. They walked through. She closed the gate but didn't lock it.

The quad was exactly where Chase had parked it, though it had tipped over.

"Do you want to walk or try to ride up to the house?"

"Ride," Nicole and Rashawn said together.

"That's what I thought," Chase said. "But the quad is going to be unstable in the wind with three people on it. We'll have to keep a low profile. If it starts to tip, just lean the opposite way. No sudden moves. We don't want to flip it."

They righted the quad. Chase swung on first, turned the key, then pushed the ignition switch. It didn't start. With the rain and being tipped over by the wind, it could have any number of problems – none of which he could repair where they were. He adjusted the choke and pushed the ignition switch again.

"We might be walking after all." He made another adjustment to the choke, then let it set for a minute before giving the switch one last try.

It started ... at least Chase thought it started. The quad was loud, but he couldn't hear the roar of the engine above the wind.

"Do you see the helmets anywhere?" He had left them hanging on the handlebars.

"They're long gone," Nicole said.

Chase laughed at himself. They had just spent half the night walking through a hurricane and he was worrying about helmets.

He pulled his headlamp off, handed it to Nicole. He told her to climb on behind him, and Rashawn to climb on behind Nicole.

"Everyone lean forward," he shouted. "Face your headlamps to the side in opposite directions and keep your eyes open. This way we'll have a hundred-and-eighty-degree view. If you see a problem, like a big branch flying in our direction, tap me on the shoulder in the direction it's coming. I'm going to drive directly to the farmhouse to check on Momma Rossi."

He leaned forward until his chin was almost touching his knees. Nicole draped herself over his back. Under other circumstances he might have felt very different about having Nicole this close to him, and he wondered if Nicole was thinking the same thing.

He started out slowly, getting a feel for the overloaded quad. The steering was sluggish in the crosswind.

Up ahead he remembered the road veering to the left. The wind would be at their backs and he might be able to pick up speed. There was standing water on the gravel road, but not nearly as much as there had been on the highway. The quad's balloon tyres cut through the water easily, but he'd have to watch out for hydroplaning, which was just as dangerous as driving on ice.

He followed the road to the left and the steering became more responsive. He increased the speed, and tried to recall if there were any other turns before they reached the buildings below the house.

He felt a tap on his right shoulder and grimaced in pain. He looked to his right, but didn't see anything. He eased off the throttle, and something very strange happened.

The wind died and the rain stopped.

Completely.

Chase shut the quad off.

It was silent except for their breathing, which they hadn't been able to hear for hours.

Chase looked up and saw stars against a black sky.

"Weird," Rashawn said.

"The eye of the storm," Chase said. "It's going to start up again, and the back end of the hurricane might be worse than the front. Do you realize that we're talking in normal voices and not shouting at each other?"

"This eye-of-the-storm thing is not why I tapped you on the shoulder," Rashawn said.

"Then why?"

"I know you'll think I'm crazy. Maybe I dozed off, or maybe I'm so worn out I'm hallucinating, but I think I saw a big spotted cat running along my side. Looked like a leopard."

Chase and Nicole stared at her, absolutely speechless.

"I told you, you'd think I was crazy. But it gets stranger. The cat was carrying what looked like a little monkey in its mouth. The monkey was limp. It looked dead."

"Poco," Nicole said.

"Hector," Chase said.

"Are you saying I did see a leopard carrying a little green monkey? What kind of a farm is this?"

"Right now, a very dangerous farm," Nicole said.

Chase started the quad, put it into gear, and pushed the throttle as far as it would go. As they sped up the road he wondered how fast a leopard could run.

03:42AM

Chase pulled up in front of the Rossis' house, or at least where it used to be. The old farmhouse looked like it had been pushed over by a bulldozer. Nicole was off the quad, screaming for Momma Rossi, before the quad came to a complete stop.

"This was their house?" Rashawn asked in shock.

"Yeah." Chase swung off the quad and stepped into half a metre of water. "Can I borrow your headlamp?" Rashawn slipped it off her forehead. "You want to stay here with the quad while I get Nicole?"

"With a leopard running around?" Rashawn said. "No, thanks."

"That's why I have to get Nicole. We can't be standing out here in the open like this with Hector running around. And this eye isn't going to last long. When the wind starts up again, this debris is going to be blowing all over the place. We have to find shelter."

"Then let's get her and get out of here," Rashawn said.

Nicole was yelling for Momma Rossi and frantically pulling up floating debris. Chase put his hand on her shoulder.

"We need to go," he said gently.

"We need to find Momma Rossi!" Nicole shouted.

"She may not be here," Chase said. "I saw a light on outside one of the buildings."

136

Nicole turned around and looked. "The circus barn!"

She ran back to the quad, with Chase and Rashawn right behind her. When they reached the barn, Nicole was off the quad again before it stopped, and running to a side door.

"A lot of water here," Rashawn said as they hurried to the entrance.

"I know," Chase said.

Inside, Nicole had her arms wrapped around Momma Rossi. They were both crying. Chase was relieved Momma Rossi had made it through the storm, but he knew they were still far from safe. A metre in from the door, there was a good ten centimetres of standing water.

"Is that an elephant?" Rashawn asked.

"Her name's Pet," Chase said.

"Nicole's mom is kind of small."

"Don't let that fool you," Chase said. "She's bigger than she looks. And older – she's actually Nicole's grandmother."

They walked over, and Momma Rossi hugged them both.

"Where's Dad?" Nicole asked.

Momma Rossi shook her head. "I don't know. He left hours ago to see if he could find you. I was sitting in the house, waiting for you, when it started to come apart. I ran down here and I've been sitting here ever since. Did you stop at the house?"

Nicole nodded, tears rolling down her cheeks. "It's gone," she said quietly.

Momma Rossi put her arms around her. "It's just a house. We can rebuild a house. Did you see Poco up there? He jumped out of my arms and disappeared into the night."

Rashawn was about to say something, but Nicole cut her off. "We didn't see him," she said. "I'm sure he's fine."

"I'm sure your father's fine too," Momma Rossi said. "He'll be back now that the storm's over."

"It's not over," Chase said. "We're in the eye of—"

His words were cut off by a gust of wind slamming into the metal building. Pet pulled on her chains and threw hay and sawdust over her back with her grey trunk.

"That wind's going to scare the baby right out of her," Momma Rossi shouted above the noise.

Chase glanced again at the door. The water was rising.

PART 2

THE
SURGE

12 HOURS

Chase Masters looked at his watch. It was hard to believe it had only been twelve hours since he, Nicole, and Rashawn had got on the ill-fated school bus at Palm Breeze Middle School.

During those terrible hours, the bus had sunk, its driver had died, and they had nearly drowned. Chase had broken a front tooth, his shoulder had been smashed by a falling chunk of asphalt road, and a thirteen-foot alligator had attacked him.

But we're alive, he thought. *Hurricane Emily didn't get us . . .*

The wind slammed into the side of the metal barn where they had taken shelter.

. . . yet.

Rashawn and Nicole jumped.

"What time is it?" Nicole asked with a nervous laugh.

Chase told her. . .

03:51 AM

"Sounds like we're trapped in a steel barrel and someone's poundin' on the side with a sledgehammer," Rashawn said, covering her ears.

That's exactly what it sounds like, Chase thought, tempted to find a steel barrel, curl up inside and stay there until Hurricane Emily blew herself out. He ran his tongue along the jagged edge of his front tooth and stretched his shoulder – both still ached. He'd hoped that when they finally reached the farm the nightmare would be over, but it wasn't. A leopard named Hector was running around the property with Nicole's grandmother's pet monkey, Poco, dangling from his mouth, and her family's house looked like it had been crushed with a wrecking ball. At first they'd thought that Nicole's grandmother, Momma Rossi, had been trapped under the rubble, but she had taken refuge down the hill in the barn just before the house collapsed.

Momma Rossi was a little person, like Nicole's father, Marco. The dwarfism gene had bypassed Nicole, so she was regular height. Chase glanced at Rashawn, who was alternating her gaze between Momma Rossi and the very large elephant chained in the middle of a sawdust-covered circus ring. It was hard to say which sight confused Rashawn more.

Momma Rossi fixed her brown eyes on Chase. "How are my treasures?"

"Uh ... I don't know. I didn't get a chance to check," he replied. Momma Rossi had predicted that the house would go down in the storm. A day earlier, she'd asked Chase to transfer dozens of boxes of memorabilia to a storage container near the swimming pool in back of the house. He'd caulked the container and wrapped it in tarps, but he doubted it had held up to Hurricane Emily's fury.

"What's important is that you're all OK," Momma Rossi said.

"What *is* this place?" Rashawn asked.

"Our farm is winter quarters for the Rossi Brothers' Circus," Momma Rossi explained. "Normally this time of year the farm would be filled with show animals and performers, but they managed to book some additional dates in Mexico, prolonging the season. Nicole's mother runs the show and her father – my son – Marco runs the farm."

"Why'd this elephant stay behind?"

"Pet? She's pregnant with her first calf," Momma Rossi said.

"Why's she chained up?"

"So she doesn't float to the ceiling," Nicole and Chase said in unison and laughed.

"You guys are hilarious," Rashawn said, rolling her eyes. "I bet she's chained so she doesn't tear this building down."

"You're right," Nicole said. "We don't have an elephant-proof building. The show elephants spend their winters in Texas with our trainer. Pet would be there now, but we didn't want to move her this close to having her calf."

"I hope the building is hurricane-proof," Rashawn said.

Chase had never been in a hurricane, but he'd seen plenty of dangerous weather. Following his father from disaster to disaster the past two years had shown him that no building was stormproof.

At that moment something heavy slammed into the side of the metal circus barn. They all jumped.

"What was that?" Rashawn shouted.

"I don't know," Nicole said. "But it sounded like it was shot out of a cannon at point-blank range."

"Storm debris," Chase said. "Probably from the house. It's upwind." By the loudness and density of the hit, he thought it might be one of the house's toilets. His father was always giving him articles about people getting killed by unusual WPPs, wind-propelled projectiles. "I think we'll be—"

The first thud was followed by a salvo of WPPs. Everyone covered their ears and backed away from the wall. Nicole huddled closer to her grandmother, and Rashawn was shaking. Chase stood frozen in place. The barrage went on for several minutes, then suddenly stopped.

They all stared at the wall. No one spoke. The wind still rattled the metal building, but the sound was nothing compared to the strikes they'd just heard.

Nicole broke the silence. "That was insane!"

"I thought the wall was going to fall down right on top of us," Rashawn said.

"So did I," Chase admitted. He walked up to the wall and checked for damage. There were a lot of dents, but nothing seemed to have pierced the metal. "Heavy-gauge steel," he said, not mentioning that if one of the panels had come loose, it would have peeled off the building like the skin from a rotten banana, with the other panels close behind. "We're safe in here," he added with more confidence than he felt.

"Are you sure?" Nicole asked.

Her long black hair was wet and tangled with twigs and dirt. Her usually bright brown eyes were dull with fatigue. Chase wasn't surprised, after the terrifying journey they'd endured to get to the farm. "Maybe you should sit down," he said.

"He's right," Momma Rossi said. "You look dead on your feet."

Nicole nodded and collapsed on the kerb of the circus ring. "I am. That last swim took a lot out of me." She looked up at Chase. "You haven't answered my question."

"I don't know if we're safe or not," Chase admitted. "There's water coming in around the door, which isn't surprising with this wind and rain. I guess I'd better check out the rest of the building, but to do that I'll need more light."

"Our generator can only power one of these rings at a time," Nicole said. "I don't know how to switch it to the other rings." She looked at her grandmother.

"I don't know either," Momma Rossi said. "The lights were on over Pet's ring when I got into here."

"I'll check it out," Chase said. "Where's the generator?"

"In the workshop – connected to the bunkhouse," Momma Rossi said.

Chase clicked on his headlamp and shined the beam

along the wall. "Battery's just about gone." He checked the second headlamp. Its beam was worse.

Momma Rossi took a flashlight out of her coat pocket. "Plenty of life left in this one. You should find batteries in the bunkhouse. I'm not sure where they keep them. If you don't find them in the kitchen, check in the workshop. Marco's been camping out in the bunkhouse for the last week to stay close to Pet. There should be plenty of food in the kitchen if any of you are hungry."

"We haven't eaten for hours," Chase said. "I'll see what I can find."

"Do you think *your* dad can find *my* dad?" Nicole asked.

"If I can get ahold of him." Chase pulled a plastic bag from his trouser pocket. Inside was a satellite phone just like the one his father and his father's partner, Tomás, carried. Chase's phone had died after the school bus sank, but it had come back to life just before they reached the farm. He'd been able to talk to his father long enough to find out that he and Tomás were stranded on the other side of the lake and were looking for a way around to reach the farm. Chase did not expect to see them anytime soon. He pushed the on button. Nothing happened.

"Still dead," Chase said.

Momma Rossi had set up a small electric heater next to the ring. Chase removed the phone battery, wiped it and the phone off as best as he could, then set both of them near the heater.

Tears formed in Nicole's eyes. "I hope Dad's not hurt."

"Marco is fine," Momma Rossi said, putting her arms around her granddaughter.

"Are you just saying that to make me feel better?" Nicole asked. "Or do you know?"

"I know," Momma Rossi said. "Just like I knew you and Chase and Rashawn were in danger."

Just like she knew the farmhouse was going to blow over and nobody believed her, Chase thought. *Just like she knew that Mom and Monica had died in a car crash on a mountain.*

"Excuse me, ma'am," Rashawn said.

"Please call me Momma Rossi."

"OK, Momma Rossi. No disrespect, but I just met you a few minutes ago when we stepped into this barn. How could you know about me before then?"

Momma Rossi smiled, but didn't answer her.

Chase looked at Rashawn. "She just knows things. Do you want to help me check out the rest of this barn?"

"Sure," Rashawn said. "But first I want to know if Momma Rossi has a bag of rice in that kitchen of hers."

"I'm sure there is, dear," Momma Rossi said. "But we don't have any way to cook it with the power out."

"I don't want to eat it," Rashawn said. "I want to use it on Chase's sat phone. My daddy is always dunkin' his phone in the water – he manages a wildlife refuge, so he's outside all day. He just puts it in a bag of uncooked rice and the grains suck the moisture right out of it. Couple hours, the phone's good as new."

"You're kidding," Chase said.

"No joke," Rashawn said. "And when you get that phone fired up, you also need to ask your daddy about *my* daddy. I'm sure he's out looking for me too."

"I will," Chase promised.

04:12 AM

Chase led Rashawn into the dark shadows of the circus barn. He didn't really need her help, but he wanted to give Nicole and Momma Rossi some time to themselves. Also, Rashawn knew things he didn't. She might *see* things he didn't as he checked the barn for hurricane damage. He'd only met Rashawn a few hours ago, but she had proven herself over and over again, just as Nicole had.

There were three brightly coloured, kerbed circus rings running down the middle of the barn. Each ring was at least a hundred metres across. Pet was chained in the centre of the first ring, and stretched across the second, a metre off the ground, was a gigantic net. Ten metres above the net, a tightrope connected two platforms. Next to the tightrope was an array of trapeze equipment.

Chase shined his light up at the ceiling. A series of catwalks crisscrossed the rafters above the equipment.

"What are those for?" Rashawn asked.

"They must use them to adjust the rigging and the lights," Chase said.

Rashawn jumped up and brushed the bottom of the net with her hand. "Guess this is in case someone does a header from that wire or a swing. When we get to the bunkhouse, I'm going to find me a blanket, climb up on this net and sleep for a week. It's like a big ol' hammock."

Chase smiled. Another thing he liked about Rashawn was her ability to joke when there was nothing to joke about. He cut across the ring to the north wall of the building and put his hands on the metal sheeting. It was vibrating in the wind, but there was no evidence of water getting in. The wind was blowing from the west, where they had entered the building, which accounted for the water pooling inside the door near the elephant ring. The fact that there was no water along this wall gave him hope that the building might hold up to Hurricane Emily. He crossed to the opposite wall, but it was blocked off by a stack of hay bales that reached almost to the rafters.

Chase and Rashawn walked down to the third ring, which held a circular cage. "I think they use this one to train the big cats," Chase said.

"How many cats do they have?" Rashawn asked.

"I'm not exactly sure," Chase said. "When I got here, Nicole showed me five lions and a leopard."

"The one named Hector?" Rashawn asked.

"Yeah. He was confiscated from a drug dealer and he's very aggressive."

"Don't you think all leopards are aggressive?"

"Good point," Chase said.

"You think the lions were born free like Hector?"

"I hope not." Chase neglected to tell her that the biggest lion, Simba, had been retired from the show the previous year after mauling his trainer.

"How come you didn't tell Momma Rossi about the dead monkey Hector was trotting around with in his mouth? Poco, right?"

"Right," Chase answered. "It's not my place to tell her. The last time I saw Poco, he was in Momma Rossi's kitchen wearing tiny diapers and eating sweet potato peels – he's her pet. I'm sure Nicole will tell her when the time is right."

"They make monkey diapers?"

"I'm guessing that Momma Rossi makes monkey diapers."

"Never heard of such a thing." Rashawn glanced back at the lighted end of the long barn. "Is Momma Rossi psychic or something?"

"I guess we'll find out," Chase said.

04:19 AM

"We can't stay here," Chase's father, John Masters, announced. He was looking at the display of his handheld GPS. "The question is, where do we go and how do we get there from here?"

Here was a two-lane country road about three miles from the same lake Chase's school bus had sunk into several hours earlier.

Chase and his friends are lucky to have survived, John thought. *If they made it to the Rossis' farm. If they're still alive.*

John Masters had tried to call Chase a half a dozen times since their garbled sat phone conversation more than an hour ago. There had been no answer. The eye of the storm had passed over, and by the look of things inside the 4x4 truck he was sitting in, the back end of Hurricane Emily was going to be just as bad as – if not worse than – the front.

Something large, heavy and black bounced off the hood of the truck.

Maybe a lot worse, John thought.

"What was that?" Mark shouted from the crew cab behind John.

"Tree stump," John said. "I think."

"It felt like a meteorite!" Mark was a cameraman from a local TV station in Saint Petersburg, Florida.

153

Sitting between John and his partner, Tomás, on the front seat was Cindy Stewart, a TV reporter who worked with Mark. John still wasn't sure why he had invited Cindy and Mark to drive along with him and Tomás into the centre of the worst hurricane in US history. They had already crashed and totalled one truck, and if they didn't get moving, the second truck was going to be history as well, along with its four occupants.

Cindy looked at the photographs stuck to Tomás's dashboard. "Are these your children, Tomás?"

"*Sí.*" Tomás smiled and listed their names as he pointed at each photo. "And my wife, Guadalupe."

"Are they here in the States?"

Tomás shook his grey head. "Mexico. I see them one time every year."

"You must miss them."

"*Sí.* Of course."

"Why don't you bring them up here?"

"Guadalupe, she loves our village in the mountains. Too expensive here with so many children."

Tomás had been working for John Masters for more than twenty years. When John sold his part of the family construction business to his brother-in-law and hit the road to chase storms, there was no question about Tomás going with him. They were closer than brothers.

John stared straight ahead through the windscreen. The path before them looked more like a stream than a road, and it was strewn with downed trees as far as he could see. With the gale-force winds pushing the water, it was impossible to tell which way it was flowing, but one thing was clear: the water was rising. They had to get to high ground. Soon.

"The surge," John said.

"What?" Mark shouted above the roaring wind.

"Storm surge," John clarified. "Flooding. It could cause more damage than the wind."

"After what we've already been through, I'd prefer not to drown if it's OK with you," Mark called from his spot in the back.

"I'll see what I can do." John leaned over Cindy and showed the GPS to Tomás.

"We can try," Tomás said, after studying the map.

"Try what?" Cindy asked.

"A detour." John leaned back into his seat and put his seat belt on. The 4x4 rocked as Tomás pulled it off the road and headed into the woods.

"What's he doing?" Mark shouted, struggling to get his seat belt on as he bounced in the jump seat like a tennis ball.

"Trying to save you from death by drowning," John said. "There's a rail line about a mile away. It should be dry and clear of downed trees. If we can reach it and get the rig up on the bed, it'll take us to the main highway."

"So now it's death by oncoming train," Mark said.

"Trains don't run during hurricanes," John said. "But there are any number of other things that could kill us on the way."

"Like death by flying tree stump," Cindy said.

"Yep, that's one of them," John said. Then he proceeded to give them a grim list of death by WPPs.

04:25 AM

A blast of windblown rain knocked Chase and Rashawn backwards as they opened the bunkhouse door.

"Window!" Chase shouted. "Over the sink!"

They hunkered down and fought their way across the room towards the opening. The window was broken. Chase grabbed a large wooden cutting board from the kitchen counter. With the wind and rain hammering their faces, it took all of their strength to wedge the board into the window frame.

"It will keep most of the rain out," Chase said, out of breath.

Rashawn leaned against the counter and wrung the water out of her hair. "And I was just getting dry!"

Chase shined the flashlight at the six centimetres of water covering the floor. An armada of plastic cups and containers bobbed on the surface like little ships. He walked cautiously to the centre of the room.

"What are you doing?" Rashawn asked.

Instead of answering, Chase bent down and pulled up a large frying pan by the handle. With the drain unplugged the water level started to drop.

"Cement floor," Chase said. "Three-inch central drain. Shouldn't be too much damage after it dries."

"What is it with you?" Rashawn asked.

"What do you mean?"

"'Cement floor. Three-inch central drain...' You sound like an architect or something. And before our bus ran off the road and sank, you sounded like you worked for FEMA. I'm not complaining, but what kind of kid carries a satellite phone, several bottles of water, two headlamps and a first aid kit to school in his backpack?"

"A very strange kid," Chase admitted, and then gave her a brief outline of what had happened to him the past two years. He finished just as the last of the water circled the drain.

"I'm sorry about your momma and sister, Chase," Rashawn said. "The last couple of years of your life sound like the water goin' down this drain."

Chase smiled. "You're right. It has kind of sucked."

"Your daddy really got hit by a lightning bolt?"

"It went right through his shoulder. Blew his boots off his feet. He was in a coma for days. When he came out of it he looked like my father, but it was like someone else had crawled into his skin."

"So now he and this Tomás guy drive around the country looking for storm damage, then charge people an arm and a leg to fix things. And drag you along with them."

"Yup, that's M.D. Emergency Services," Chase said.

"M.D., like in doctor?"

Chase shook his head. "M.D., like in *Masters of Disaster*."

"At least your daddy has a sense of humour."

"Not really," Chase said. "Not any more. But he's a good contractor and he's taught me a lot."

"What happens to you after Emily blows through?"

"Hopefully we'll stick around awhile. I like it here. But my father doesn't spend too much time in one spot."

"Your daddy sounds a lot like *my* daddy. I bet my daddy's worked at a dozen wildlife refuges from here to Oregon. Our last name is Stone. Momma calls him Mr Rollin' Stone, but I think she likes movin' around just as much he does." Rashawn glanced at the rain blowing through a gap in the window. "I just hope they had the sense to stay out of this mess and not go out looking for me."

"Do you have brothers or sisters?"

"A little brother, Randall . . . two years old."

"You live on the wildlife refuge?"

"Smack-dab in the middle of it. The job always comes with a house."

"A sturdy house?"

Rashawn laughed. "Brick. I made fun of it when we moved in. Called it the Three Little Pigs' House. If it's standing when this is over and my family's OK, I won't be making fun of that house any more."

"I think they'll be fine. I'm sure your parents have seen plenty of bad weather living out in the woods."

Rashawn stole another glance at the window. "I don't think anybody's seen weather like this before."

"You're probably right," Chase agreed. He switched on the headlamp and handed it to her. "Not much light. Think you can manage to find some batteries while I look for the generator?"

"No problem," Rashawn said, slipping the headlamp over her forehead. "I'll raid the cupboards for food too, and find some rice for that satellite phone of yours."

Chase shined his light around the room, which was a lot bigger and nicer than he'd expected. It was a combination kitchen/recreation room. The kitchen was equipped with shiny stainless steel appliances, granite countertops and a commercial refrigerator big enough to hang a cow in. The recreation room had a pool table, leather sofas and chairs, and two gigantic flat-screen TVs.

"Whoa!" Rashawn said. "When Momma Rossi said 'bunkhouse' I was thinking bunk beds, cowboys and a potbellied ol' stove ... but this is nice! Makes me want to switch my dream of becoming a biologist like my daddy and join the circus instead."

Chase smiled. He'd said almost the same thing to Nicole the day before. He opened the door to the right of the recreation room. It led to a hallway with several doors running along the left side and another door at the end. As he walked down the hall, he tried the doors on the left and found them all locked except for one. It opened into a furnished apartment with a sitting room, a bedroom and a bathroom. There were no personal effects, which led Chase to believe the locked doors were for occupied apartments.

The Rossis take good care of their roughnecks, he thought.

He continued down to the door at the end, which opened on to the workshop. Like the kitchen/recreation room and the apartments, it wasn't what he'd expected. It was almost as big as the circus barn, well equipped, and immaculately clean. With the assortment of tools hanging above the long workbench, the roughnecks could repair anything. Along another wall were three garage doors rattling loudly in the wind, each big enough to back a semi-trailer through.

The generator was in the corner along the common wall between the barn and the workshop. Chase knew the generator was on by the green light, but he couldn't hear it above the wind. He walked over and checked the gas. It was close to empty. He picked up the gas can next to it and his heart sank. It was completely dry, as were the two other cans he found along the wall. It took him nearly twenty minutes to discover that there wasn't a drop of gasoline in the workshop.

Rashawn came in with her headlamp shining brightly again.

"I see you found batteries," Chase shouted above the rumbling garage doors.

"And food, and blankets, and pillows, and towels and a bag of rice for that phone of yours."

"Good job," he said, then frowned.

"Everything OK?" she asked.

"Yeah," Chase said, although he knew it wouldn't be OK if he didn't find some gasoline. In a little while it was going to be as dark inside the barn as a mine shaft. Chase looked at his watch. It was 5:01 a.m.

05:01 AM

Tomás's 4x4 bouncing along the slick railroad ties was like an amusement park ride for the occupants – minus the amusement.

"How much further?" Mark shouted from the jump seat in back, where he was getting the brunt of the bounce.

"About half a mile," John shouted back.

"How far have we gone?"

"About a half a mile."

"You gotta be kidding me! I'm getting pounded back here. I need a helmet!"

John turned. Mark was cradling the video camera like it was an infant. "You might want to let go of that camera and hang on."

"This camera is worth more than my life."

"It doesn't even belong to you," Cindy pointed out. "The station owns it."

"Yeah, but if I break it, I *will* own it," Mark said. "And a busted camera won't do me much good considering that in a couple hours, when I don't show up at the station for work, I'll be unemployed."

"So will I," Cindy said.

Cindy and Mark had both known when they climbed into John Masters's truck and headed towards Hurricane Emily that there was a good chance they would not make it back to Saint Petersburg by morning. Cindy had accepted John's invitation because, after spending half the previous day watching him work, she was curious about him. Mark had tagged along because he was curious about the hurricane. They had both got what they wanted. Cindy had interviewed John during the terrifying ride into the storm, and she'd learned enough about him to know that he would make a very interesting subject of a documentary. She was thinking of calling it *The Man Who Got Struck by Lightning*. Mark had shot some amazing footage of Emily's fury, but the only way to save his job was to get that footage on the air. Without power there was no way to do this.

"It was a lousy television station anyway," Cindy said. "Look on the bright side. We won't have to put up with Richard Krupp any more."

Richard Krupp was the station's lead anchorman and the most popular television personality in Saint Petersburg.

"It'll be nice not to have to deal with that gasbag any more," Mark admitted. "But how am I going to make a living?"

"With me," Cindy said. "We'll go freelance."

"Without a camera?"

"I have some money put away. I'll get you a camera. In the meantime hand the station's camera up front. We'll hang on to it while you get a grip."

Mark happily gave Cindy and John the expensive camera to guard for a while.

John looked over at Tomás, who was hunched over the steering wheel, trying to see through the watery windscreen. He'd offered to take over the driving again, but Tomás shook his head just as he had every time John had suggested it.

Three minutes later they hit something lying across the track. The truck went airborne, rolled anticlockwise, slammed back on to the track on the driver's side, then slid for ten metres between the rails, with the air bags deployed, before coming to a teetering stop.

"Is everyone OK?" John asked.

"I'm good," Cindy said.

"OK," Tomás said.

"Soiled underpants," Mark said.

"Too much information," Cindy said.

"How's the camera?" Mark asked.

"It's jammed between Tomás's shoulder and my ear," Cindy answered. "But I think it's fine."

"Put it in park, Tomás," John said. "Don't turn the engine off. We may not be able to get it started again."

"That seems moot since the truck is lying on its side," Mark said.

"With some luck we might be able to right it," John said. "I'm going to try to climb out through the window. Nobody move. I don't want to flip it over on the roof, on top of me, or over the trestle."

"As in bridge?" Mark asked.

"I can't see very clearly through the windscreen, but it looks like this section of track is ten to twelve feet above a swamp. If we go into the drink, we'll be on foot."

"Providing we don't drown," Mark added.

"Exactly."

"Just so you know, I can't swim."

"That's good to know."

John slipped his headlamp on and opened the passenger window. When he stuck his head outside, the wind nearly pulled him out of the cab.

Ø5:13AM

Chase put the battery back into the satellite phone, then turned it on.

"No go," he said.

"Rice time." Rashawn took the phone and put it into a Ziploc bag filled with uncooked rice. "You'll be talking to your dad before you know it."

"I hope it works," Nicole said.

"I've never seen this fail." Rashawn started unloading the other goodies from the large box she'd brought from the bunkhouse kitchen.

Chase looked at the electric heater, then at Momma Rossi. "Maybe we should switch the heater off to conserve power."

"Not until you dry off," Momma Rossi said. "How did you and Rashawn get so wet?"

Chase told her about the broken window.

"Did you top the generator off?" Nicole asked.

"I would have, but there wasn't any gas. The cans were all empty." Chase walked over to the heater and put his cold hands in front of it.

"You didn't tell me that," Rashawn said, joining him in front of the heater.

"I thought I'd let everyone know at once." Chase looked at Nicole. "I searched all over the workshop. Is there anyplace else your dad might store it?"

Nicole shook her head. "There are three cans next to the generator. He fills them in town when they're empty."

"There *were* three cans," Chase said. "And they're all empty. Unfortunately, the generator is just about empty too. I'd guess we have about an hour before the lights go off. Maybe less."

"Not good," Nicole said, glancing at Pet. "This barn is dark as a tomb, even during the day." She pointed at a small window to the side of the ring. "That's it for daylight. Dad's been so busy with Pet and taking care of the farm, I guess he forgot to pick up gas."

"You open that big door after sun-up," Rashawn said. "There'd be plenty of light."

"The storm might not be over by sunrise," Chase pointed out. "Which would mean no light, or at least not very much."

"And if Pet saw an opening that big," Nicole added, "she'd try to pull her leg off trying to get to it."

"We have plenty of gas in the Shack and Shop," Chase said.

The Shack was the fifth-wheel where Chase and his father lived. The Shop was his father's tractor-trailer rig. It was filled with tools and building supplies. Tomás had a small apartment built into the front end of the Shop.

"You can't go out in this," Nicole said.

"It's either that or we'll be sitting here in the dark *listening* to an elephant being born," Chase said.

"We have flashlights."

"We have one flashlight and two headlamps," Chase corrected. "Which aren't going to do us much good if there's a problem with the calf."

"What about the four-wheeler?" Rashawn said.

"What about it?" Chase asked.

"I don't know what the Shack and Shop is, or where it is, but we rode down here on a four-wheeler and it's parked right outside the door we came through to get into the barn."

Chase smiled. *Rashawn. Always thinking.* He had no desire to fight his way on foot to the Shop to get gas, especially in the dark.

"Is the tank full?" Nicole asked, looking as relieved as he felt.

"Yeah," Chase answered. "Or pretty close to full." One of his father's many rules was that all gas tanks were to be kept full at all times for situations just like this. He had topped the four-wheeler's tank off the previous morning before he'd picked up Nicole and driven her to the road to catch the school bus. "It has a five-gallon tank. We could siphon it into one of the cans and we'd have enough to keep us going for several hours."

"Let's get it inside," Nicole said. "We can crack the big door open and pull it in."

The big door was in fact big enough to drive a semi-truck through. But the door wouldn't budge, even with all four of them pushing and pulling on it.

"The wind's too strong out there," Chase said. "We'll never get it open. I'll have to use the small door."

"The four-wheeler won't fit through that door," Nicole said.

"You're right. But I can push it up to the door, and we have to siphon the gas out anyway."

"I'll get the hose and a can," Rashawn said, hurrying off into the darkness towards the bunkhouse.

"That Rashawn's a go-getter," Momma Rossi said. "I like her."

"So do I," Nicole agreed.

"Where does she live?"

"Up the road a few miles. Her dad's the refuge manager."

"We need to turn the heater off," Chase said. "And any lights we don't absolutely need."

Momma Rossi walked over and unplugged the heater. Nicole opened a panel on the wall and switched off everything except for a couple of spotlights over the ring.

A few minutes later, Rashawn returned with a watering hose, an empty gas can, and an armful of pillows and blankets.

"Don't know about you, but I'm going to take a nap after we get the generator gassed up."

"On the big ol' hammock?" Chase asked, taking the gas can from her.

"Yep."

"What are you two talking about?" Nicole asked.

Momma Rossi laughed. "I think they're talking about the catch net for the fliers."

"Fliers?" Rashawn said.

"The trapeze artists," Nicole explained.

Chase took out his pocketknife, cut a length of hose, and walked over to the door with Nicole and Rashawn. "I'll get the four-wheeler as close as I can, and we'll figure out what to do from there. Ready?"

He turned the handle. The door banged open, nearly

dislocating his arm. Water and debris flew through the opening.

"Watch out!"

Nicole and Rashawn ducked to either side. Chase dropped to his knees to give the wind a smaller target and peered outside with his headlamp. Shingles, broken furniture and other house debris lined the outside walls like a metre-high snowdrift of rubbish.

WPPs, thought Chase. *We were lucky to get inside the barn when we did.*

The four-wheeler was nowhere to be seen. Chase swore, but the word was lost in the wind. Perhaps more disturbing was the amount of water outside. The side of the barn looked like the bow of a ship slicing through flotsam and jetsam on a rough sea. He pulled his head back inside and struggled to close the door, but could barely move it. Nicole and Rashawn leapt to their feet to help him, and after what seemed like for ever, they managed to shut the door, getting themselves drenched once again.

"What happened?" Nicole asked.

"The four-wheeler must be buried under debris," Chase answered. "Or maybe it floated away. The balloon tyres could have lifted it like a boat in the current."

"What do you mean by the current?" Rashawn asked.

"There's a lot of water out there. The surge. Flooding. Right now, the only thing keeping the water out of the barn – or most of the water anyway – is the debris. It's formed a dam."

"What are we going to do?" Nicole asked.

"I guess I'm going to have to make my way to the Shop after all."

"I'll go with you," Nicole said.

"There's no point in that. It won't take two of us to bring back a can of gas."

"What's it like out there?" Rashawn asked.

"Not too bad," Chase lied.

05:41 AM

John Masters crawled on his stomach, playing out the steel cable from the power winch bolted to the front of Tomás's truck, which was still precariously balanced on its side on the old railroad bridge. Cindy and Mark had crept ahead to the end of the trestle and were crouched behind an uprooted tree in a futile attempt to stay out of the vicious wind. The only person who was out of the wind was Tomás. He was behind the steering wheel, waiting for his partner to right the truck. Engines were not designed to operate sideways. Someone had to stay in the cab and play with the accelerator to keep the engine idling. John had once again offered to spell him from behind the wheel, and once again Tomás had refused, adding in Spanglish that he would be grateful if John could get the truck to tip on to the tracks rather than into the swamp.

John was doing his best. The water was rising quickly. It had almost reached the bottom of the ties. John hoped he had the cable angles figured correctly. He fished the hook under the second rail, attached it back on to the cable, then crawled back to the truck and spoke to Tomás through the smashed windscreen.

"You ready, amigo?"

"Minute," Tomás said. He pulled the last two

photographs of his family off the dash and put them with the others in a Ziploc bag. "*Sí*. Ready."

"When I get it righted, drive forward just enough to loosen the slack. I'll spool the cable and jump in the cab."

"*Vaya con Dios,*" Tomás said.

"*Gracias,*" John replied.

He started the winch.

"Are you sure the camera's safe?" Mark asked.

"Strapped in like a toddler," Cindy answered as she watched John's headlamp bobbing around the tracks in the dark and the two truck headlights vertical rather than horizontal.

"You really think we can make a living going freelance?"

"You mean if we live through this storm?"

"Right."

"Well, it won't be easy, but I think we can make a living … eventually."

"And you think John Masters is a worthy subject of a documentary?"

"Maybe," Cindy said. "We'll have to see how the story develops. You have to admit that it's been pretty dramatic so far."

"I've never been more scared in my life," Mark said. "If that's what you mean."

"Me too," Cindy admitted. "I don't think I would have tagged along if I'd known how bad this hurricane was going to be, yet John and Tomás don't appear the least bit worried."

"That's because they are insane," Mark said.

"You've got a point, but they have managed to keep us alive."

"So far," Mark said. "But if we don't get out of here soon, we'll be swimming to the highway. Did I mention that I can't swim?"

"A few dozen times. Look!" Cindy said. "The headlights are horizontal."

"Yeah," Mark said. "But are they right side up?"

John Masters let out a sigh of relief as Tomás drove the truck forward to give him enough slack to unhook the cable. He spooled it up and climbed into the cab. Inside, Tomás was reattaching his family to the dash.

05:48 AM

"You can't go out there alone," Nicole insisted.

She had followed Chase to the door at the far end of the barn.

"Believe me," Chase said, "I don't want to go out there whether it's with you or without you, but I don't see any other choice. You and Momma Rossi said there could be a problem if Pet has her calf in the dark."

"A two-hundred-and-twenty-five-pound problem," Nicole said.

"That's how much a baby elephant weighs when it's born?"

"Give or take a few pounds."

"We need light," Chase said.

"Let me get the gas," Nicole said. "I know the farm a lot better than you do."

"But you don't know the Shop."

"Back to my original argument," Nicole said. "We should both go."

Chase didn't like it, but Nicole had a good point. He'd only been on the Rossi farm a day before the hurricane struck. He was certain he could find the building where they had parked their rigs, but if he ran into trouble getting there, or getting back, Nicole would have a better idea about how to get around the problem.

"And there's Hector," Nicole added.

Chase had forgotten about Hector, or perhaps he had intentionally put him out of his mind. Having an aggressive leopard running loose was something he didn't want to think about.

"What are the chances of running into him?" Chase asked.

Nicole shrugged her shoulders. "Hard to say. With luck he might be hunkered down somewhere waiting the storm out."

"And eating Poco," Chase added.

"Unfortunately, that meal is probably long over."

"What could you do that I couldn't do if I was unlucky enough to run into Hector?" Chase asked.

"Hector is not the only reason I want to go with you," Nicole said. "I need to check on the other animals. If Hector's out, there's a good chance other animals are loose too."

Suddenly, sitting in a dark barn with a pregnant elephant seemed a lot more attractive to Chase. "What are the chances of Pet having her calf in the next few hours?"

"Good, according to Momma Rossi," Nicole answered. "And she thinks there's a very good chance that Pet isn't going to take care of her calf. These are not ideal circumstances to have your first baby. If there's a problem, we'll have to catch the calf and take it away so it doesn't get stepped on."

"Hard to do in the dark," Chase said.

"Hard to do in the *light*," Nicole pointed out. "Wait here."

"Where are you going?"

"I have to get something from the bunkhouse." She hurried away.

While he waited, Chase slowly turned the door handle, expecting the door to fly open and hit him in the face. It didn't. Cautiously he peered out into the darkness with his headlamp, and was pleased to see the downwind side was calm compared to the opposite end of the circus barn. They wouldn't have to worry about WPPs until they stepped out from the shelter of the wall. There was a lot of water buildup to his left – the same direction they'd have to travel to reach the barn where the Shack & Shop was parked. Between the Shack & Shop and the circus barn were two other barns, one of which was the barn where Hector *used* to live. Chase's father had taught him hundreds of survival techniques over the past couple of years, but how to survive a leopard attack was not one of them.

Chase slowly scanned the windblown darkness with his headlamp, hoping to see the four-wheeler with its precious load of fuel. There was no sign of it. He was kicking himself for not having had the sense to put it inside the barn when he felt a tap on his shoulder. He ducked back inside and closed the door.

"How is it out there?" Nicole asked.

"Not as bad as it is on the other end," Chase answered as he shook the rain out of his hair. "I should have at least tied the four-wheeler down. There was plenty of time before the wind started up again after the eye."

"You couldn't have known that it would be buried or blown away," Nicole said.

"I should have known." He turned and looked at her. "Is that a—"

"Shotgun," Nicole said. "With twelve-gauge double-ought shells. Just in case."

"In case of what?"

"In case of Hector."

"Do you know how to use that thing?"

Nicole pumped a shell into the breech. "Yes, I do, but I hope I don't have to use it." She reached behind her back and pulled out a pistol. "If we run into Hector, I'd prefer to use this, but he may not give us a chance. It's a tranquillizer pistol. I think it'll fit into one of your pockets. The safety's on. It won't go off."

"I'm glad to hear that." Chase put the pistol in his pocket.

"Momma Rossi won't want me to go," Nicole said. "So I'm not going to tell her until just before we head out."

"I don't want you to go either," Chase said.

"I'm going. Ready?"

Chase turned the handle.

"I'm going with Chase to get gas," Nicole shouted over her shoulder as they stepped out into Hurricane Emily.

"Big surprise," Momma Rossi said after the door closed.

"I knew she was going too," Rashawn said.

Momma Rossi fixed her dark eyes on Rashawn. "Now that we're alone, tell me what you and Nicole and Chase are keeping from me."

Reluctantly, Rashawn told her about Poco and Hector.

"Poor little Poco," Momma Rossi said. "I didn't see that coming."

"I'm sorry about your monkey," Rashawn said.

"Exactly where did you see Hector?"

"I can't say *exactly* because I've never been here before, but it wasn't far from the gate we came through. He was headed the same way we were going, but we were faster on the four-wheeler."

"He was probably looking for shelter just like you were," Momma Rossi said.

"What did you mean by you didn't *see* that coming?" Rashawn asked.

"My mother and her mother had second sight, and it was passed on to me," Momma Rossi answered. "Their sight was much clearer than mine."

"So, you're a psychic?"

Momma Rossi smiled. "Part-time, and I'm afraid I'm not very talented at it."

"Chase said that you knew Hurricane Emily was going to get your house."

"*Knew* is too strong of a word. If I had *known*, I wouldn't have been inside the house when the wind started to take it apart. I would have put Poco in a crate so he couldn't have run out the front door when we escaped. I would have known that Hector was on the loose."

"Stay next to the wall!" Chase shouted. "I'll lead us to the edge of the building, then you can take over."

The barn protected them from the brunt of the savage wind, but it was still strong enough to knock them down if they weren't careful.

"There's a lot of water," Nicole said.

"I know. I'm worried about it." It looked like the barn was on the bank of a flooding river. Chase bent closer to Nicole. "The only higher ground than this is where your house is – or was. What's behind the house?"

"Woods," Nicole answered. "And a lake."

Chase hadn't seen the lake the day before. That explained where the water was coming from. "How big is it?"

"Big. But it's never overflowed before, and our family has lived here for seventy years."

It's flooding now, Chase thought. *Big-time.* He visualized the lay of the land, thinking back to the tour Nicole had given him upon his arrival just two days earlier. The road to the farm was below them, which meant that it was probably swamped with water running down to the other lake, where their school bus had sunk. His father and Tomás were not going to have an easy time getting to the farm.

Chase and Nicole inched their way along the wall to where Chase hoped they'd find the four-wheeler around the corner of the building. What they found instead was a dead giraffe.

"Gertrude!" Nicole shouted above the howling wind.

Chase had seen a lot of bad things the past couple years, but the dead giraffe was the worst. There was something terribly wrong with the sight of a four-metre-tall giraffe lying on the ground with floodwater sluicing around it.

Nicole waded out and put her arms around Gertrude's long neck, totally ignoring the wind and flying debris. Hesitantly, Chase joined her. He felt bad about Gertrude, but now was not the time for either of them to pay their last respects. He needed to get Nicole out of there.

"I'm sorry about Gertrude," Chase said. "But we can't stay here. We have to move."

He glanced to his left just in time to see the farmhouse's heavy front door and frame cartwheeling its way directly at them. He grabbed Nicole by the arm and yanked her to the side. The door clipped one of Gertrude's front legs, snapping it like a brittle branch, then sailed off into the night.

"That was close." Nicole shuddered. "Thank you."

"No problem. Now let's get out of here before the next WPP comes barrelling down this wind tunnel."

"Gertrude's still warm. She couldn't have been dead very long."

"Can we talk about Gertrude once we get inside the next building?"

"Sorry."

They didn't get very far. Halfway to the second building, they came across a lion. It was not dead.

05:53 AM

"I vote for going to the shelter," Mark said. "At least long enough to get some coffee and use the bathroom."

"It *would* give us a chance to check up on the latest hurricane reports," Cindy added.

John hated to backtrack, but he had to agree: going to the emergency shelter was probably their best option at the moment. They needed to check the truck out. Something was wrong with the steering. Tomás was having a difficult time keeping the 4x4 on the highway, and it wasn't just because of Hurricane Emily.

A police cruiser with flashing lights marked the road to the emergency shelter. The policeman stayed inside his car, waving them past with a flashlight. The road led them to a large high school gymnasium. The car park looked as if the state basketball tournament were being played.

"A lot of people didn't make it home," Cindy said.

Mark pointed. "There's a parking spot."

Tomás drove by the empty spot, then passed up three more.

"Where are you going?" Cindy asked.

Tomás didn't answer.

John switched on a spotlight outside the passenger window. "Before we go inside we need to circle the building and check for structural damage."

"The gym's made out of concrete," Mark pointed out.

"Water can take down any building regardless of the material," John said. "Water's the most powerful thing on earth. The Grand Canyon was created by water." He swung the spotlight between the foundation and the roofline as they slowly circled the building. When they got back to the car park he switched the spot off.

"Well?" Mark asked.

"So far so good," John answered. "Hope you brought wellies."

"I can't remember the last time I was dry," Mark said.

Tomás parked the truck, jumped out, then disappeared from sight.

"Where'd he go?" Cindy asked.

"Under the truck. Something's broken. Why don't you and Mark head into the gym? Tomás and I will be in after we figure out the problem. Watch out for WPPs. And when you get inside find a spot near one of the exits to hang out. You'll want to be near a door if the building starts to collapse."

"Good safety tip," Mark said.

He and Cindy waded through the ankle-deep water to the gymnasium.

05:56 AM

"Don't move," Nicole said.

Chase wasn't sure if she was talking to him or to the lion, but he froze in midstep just to be safe.

Nicole put her lips close to his ear and whispered, "It's Simba. He can't see us." Her warm breath sent a shiver down his neck, or maybe it was the lion's unblinking eyes drilling into him. "Our headlamps are blinding him," Nicole continued. "We're downwind, so he can't smell us either. And he can't hear us with the wind rattling the metal buildings. He's as confused and frightened as we are."

Simba was standing five metres away and did not look confused or frightened to Chase. He looked hungry and impossibly big. Nicole had told him the day before that Simba had been retired from the circus after mauling his trainer. If Simba was loose, the other lions might be loose as well. Three females and one immature male. Simba was twice as big as the young male. Right now, he looked like he was ready to pounce and tear them to shreds.

"On the count of three we'll turn our headlamps off," Nicole whispered. "While Simba's eyes adjust back to the dark, he'll be temporarily blinded and we'll run over to the next building."

Temporarily blinded? Chase thought. *How long does temporary last?*

Nicole was cradling the shotgun in her arms, which seemed like a better, and more permanent, solution to their lion problem than turning their headlamps off.

"...three," Nicole said.

What happened to one and two?

Chase switched his headlamp off a second behind Nicole. She grabbed his arm and pulled him to the left. Simba might have been temporarily blinded, but so were they. Chase couldn't see a thing. He allowed Nicole to drag him into the darkness.

They got to the wall of the second building and started inching along it with the wind at their backs. Chase hoped there weren't four lions in front of them.

06:00 AM

"What are you two doing here?" Richard Krupp shouted across the crowded gymnasium.

Cindy and Mark had not even checked in with the emergency worker at the table near the entrance when Richard Krupp, the number one news anchor in Saint Petersburg, Florida, barrelled his way to the front of the line.

"We're here for the basketball game," Mark said. "The weather slowed us down a bit. Who's winning?"

"I'm serious," Richard said.

"So am I." Mark glanced at the emblem on the wall of the dimly lit gym. "I never miss a Florida Hams game."

"I think it says *Rams*," Cindy said.

"Whatever. I never miss one of their games. Hey! What's with all the camp beds on the court?"

Cindy laughed.

Richard glowered. "You won't be cracking jokes in a couple hours when you get fired for not showing up for work."

"No worries," Mark said. "We resigned."

"Really."

"Yep."

"When?"

"A couple hours ago. We dropped by to let you know."

"I thought you said you came here for a basketball game."

"That too."

"Why'd you quit?"

"We had an epiphany."

"That's a big word, Mark."

"It was a big feeling, Richard."

"How'd you get here?"

"Drove."

"Station vehicle?"

"Private vehicle."

"But you still have the station camera. Give it to me and I'll take it back."

"No can do, Richard. I signed my life away for this thing. I'll return it personally."

"What about the video inside?"

"That too."

"I can take it from you."

"You can try." Mark smiled.

"Back off, both of you," Cindy said. "We're wet, we're tired and we're hungry." She looked at Richard. "And we are not giving you the video we shot."

Richard Krupp backed off, but not very far. He pulled his sat phone out and woke the station manager from a very sound sleep.

06:01AM

The walk to the end of the second barn seemed to take an hour, but according to Chase's watch it was less than five minutes. The luminous hands looked as bright as the sun in the pitch dark.

If I can see the hands, Simba can see the hands.

Chase slipped the watch off his wrist and stuffed it into his pocket, next to the tranquillizer gun.

He and Nicole found the door to the barn open, banging against the metal side. Chase went over the list of animals Nicole had shown him during his tour of the barn.

One brown bear. Three zebras. Four ostriches. Some parrots. And Hector...

Nicole started to go in, but Chase put his hand on her shoulder. "What are the chances of Hector sneaking back inside here to get away from the hurricane?"

Nicole stopped and frowned.

"So there is a chance that we are standing between a lion and a leopard," Chase continued. "Is there any gas inside the barn?"

Nicole shook her head.

"Maybe we should skip inspecting this barn and go directly to the barn where the Shack and Shop is parked. We don't have a lot of time before the generator runs dry."

"I need to check on the animals," Nicole said. "If I'd checked earlier, Gertrude might still be alive."

"What could you have done?"

"That's the problem," Nicole said. "I'll never know."

"We also don't *know* if Hector is inside here waiting for us. The door's wide open. Simba might be waiting inside for us as well."

"I doubt Simba slipped in front of us."

"No problem, then," Chase said. "We'll just walk into a dark barn with a bear, a few zebras, some ostriches and parrots, and maybe a killer leopard."

"I get your point," Nicole said with a slight smile. "It's not a smart move. Why don't you go get the gas and pick me up on your way back?"

"No. We're sticking together."

"Well, then *we* need to check on the animals."

Chase knew there was no point in arguing with her further, and they were wasting time.

"I'll go in first," Nicole said.

"Be my guest. You're the one with the shotgun."

Nicole took two steps into the barn and stopped. Chase followed and closed the door firmly so Simba couldn't sneak in behind them.

Providing he isn't already in the barn waiting to devour us.

Chase looked around nervously, slicing his headlamp back and forth through the darkness. Any second, he expected Hector to attack, or the bear to run out of the shadows and tear his head off.

They stepped deeper into the darkness. Chase glanced

down to see five centimetres of standing water covering the cement floor.

"How far are we from the coast?" Chase asked.

"What?"

"The surge," Chase said. "This water isn't just coming from the lake in back of your house. There's too much of it. I think we're getting floodwaters from two directions."

"The gulf is three miles away as the crow flies," Nicole said. "Maybe a little less."

She took a few more tentative steps forward. Something moved to their left. Something big.

"Bear," Nicole said.

Chase swung his headlamp in the direction of the movement. The bear was six metres away from them, pushing on the metal wall with his giant paw.

"We'll be OK," Nicole said calmly.

"I guess that depends on your definition of *OK*," Chase said.

06:07 AM

John and Tomás stepped into the gymnasium.

Organized, John thought. *And relatively calm. Probably about two hundred people.* He had been in a dozen shelters over the past two years, in gymnasiums, sports arenas and convention centres. When he and Tomás had first started following weather disasters, they had gone to shelters to solicit work but quickly learned that most of the people in shelters had nowhere else to go. Business owners and wealthy people stayed on their properties, checked into high-end hotels or left town altogether.

John and Tomás had entered the gym near the makeshift hospital area, where people were being treated for all sorts of weather injuries: lacerations, bruises, broken bones, heart attacks, nervous breakdowns... Nurses and doctors scurried between camp beds treating wounds, checking IV fluids, replacing ice packs and handing out medications.

A food and water station had been set up in the middle of the gym so everyone could get to it easily. It was crowded with people grabbing doughnuts, pizza, water and coffee.

Breakfast of champions.

Surrounding the station was a sea of camp beds and folding chairs filled with people wondering how long it would be before they could go home, assuming they still had homes. At their feet were boxes and bags of precious possessions they could not leave behind.

"Name, address, social security number," the emergency worker said, sliding two clipboards to them. "I'll need to see some identification too if you have it."

Their IDs were wet. They flipped open their swollen wallets and filled out the forms.

The emergency worker looked at the licences. "Whoa, a long way from home. What brings you to this neck of the woods?"

"Just passing through," John said.

"Bad timing."

"Tell me about it."

"Are either of you injured?"

"No. Just tired and wet."

"The locker room is open if you don't mind a cold shower. We're using generators for the lights and heat. Not enough juice to warm the water, but you'll find plenty of towels. I'm afraid there are no dry clothes. We brought in a big load, but they were all used up by the first wave."

"We'll be fine." John scanned the gym for Cindy and Mark, but he didn't see them.

"What's it like out there?" the emergency worker asked, as John and Tomás headed towards the locker room.

"Breezy," John said. "Wet."

06:09 AM

"Brutus," Nicole said. "He's been on the farm longer than I have."

"Has he ever mauled anyone?" Chase asked.

"No," Nicole answered. "I'm not saying that we should walk up and scratch his belly, but he's not aggressive."

"He's not in his cage either."

"Brutus is more afraid of us than we are of him."

"Speak for yourself."

Brutus didn't look the least bit afraid. He had managed to loosen the corner of one of the metal panels and was trying to tear it off the wall.

Why didn't he just walk through the open door? Chase thought. *Maybe Brutus isn't as bright as he is big.*

"Do you think he'll get that panel off?" Nicole asked.

Chase shook his head. "The panels are attached with long bolts screwed into treated posts. For the time being he's not going anywhere unless he knows how to open a door, which reminds me... Who opened the door?"

"I've been thinking about that. It had to be Hector."

"How does a leopard open a door?"

"It's a bar handle on the inside. All he'd have to do is jump up and give it a swipe with his paw."

"Lucky swipe," Chase said.

"Maybe not."

"What do you mean?"

"Hector is smarter than your average cat. He's a watcher. He's seen me come in and out through that door hundreds of times. I think he's been waiting for the opportunity."

Chase shined his headlamp at Hector's cage. The door was closed, but the chain-link fencing was hanging down. "How'd that happen?"

Nicole pointed at the bear cage. The door was gone. "I'd say that Brutus managed to tear his door off. Probably in a panic from the sound of the wind. He must have torn into the chain link on Hector's cage."

Chase glanced back at the door they'd walked through. "You think Hector's figured out how to open it from the outside?"

Nicole shook her head. "It's a twist knob on the outside. As long as Hector isn't in here, we're safe."

"Except for the bear," Chase said.

Rashawn broke off a flake of hay and threw it to the elephant. Pet picked the flake up with her trunk and tossed it over her back.

"Guess she's not hungry," Rashawn said.

Momma Rossi smiled. "She's been off her feed for days. We're just giving her food to keep her mind off her discomfort and the wind."

Pet yanked on the chains around her left front ankle and right rear ankle.

"Doesn't look like it's working," Rashawn said.

A far-off look clouded Momma Rossi's face.

"What's wrong?" Rashawn asked.

Momma Rossi didn't answer. Her distant expression deepened.

"Momma Rossi?"

Rashawn glanced over at Pet. The elephant was standing perfectly still for the first time since they'd stepped into the barn. She was staring at Momma Rossi as if she could see right through her.

"Are you OK, Momma Rossi?" Rashawn tried to stay calm, hoping the old woman wasn't having a stroke or something. "Can you hear me? Is anyone home? Earth to Momma—"

Momma Rossi blinked, then sighed, and said, "That was a strong one."

She looked a little wobbly, almost as if she might collapse.

Rashawn rushed forward and took her arm. "Is it your heart?"

"Oh no, dear. It wasn't my heart. It was a... Well, for lack of a better word, a premonition."

"You mean you had a vision?"

"*Vision* is too clear of a word. It's more like a flash of insight."

"What did you see?"

"It's too early to tell. It takes awhile for my old brain to catch up with the sight and define it."

"Are Chase and Nicole all right?"

"I think I'd know if they weren't. I didn't get the sense that they were in trouble. At least at this moment."

"What's that mean?"

"I'm not sure. I have a feeling that things are going to get worse before they get better. Much worse."

"Did you get any ... uh ... vibes about your son?"

"Marco?" Momma Rossi closed her eyes for a few seconds, then opened them again. "Nothing."

Rashawn took a deep breath. "What about my family?"

"Give me your hand."

Rashawn placed her hand in Momma Rossi's tiny one. The old woman fixed her dark eyes on Rashawn's for a full minute before saying anything.

"They are in a kitchen. All three of them. Your mother is asleep in a green leather chair with her feet up. She's holding a young boy in her lap."

"That's my daddy's green recliner! They must have dragged it into the kitchen from the living room. My momma and little brother nap in it all the time. What was my daddy doing?"

"Playing cards at a table."

"Solitaire! He always plays when he's stressed or thinking about something."

"I can't pick up people's thoughts," Momma Rossi said. "But I bet he's worrying about you."

"I bet he is too," Rashawn said. "It's kind of weird that you can see our kitchen without ever having been in it." She took her hand away. "But I'm glad they're OK."

"I'm glad too," Momma Rossi said. "Do you think your rice trick has fixed the phone?"

"Only one way to find out." Rashawn took the satellite phone out of the plastic bag and snapped in the battery. "Here goes nothing."

She pressed the button. The orange display came on.

"No signal," Rashawn said. "I don't know much about these things. I wonder if you have to point them at the sky for them to work."

She walked over to the small window by Pet's ring, holding the phone out in front of her.

"Two bars! Now if we only had someone to call. My daddy just has a regular phone, and no one's been able to get a mobile signal since yesterday."

"The towers were probably damaged because of Emily," Momma Rossi pointed out.

"Maybe I can hit the redial button and get ahold of Chase's dad," Rashawn said.

She didn't have to. The satellite phone rang.

06:19 AM

"What time is it?"

"Ummm ... I don't know," Rashawn said slowly. "I don't wear a watch."

"Sorry ... uh ... that's a game that Chase and I play. Is this Nicole?"

"Rashawn."

"Hi, Rashawn. This is John Masters. Can I speak to Chase?"

"He's not here."

"Where is he?"

"Out trying to find gas for the generator."

"You mean *outside*?"

"Yes, sir, with Nicole."

"It's going to be light soon, and it's not that cold. Why did he go outside in the middle of a hurricane to get gas?"

"Sun's not going to shine where we are even after it comes up."

"Are you in the basement of the Rossis' house?"

"We're in the barn. There *is* no house. Emily turned it into sticks."

"Which barn are you in?"

"The one with Pet."

"Pet?"

"The elephant."

"Did you say *elephant*?"

"Yeah, you know ... the one that's pregnant. She's supposed to have her baby any moment now. Be bad if she had it in the pitch dark. If there was a problem, we wouldn't be able to get the baby away from her. The wind has Pet all agitated, as you can probably imagine," Rashawn concluded matter-of-factly.

"It's hard to imagine any of this. I didn't know the Rossis had an elephant on their farm."

"It's a circus."

"Sounds like it. Is Marco there?"

"No, sir. We don't know where he is, and Nicole is sick over it. Chase said you might be able to find him."

"I can try. Do you know what kind of vehicle he's driving?"

"Just a minute... White Chevy Tahoe."

"What's the condition of the building you're in?"

"It's holding up, but the wind is slamming into the sides. There's water coming in on one end."

"The windward side?"

"I guess."

"How much water?"

"There's fifteen centimetres on the cement. Maybe a little more, but most of the barn is dry."

"What's your backup shelter?"

Rashawn hesitated. "What do you mean?"

"Where are you going to go if the building you're in starts to collapse?"

"I don't know."

"I'm sure Chase has thought of a backup."

"I'm sure he has. He's like some kind of storm superhero. He knows exactly what to do ... well, most of the time he does. None of us knows what to do about Hector."

"Who's Hector?"

"The leopard."

"As in big cat?"

"Big enough. And he killed Poco."

"Slow down, Rashawn. Who's Poco?"

"Momma Rossi's monkey."

"Momma Rossi?"

"You don't know much about the farm, do you?"

"Apparently not."

"Momma Rossi is Marco's mom."

"And she has a monkey?"

"She *had* a monkey until Hector killed it."

"Is Momma Rossi there?"

"She's standing right here. You want to talk to her?"

"I guess I'd better, but before you hand the phone over to her, check the battery level."

"Hang on... It's in the red."

"I was afraid of that. There's a charger and spare battery in Chase's go bag."

"You mean his backpack?"

"Right."

"He dumped it after our school bus sank. He stuffed some things in those big pockets he has on his trousers, but I don't know what they were."

"How long has he been gone?"

"I can't say exactly. Maybe a half an hour. This is my first time on this farm. Chase said something about a shack and a shop? I don't know how far they are from here."

"It can't be far. You be careful, Rashawn. Let me talk to Mrs Rossi."

"You be careful too, Mr Masters. Nice talking to you."

06:23 AM

A terrible scream rose above the clattering wind. Chase's knees nearly buckled at the sound.

"What—?"

"Sulfur-crested cockatoo," Nicole said. "Nothing to worry – watch out!" She tackled Chase. A charging ostrich missed them by centimetres, then hit the wall behind them with a loud bang.

Nicole was up on her feet and running back to the door before Chase could piece together what had happened. He checked on Brutus, making sure the bear was still worrying the metal panel, before getting to his feet and following her.

The hundred-kilo ostrich was thrashing on the cement floor, trying to get up, which was not going to happen with two broken legs.

"I hate this hurricane!" Nicole shouted bitterly as she dodged the bird's flailing feet.

With tears running down her face, she pointed the shotgun at the ostrich's head and pulled the trigger. The bird continued to thrash for several seconds, then stopped. Nicole walked outside.

Chase found her leaning against the wall, sobbing. The shotgun was on the ground at her feet. He picked it up and waited.

Nicole wiped her tears on her sleeve. "You were right," she said.

"About what?"

"About the animals. There's nothing we can do to help them in the dark. We need to get the gas and go back to the circus barn. The only animal we can help at this point is Pet."

"Why don't you go back to the barn?" Chase said. "I can get the gas on my own."

Nicole took the shotgun. She ejected the spent shell and jacked a fresh one into the breech. "Not with Simba and Hector running around, you can't. And who knows what else has escaped. We have four other lions besides Simba, you know."

"Yeah, I know," Chase said. "You think they're out too?"

"They were in the same barn as Simba."

Just the mention of Simba's name sent a chill down Chase's back.

"Gertrude – the giraffe – she was in that barn too," Nicole continued. "At fourteen feet, the only way she could have gotten out is if the big door was open."

"Or if the building collapsed," Chase added. He looked up at the sky. "Eventually the storm's going to pass. I think the winds have already died down."

The diving board from the Rossis' swimming pool tumbled through the open area before them and disappeared into the dark.

Nicole grinned. "You were saying?"

"I didn't say the winds had stopped," Chase said. "What do you usually do with escaped man-eaters?"

"They aren't man-eaters, but they are potentially dangerous. We've had a few escapes inside the barn, but they've never gotten outside the barn. The important thing now is containment."

"We're way past containment." Chase looked out at the Rossis' land. "We're in out-of-control."

06:24 AM

John found Cindy and Mark sitting on a camp bed with towels around their necks, drinking coffee and eating doughnuts. Mark had the precious TV station camera in his lap.

"How's the truck?" Mark asked.

"Beyond our ability to repair without new parts. We were lucky to have gotten this far."

"Did you try to reach Chase again?" Cindy asked.

John nodded. "His phone's working, but he didn't answer. A girl picked up, Rashawn. She was on the bus with them. I spoke to Marco's mother too, but only for a minute or two. The phone battery was going dead, but it sounds like there are some other problems on the farm."

John went on to explain what Rashawn and Mrs Rossi had told him. Cindy and Mark stared at him in complete silence.

Mark shook his head. "I'm sorry," he said slowly. "I don't understand. You mean like an African leopard, spotted, with fangs and claws?"

"It could be an Asian leopard," Cindy said. "They have them too, although not as many as they have in Africa."

Mark looked at Cindy. "Thanks, Mother Nature." He turned to John. "There's a leopard running around this farm your son is on, and it's carrying a dead monkey in its mouth?"

"That's right."

"And your son is running around looking for gas so that the elephant that lives on this so-called farm doesn't have to give birth in the dark?"

John nodded. "That about sums it up. Except Marco was out looking for the kids and didn't make it back home. I promised his mother I'd try to find him."

"Does he know that he doesn't have a home?" Cindy asked.

"I doubt it. Mrs Rossi said he left before the wind took it down. She barely made it out herself before it collapsed. I have to get back to the farm. Tomás is trying to find someone to lend us a vehicle."

"You really think someone is going to give you their wheels to drive around in a hurricane?" Mark asked.

"We'll pay them of course," John said.

"Pay for what?" Richard Krupp appeared as if out of nowhere. "Aren't you that construction guy Cindy was interviewing on my news show?"

John turned to the news anchor. He was shorter and thinner than he looked on television. "I'm that guy," he said.

"Did you drive Cindy and Mark here?"

"My partner Tomás and I did."

"Why?"

"We were headed in the same direction. How did *you* get here?"

"A television van. We would have made it all the way to

Palm Breeze if we hadn't been turned back at the roadblock. I live in Palm Breeze. My wife's the headteacher at Palm Breeze Middle School."

Cindy rolled her eyes. "What do you want now, Richard?"

"The video you shot on the way here, for one." Richard looked at Mark. "And the camera on your lap. I just got off the phone with your boss."

"He's your boss too," Mark said.

"Whatever. He was surprised to hear you two had quit, but he wasn't upset. He already has people in mind to take your places. I think his exact words were: 'No big deal. There's a dynamite reporter up in Tallahassee who wants to come south. And cameramen are a dime a dozen.'"

"Ouch," Mark said.

"He also told me to get the camera and video. And before you say no, I've talked with the police here at the shelter." Richard tilted his head. Two uniformed police officers stood six metres behind him, staring at them. "They'd be happy to take the camera away from you if you want to play it that way."

"We haven't officially resigned yet," Cindy said.

"Doesn't matter. The station wants the camera and video until you work this out *officially*. Can't blame them. The camera is worth a lot of money."

Cindy looked at her watch. "Technically we aren't even late for work ... yet."

"Technically you've violated policy by using station equipment without authorization. Listen, we can do it the easy way or the hard way. It's up to you."

The officers took a step forward as if on cue.

"Can we borrow your television van?" John asked.

"What?" Richard said.

"We need it," John said. "Our vehicle is out of commission."

Richard smiled at Cindy and Mark. "Lucky you two made it this far safely. Your driver's nuts."

John returned the smile. "Didn't you say your wife is the headteacher at Palm Breeze Middle School?"

"What does that have to do with your needing my news van?"

John glanced at the officers, then lowered his voice. "You might want to have your guys back off before I answer that question. And don't worry, Mark isn't going to run out into Hurricane Emily with your camera."

Richard thought about it for a second, then turned around and held up his hand to keep the officers at bay. "What's this all about?" he asked quietly. "And make it quick. I have to do a stand-up for the morning news in a few minutes."

"When's the last time you talked to your wife?" John asked.

"Yesterday afternoon just before school got out. She was checking on Hurricane Emily. Why?"

"Where did you tell her Emily was going to hit?"

"Saint Pete. That's where we thought it was going to land at the time. Then the power went out, and we lost phone service, and I was unable to reach her. What does this have to do with—"

"She put the kids on the bus," John interrupted.

"*Two* buses," Richard said. "Most of the kids at the school were picked up and driven home by their parents, or driven out of town ahead of the storm."

"Well, *one* bus didn't make it," John said. "It sank in a lake with three kids and the bus driver."

Richard turned pale. "I didn't hear anything about this, and we've been monitoring police and emergency bands all night. How do you know?"

"Because my son was one of the three kids on that bus when it sank. Your wife should have never put them on that bus, but she's not the one I blame. Her husband, the number one news anchor in Saint Pete, told her the hurricane of the century was not going to hit Palm Breeze."

"Is your son OK?"

"He didn't drown, if that's what you mean, but the driver did."

"The driver's dead?"

John nodded.

Richard gave a cheery wave to the police officers. "We're good here," he said. "Everything is resolved. It was just a misunderstanding. Thanks."

The two officers shrugged and walked away. Richard sat down on the edge of the camp bed. "Are the kids here?"

"No. Chase and the two girls made their way from the lake to the Rossi farm."

"The circus Rossis?"

"You know them?"

"Palm Breeze isn't that big," Richard said. "And the Rossis are kind of . . . well, unusual. Have you told Marco?"

"No. I talked to one of the girls and Marco's mother on my sat phone. Their house is gone."

Richard shook his head. "So, where are they now?"

"Holed up in a barn with a pregnant elephant and a leopard on the loose," Cindy said.

"We did a report on that cat," Richard said slowly. "Animal control wanted to euthanize it, but Marco stepped in and said he would take it. That's one dangerous creature on the loose."

"I'm aware of that," John said. "Listen, I know that you and your wife didn't mean to cause any harm, but you both made a terrible mistake. A man's dead. We need to get to the Rossis' before anyone else gets killed or injured, and we need your van to do it."

"All right," Richard said. "But my crew and I are going with you."

Cindy shook her head. "Sorry, Richard. No room. This is Mark's and my story. After what we've gone through, we're not about to give it to you. With John, Tomás and the two of us that's almost a full boat."

"There's room in the van for one more, and it's my van," Richard said quietly. "I'm going with you."

John shrugged.

"The roadblocks are still up," Richard said. "They aren't even letting FEMA through. Do you have any idea how you're going to get to the Rossis' farm?"

"I know where *not* to go," John said.

"We should ask Marco," Richard said. "The Rossis have been in this area for decades. At one time they owned a big chunk of the county."

"If we could get him on the phone, I would," John said.

Richard looked confused. "I guess you didn't understand when I asked if you had *told* Marco. He's here."

"At the shelter?"

"I saw him twenty minutes ago on the far side of the gym carrying a bottle of water and a slice of pizza. I didn't talk to him, but it was definitely Marco. The Rossis are the only little people around here. I assumed he was here with his whole family."

"I'll find him," John said, starting across the gym.

"I guess I'd better tell my crew there's been a change of plans," Richard said, and walked off.

"Was Richard actually acting like a human being for a second?" Mark asked.

"Surprised me too," Cindy said.

"Does this mean we still have jobs?"

"It might," Cindy answered. "But I'm not feeling like much of a reporter at the moment. I can't believe I didn't put together the connection between Richard's wife and Chase's school bus."

"You got bested by a builder."

"I told you there was more to John Masters than meets the eye."

"I still think he's a little crazy."

"You probably would be too if you'd been struck by lightning."

06:33AM

The sat phone rang. Rashawn rushed over to grab it from the window sill and answered it before the second ring. Momma Rossi was curled up, asleep on two bales of hay Rashawn had dragged over from the stack.

"Hello?" she said quietly.

"John Masters. Rashawn?"

"Yes, sir."

"Can I speak to Mrs Rossi?"

"She's taking a nap, but I can wake her."

"Hang on... Marco says to let her sleep."

"You found Mr Rossi?"

"He's standing right next to me and he's fine."

Rashawn smiled. "Nicole will be so relieved! I just hope my family is OK too. I haven't heard from them since this whole thing started."

"What's your last name? We're at a shelter. We can check to see if they're here."

"I think they're home," Rashawn said, recalling Momma Rossi's vision. "But it would be good if you could check. Our last name is Stone."

John said something to someone, then got back on the line.

"Are Chase and Nicole back?"

Rashawn's smile faded. "Not yet. And I'm worried."

"Moving around in this kind of weather is not like moving around in regular weather."

"I know. It took us nearly twelve hours to go five miles last night, but I'm still worried."

"Hang on a second," John said. After a moment he got back on. "Your family's not here. So you're probably right. They're at home riding the storm out."

"I hope so," Rashawn said.

"How's the barn holding up?"

"It's in one piece, but there's still water coming in on the one side I told you about."

"No structural damage?"

"Nothing I can see."

"Remind Chase to check the barn out when he comes back. He'll know what to look for."

"I'm sure he will. Before they left he went over the barn with a fine-tooth comb."

"We're going to try to get to you. I'm not sure if we'll succeed, but we'll give it our best shot."

"That's all anyone can do," Rashawn said. "Don't kill yourself trying to get here. That won't do anyone any good."

John laughed.

"What's so funny?"

"Nothing really. It's just something I've told Chase a hundred times. You're no good to anybody if you're dead ... including yourself. I hope to meet you soon in person, Rashawn. Have Chase call me when he gets back. And again, don't worry. He'll be fine. I've got to go now."

Rashawn put the phone back on the window sill and

looked over at Momma Rossi. She was still curled up on the hay bales sound asleep. Pet was swaying back and forth looking like a grey balloon ready to burst. The wind was still battering the barn but it didn't seem nearly as noisy to Rashawn.

"Maybe I'm getting used to the racket, or maybe I'm going deaf," she said to the elephant.

She walked past the light of Pet's ring into the dark.

I'll just poke my head outside and see what I can see.

Halfway to the door something bumped into her leg. She screamed. Pet trumpeted. Momma Rossi woke up.

"What is it, dear?"

Rashawn shined her flashlight at the ground. "It's a little green monkey no bigger than a squirrel."

"Poco!"

Momma Rossi ran over and gently scooped Poco up. The tiny monkey fit easily into the palms of her small hands.

"He's bleeding," Rashawn said.

"I see that. Let's get him to the ring."

In the light, they discovered that Poco's injuries were worse than they had first appeared. His right arm was broken and there was a gash on his back.

"There's a first aid kit hanging on the wall below the window," Momma Rossi said.

Rashawn ran over and got it.

"We're going to have to set his arm," Momma Rossi said. "Then we'll have to suture the wound and warm him up so he doesn't go into shock."

"Do you think he'll be OK?"

"I don't know. He's had a terrible night."

06:38 AM

Chase and Nicole stood outside the third barn, or what was left of it. Two of its walls had collapsed and the roof was completely gone. There was no sign of the other lions. They had either escaped or were stuck under one of the walls. Chase hoped it was the latter.

"It's possible they're OK under there," he said. "There's a lot of hollow space. The side wall went down first, then the windward wall fell on top of it, forming a sort of a wind foil. See the angle?"

Nicole nodded.

"That might have protected them," Chase said.

Nicole pointed at the cage that had held Simba. The door was gone. "There's no doubt about how Simba got out."

"I hope he found another place to crawl into to get out of the rain," Chase said.

"He doesn't seem to be following us at the moment."

"You mean stalking us."

"I guess," Nicole said.

The wind had dropped off dramatically, but it was still raining hard, which meant the water was still rising. Chase was also worried about the barn where the Shack & Shop was parked. It might have collapsed too. He pulled his watch out of his pocket, surprised to see that they had been gone almost forty-five minutes.

Chase slipped the watch back on to his wrist, wincing at the pain in his shoulder.

"You OK?" Nicole asked.

"Yeah. My shoulder hurts a little in certain positions."

She gave him a doubtful look. "Like when you put your watch on?"

"I'll be fine. We need to keep moving. We've already been gone too long."

Nicole nodded and started towards the last barn. The rain pummelled them so hard they had to keep their heads down to breathe. The closer they got to the last barn, the deeper the water became. By the time they reached the door, the water was up to their knees.

"The barn's completely flooded," Nicole said.

"But it's still standing," Chase said. "Do lions like water?"

"No."

"Good. Let's get the gas and get out of here."

They waded inside, bumping debris away with their knees. Chase shined his light along the side of the fifth-wheel that he and his father had nicknamed the Shack. Water lapped against the bottom of the door.

"There's water inside," he said. "It's ruined." He looked at the side of the semi-trailer they called the Shop. It sat higher than the fifth-wheel, so the water hadn't reached its threshold yet.

"We're going to have to move the Shop to higher ground," Chase said.

"You're kidding, right?"

"I'm serious."

"I thought we were in a hurry to get the gas back to the circus barn."

"We are. But along with the gas there's a hundred thousand dollars of tools and building supplies in there. If we leave the trailer here, we can kiss the contents goodbye."

"Do you know how to drive an eighteen-wheeler?" Nicole asked.

"I know how to start it, put it into gear, and step on the gas," Chase answered.

"And do you also know how to back one up?"

Tomás had pulled the semi into the barn tractor-first so they could get to the tools and supplies in the trailer easily.

"How hard can it be?" Chase said.

"A lot harder than going forward," Nicole said. "I'll drive."

"Now you're kidding?" Chase said.

"I'm a circus girl. I've been driving big rigs around the farm since I was eight."

"You couldn't even reach the pedals at eight," Chase protested.

"I was as tall as my father when I was eight," Nicole shot back.

"No offence," Chase said. "But your father isn't very tall."

"Exactly," Nicole said. "Neither is my mother or my grandmother. Which means every truck on the circus is equipped with pedal extenders, which is how I was able to drive a semi when I was eight years old. I *know* how to back a semi."

"OK," Chase said. "You win. You're driving."

"We may not get very far with this much water on the ground," Nicole said.

"It can't be worse than leaving the rig where it is," Chase said. "I'll stand behind the trailer and flip on the headlamp's emergency flasher if you're going to slam into something. Are you sure you can do this?"

"I think so," Nicole answered, sounding a little less confident than she had a minute earlier. "I'll be OK if I can see your headlamp in the side mirror."

"The spare key's above the visor. Good luck."

They waded in opposite directions.

As Chase passed the fifth-wheel he wondered if there was anything he should grab before water got to it. He and his father had lived inside the Shack for two years. He couldn't think of one thing inside that could not be easily replaced at a Walmart. There were no photographs of his mother or sister, no mementos from the house they'd lived in before the accident, nothing from their past. Chase's father had told him that everything was in storage to protect it, but Chase wasn't convinced. He and his father rarely talked about their life before they started running towards storms.

It's as if we never had another life. As if we've always been on the—

His foot connected with something underwater and he fell forward with a splash. He got up choking on oily and gritty floodwater, one of his father's favourite sayings echoing in his head: *In an emergency you must focus. The moment you leave the moment could be the last moment of your life.*

Chase wiped away the water and grime from his face, along with any thoughts of his past.

Focus.

Nicole pulled open the heavy driver's door and clambered into the cab. It smelled like sweat, coffee and fast food. She loved the scent. It reminded her of travelling with the circus – something she rarely got to do any more because of school. She wondered if her mother even knew about Hurricane Emily. Probably not. With the show in Mexico, her mother was juggling a thousand tasks, made harder by being in a foreign country. She rarely called home when she was away because Nicole's father was notorious for misplacing his mobile phone, running the battery dry or turning the ringer off.

She pulled the visor down and the keys dropped into her lap. She made sure the semi was in park before putting the key into the ignition. The powerful diesel engine roared to life. She put on her seat belt, then adjusted the seat and side mirrors as the engine warmed.

Chase's headlamp looked like it was a mile away behind her.

"Here we go," she said. "Nice and slow. I don't want to run over my boyfriend…"

Nicole blushed.

I haven't even known Chase for forty-eight hours. We're not boyfriend-girlfriend.

"Not yet," she said with a slight smile. "But I better slow that idea down too."

She took a deep breath, let it out, then eased the gear into reverse.

06:47 AM

"Marco thinks he knows a way to get us to the farm," John said.

Cindy, Mark, Richard and Tomás were gathered next to the camp bed.

"I was going to try it myself," Marco said. "But I had a blowout. The police picked me up while I was changing the tyre. I didn't want to go with them, but they threatened to slap the cuffs on me, so here I am. Frustrating. And now you tell me Hector's out. It can't get worse than that. He's the most dangerous animal we have on the farm."

"I did a report on him," Richard said.

"I saw it," Marco said. "But you don't know half the story about that cat. I should have never left my mother in the house by herself. I should have stayed on the farm and made sure the animals were secure."

"We need to get moving," John said.

"If we all try to leave at once, the police will try to stop us," Marco said. He looked at Richard. "Where's your van parked?"

"Out front."

"You need to pull it around back. There's an exit in the locker room the police aren't monitoring."

John held his hand out for the keys. "I'll drive."

Richard shook his head. "That's against company policy."

"I'm not driving," Cindy said.

"Neither am I," Mark said. "Not in this weather."

"I guess you'll have to take the wheel, Richard," Cindy said. "Have you ever driven in a hurricane?"

Richard tossed the keys to John. "If something happens, I was driving."

"Fine," John said, and gave the keys to Tomás.

They headed towards the locker room.

"You think he'll be OK?" Rashawn asked.

Momma Rossi had managed to set Poco's arm with a makeshift splint made out of a tongue depressor. Then she'd laid him in a nest of hay and covered him with a dry towel to keep him warm.

"It's a miracle he's alive," Momma Rossi said. "Not many animals survive a leopard attack."

"When I saw him hanging all limp from that leopard's mouth last night, I thought for sure he was dead. I didn't even know what kind of farm this was. I thought I was seeing things."

"I wonder how Hector got out of his cage," Momma Rossi said.

"I hear you. I wonder how Poco got..." Rashawn looked out into the darkness. "The window."

"What are you talking about?"

"The broken window in the bunkhouse," Rashawn said, trying to keep her voice from shaking. "It's a good four feet off the ground. How'd Poco get through it with his arm all busted up?"

"He couldn't have," Momma Rossi said.

"Unless that leopard jumped through the window with him in his mouth," Rashawn said.

They both stared beyond the light with the same question: was there a leopard staring back at them?

06:51 AM

Chase was walking back and forth several metres behind the semi, checking the clearance as Nicole reversed the rig in slow motion, when a strange feeling crept up the back of his neck. At first he ignored it, thinking it was cold rain running under his shirt collar, but the feeling persisted. He turned his head and froze. Simba was standing six metres behind him in water up to his golden belly.

Simba bared his yellowed teeth and roared.

I'm going to die, Chase thought. Slowly he reached up and switched off his headlamp, but he was far from invisible in the glow of the rig's tail lights. Nicole continued to back the truck towards him. If he stayed put, the semi would run him over. If he moved, Simba would attack him.

I thought Nicole said cats don't like the water!

Simba looked as comfortable as a shark.

Why is Nicole still backing up? She can't see my headlamp. Why doesn't she stop? Why. . .

Chase realized that if Nicole stopped, the rig might lose momentum and get mired in the soft ground. He could see Simba clearly thanks to the tail lights that were now only four feet away. His body was shouting RUN. But his brain was telling him to FREEZE.

Simba is just waiting for me to move.

Three feet.

Nicole continued to back up the truck at a steady rate. Chase slowly looked away from Simba and focused on the back of the trailer.

Two feet.

He put his arms out and laid his hands flat against the trailer doors.

One foot.

He felt the powerful truck push him over backwards. He planted his feet and let the truck take him down into the water, which came nearly up to the undercarriage. He tried not to think of Simba's fangs sinking into his neck.

Concentrate. Keep your legs between the tyres. Keep your head above the water.

He stretched his hands above his chest and let them play along the undercarriage until he found a strut he could grab. He felt his heels making furrows in the soft ground beneath the water as he was dragged along. A searing pain shot through his injured shoulder.

The trailer began to veer to the right.

She's cleared the barn. She's turning the rig so we have a straight shot to the circus barn. She's wondering where I am. Don't stop, Nicole! Keep cranking it!

The trailer stopped for a moment, then started forward. Chase managed to spin around so his heels were dragging again. The truck started to slow. Chase let go of the strut he'd been clinging to and rolled to his right, narrowly clearing the rear tyres. He stumbled to his feet, wiping the water from his eyes in time to see the cab lights blink on as Nicole opened the door.

He splashed forward. "Stay in the cab!"

"What?"

"Simba!"

Nicole turned her headlamp on.

Chase glanced behind him and saw Simba come around the end of the trailer.

"You'll make it!" Nicole shouted.

Not if I trip or faint. Not if you slam the door.

Simba had cut the distance between them by half.

I'm not going to make it.

Nicole jumped out of the cab with the shotgun. She put it to her shoulder and pulled the trigger. A red flame came out of the barrel, followed by a deafening *BOOM*.

Chase glanced back at Simba. The lion was standing still, staring past him at Nicole. Chase threw himself into the cab, and Nicole clambered in next to him, slamming the door closed. A second later Simba's head appeared outside the passenger window. Nicole shrank back, practically landing in Chase's lap.

Simba roared, then his head disappeared.

Chase and Nicole stared at the window for a full minute before realizing they were both sitting in the passenger seat holding each other. Nicole flushed, then climbed back into the driver's seat.

"That was scary," she said.

Chase wondered if she was talking about them holding each other or the lion.

"It's still scary," he said. "Can he get in here?"

"No."

"Did you wound him?"

Nicole shook her head. "I fired into the water at his

225

feet, or I guess his paws. It was enough to make him ...
pause."

"Funny."

"Where are your shoes?"

Chase looked down at his feet. Not only had he lost his
shoes, but his socks had been pulled off too. "I guess they
came off under the truck."

Nicole smiled. "Wanna try to find them?"

Chase smiled back. "Nah, I'm good."

Nicole released the brake and put the truck into gear.

06:59 AM

Tomás put the van into drive and pulled out of the high school car park. John was in the passenger seat with Marco sitting next to him. Cindy, Mark and Richard were in the back, wedged between expensive television equipment.

Richard looked at Cindy and Mark. "Now that we're partners, let's take a look at that hurricane footage."

"Partners?" Mark asked.

Richard flashed his best anchorman smile. "OK. How about colleagues, then? We still work for the same station."

"You told the boss that we resigned," Cindy pointed out.

"I can smooth out that misunderstanding."

"Maybe we don't want it smoothed out," Mark said.

"Whatever," Richard said. "We have nothing else to do. Let's see what you have."

Cindy nodded at Mark. He pulled a memory card out of his pocket and popped it into a laptop.

"How is it out there?" Cindy called up to John.

"Wet. Treacherous. But the rain has died down. I'd guess it's seventy miles an hour sustained, which puts Emily back into the tropical storm category. The bad news is that there's a lot of water on the road. The good news, at least for us, is that it's washing the lighter debris out of our way."

"This hurricane footage is fantastic!" Richard said. "We need to get it on the air right away."

"We'd have to stop to position the satellite dish," Mark said.

"Someplace with shelter," Cindy added. "This wind would rip the dish off the van."

"Turn right up ahead," Marco said.

"And pull over," Richard added.

"No," John said. "We're not here to get video on the air for the morning news. We have to get to the Rossis' farm."

Tomás turned the van right and ran over several small palmetto bushes.

"Is this even a road?" Richard said.

"Used to be," Marco answered. "They closed it down years ago after the highway opened. If we can get through, it will take us into Palm Breeze, and there are several ways to get to the farm from there."

"And if we can't?" Cindy asked.

"Then it's back to the shelter," John said. "This is our last shot."

07:02 AM

Chase looked out at the passenger side mirror. There was no sign of Simba, but that didn't mean the lion wasn't trotting behind the rig in the dark.

They had just reached the second barn, and Chase could see that another challenge was still ahead. To reach the circus barn they would have to drive across the water rushing between the two buildings.

"Stop here," he said.

"Why?"

"Just stop for a second."

Nicole stepped on the brake and took the truck out of gear. "What's the matter? We're almost there. It's only fifty yards away."

"It might as well be fifty miles away," Chase said. "Look at the water in front of us."

"I see it," Nicole said. "It doesn't look nearly as wide as it was before."

"But it's moving faster now and I'm guessing that's because it's deeper."

"I think we can make it across," Nicole said. "If we get bogged down, we'll still be closer to the barn."

"This rig is worth a lot of money. To say nothing about the stuff inside the trailer."

"What do you want to do?"

"I think we should get that gas out of the back and wade across. If we find that it's not too deep, we can get back in and drive across instead."

"You're barefoot," Nicole said.

"I'll have to be careful where I step."

"And Simba is out there."

"Believe me," Chase said, "I'd rather drive too. And if we could get the rig there, I might be able to hook up the two generators we have in back to the barn. We'd have power for a week. But if the truck gets stuck, we might lose everything inside."

Chase looked at his watch. They had been gone for more than an hour. He wondered if the generator in the barn was still working.

07:04 AM

Inside the circus barn, the lights flickered and then went out.

Pet trumpeted. Rashawn screamed.

Momma Rossi put her hand on Rashawn's arm and said, "Be calm, dear."

"Sorry," Rashawn said. "It's embarrassing but I'm kind of afraid of the dark. Add a leopard to that and I'm petrified."

"We don't know if Hector's out there," Momma Rossi said. "You said you closed the bunkhouse door when you came back into the barn."

"I did," Rashawn said. "But it was open the whole time Chase and I were in there. Hector could have slipped into the barn anytime."

"We've already been over this," Momma Rossi said. "You and Chase didn't see Hector in the bunkhouse."

Rashawn took a deep breath to calm herself. "No, ma'am, we didn't, but he could have gone through the door when we weren't looking."

"Right," Momma Rossi said. "But if he had, it means he was more interested in getting into the barn than he was in attacking you and Chase."

"I guess," Rashawn said.

"You're standing here. No scratches that I can see."

"It's dark," Rashawn said. "We can't see anything."

Momma Rossi laughed. "You know what I mean, Rashawn."

"What are we going to do now?"

"There's nothing we can do for Pet without light. So as a precaution, and it's just a precaution, I think we should head down to the cat cage. It's made to keep the cats in, but it will work just as well to keep a cat out. I'm going to let your arm go. Do you think you can find the flashlight?"

"I think so. I'm trying to remember where I saw it before the lights went out."

"Be careful not to stumble over Poco. And whatever you do, don't step into the ring with Pet."

"Are you afraid that ol' elephant might punch me out?"

"No, I'm afraid that she might kill you."

"You're not kidding, are you?" Rashawn said. "I guess it'd be a shame to be killed by a pregnant pachyderm after surviving the storm of the century."

07:06 AM

Chase and Nicole sloshed to the end of the trailer in water up to their calves. Nicole took the lead with the shotgun. Chase followed, keeping an eye out from behind, with his bare feet numbed by the cold water.

"Anything?" Nicole asked.

"Trust me," Chase said. "I'll scream if I see a lion."

"We're almost there."

Nicole stopped. Chase bumped into her. Neither of them laughed.

"I'm going to step out from the trailer and circle around for a wider view. Watch my back."

"Sure," Chase said, although he had no idea what he could do to protect her from a lion attack.

When they had climbed out of the truck, Chase had taken the tranquillizer pistol out of his pocket. Nicole had told him to put it back. She'd said that it would only work at close range. "Also, tranquillizer darts only work fast in the movies," she'd added. "In real life, it can take twenty minutes for an animal to go down."

Nicole slowly stepped around the trailer with the shotgun ready. She and Chase shined their headlamps back and forth through the darkness. Simba was not there.

"Let's get the gas and get out of here," Nicole said.

Chase released the latch, swung the door open and switched on the interior lights.

"Wow," Nicole said.

"Yeah," Chase agreed, looking at the well-organized workshop running almost the entire length of the trailer. He pointed at the far end. "That door past the workbench and tools leads to Tomás's apartment."

"But there's a sleeper in the truck."

"Not very comfortable as permanent sleeping quarters."

Chase climbed into the trailer and made his way to the generator while Nicole watched from the door. There were two five-gallon gas cans next to it. He picked them both up, but immediately dropped one as pain shot to his right shoulder.

I can't carry both of them, Chase thought. *And I can't let Nicole carry the other. She needs both her hands for the shotgun.*

He walked back to the door with one can.

Nicole stood on the ground with her elbows resting on the trailer floorboards. She looked as if she were about ready to fall asleep.

"I thought there were two cans," she said wearily.

"One will do. It'll keep us going for hours. We can come back and get the other one when it gets—"

Simba was airborne and flying right at him.

Chase dived down towards Nicole and pushed her to the side. Simba hit the shop floor three metres past him and slid. Chase rolled out of the trailer and managed to land on his feet. He caught the edge of the door and slammed it shut just as Simba turned around and started his second charge.

Chase jammed the locking bolt into place and stumbled backwards. His knees buckled. He sat down in fifteen centimetres of water, hyperventilating.

"Why did you knock me down?" Nicole asked indignantly.

Chase couldn't inhale enough air into his lungs to answer her. His heart was beating so hard he thought it was going to explode.

Simba hit the door from inside and roared. The door rattled but held.

Nicole jumped back from the trailer, then stared at Chase. "How did—"

Chase held his hand up for her to wait and slowly got to his feet. He took a couple of deep breaths. "I didn't knock you down for the fun of it. You missed the leaping lion act. It was pretty spectacular."

"What are you talking about?" Nicole said.

"I saw Simba leaping towards the trailer. I pushed you down and rolled out. I don't know how I got the door closed behind me. It all happened so fast. If you blinked, you would have missed it."

"Lucky you didn't blink," Nicole said.

Chase almost wished he had. The image of Simba flying over his head was going to haunt him for the rest of his life. "I blew it," he said. "The gas can." He looked at the trailer door. "I'm not going back in there to get it."

"You don't have to." Nicole reached under the trailer and picked up the can. "It must have fallen out when you jumped."

The trailer door rattled again. "What do you think he's doing in there?" Chase asked.

"Looking for a way out."

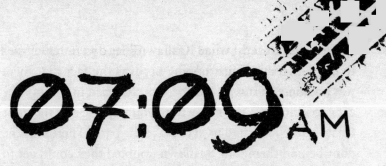

07:09 AM

Rashawn and Momma Rossi slowly made their way towards the big cat cage at the far end of the circus barn. Rashawn held the flashlight. Momma Rossi held Poco.

Eyeshine, Rashawn thought. *Yellow. I think.*

Rashawn's father had taught her a lot about *tapetum lucidum*, or eyeshine, in animals. One of her favourite things to do was drive around with him at night spotlighting wildlife. One of her father's responsibilities as refuge manager was to determine which animals lived on the refuge. Raccoon, dog and cat eyes reflected yellow light. Rashawn and her father could tell what an animal was by the height of its eyes off the ground and by how far apart they were.

She swept the flashlight back and forth. "I just hope that two yellow eyes don't shine back at me."

"What's that, dear?" Momma Rossi asked.

"Just talking to myself. I do that when I'm nervous."

"I'm nervous too," Momma Rossi admitted. "But I think we'll be fine. We're halfway there. If Hector was in the—"

Rashawn had stopped. The beam of her flashlight shined on two yellow eyes and a spotted face.

"Oh my," Momma Rossi whispered.

"What do we do?" Rashawn whispered back.

"No matter what your legs are telling you," Momma Rossi said firmly, "do not run."

That was exactly what Rashawn's legs were telling her to do. The only thing stopping her was the fact that there was nowhere to run to. Hector was crouched in front of the cat cage, blocking their way to the bunkhouse and the door Chase and Nicole had used to leave the barn. There was the door behind them, but Rashawn doubted they could get to it before the leopard got to them.

"I'll take the flashlight. You take Poco," Momma Rossi said.

"What's the plan?"

"I want you to head over to the ladder by the flier ring and climb up to the platform."

"Aren't leopards good climbers?" Rashawn asked.

"They are, but they have to have something to sink their claws into. The ladder is made out of metal. Do you think you can get up there holding Poco?"

"I think so."

"Good." Momma Rossi took the flashlight and gently handed Poco to her. "I'll shine the light on the ladder until you start up. Do you think you'll have a problem climbing in the dark?"

"I should be OK," Rashawn said. "If I run into a snag, I'll tell you and you can switch it on behind me."

"Oh, I won't be behind you, dear."

"Huh?"

"I'll stay down here and distract Hector while you get up to that platform."

"No way," Rashawn said.

"There's no time to debate," Momma Rossi said. "I'm too old to climb that ladder. I've been working with cats

238

since I was a little girl. I can save myself, but I don't think I can save all three of us. Now go!"

Rashawn went, but she didn't feel right about it. As soon as she grabbed the first rung, Momma Rossi swung the flashlight beam away. Climbing in the pitch dark with an injured monkey in the crook of her arm was nearly impossible. Three metres up Rashawn was sweating and out of breath. She paused and looked down – and what she saw nearly caused her to fall off the ladder. Hector was batting the flashlight around the floor like a cat torturing a mouse.

The beam went out.

"Momma Rossi?" Rashawn shouted. "Momma Rossi?"

There was no answer.

07:15 AM

"Stop here," John said.

Tomás pulled the van over to what might have been the kerb, though it was difficult to tell under half a metre of water. They had reached the town of Palm Breeze.

"I want to check something out," John said. "It will only take a minute." He got out of the van, and Tomás and Marco joined him.

"Let's see if we can beam some of this video to the station," Richard said.

"What do you think?" Mark asked Cindy.

"I guess it won't hurt," Cindy answered. "But I want to be on camera."

"We'll both do the stand-up," Richard said.

"Fine."

They started putting the gear together while Mark set up the satellite dish.

John, Tomás and Marco waded over to a building. John shined his flashlight on the sign.

"Palm Breeze Middle School," Marco said. "All my kids have gone here."

There was wind and water damage to the main building, but it was in pretty good shape compared to some of the other buildings they had passed driving through town. They wandered further into the school complex.

Marco pointed. "That's the cafetorium."

They walked over and John shined his flashlight through the window. "Dry as a bone," he said. "That's the strange thing about storm surge. You never know how the water is going to flow."

"And hindsight is perfect," Marco said.

"Yep," John agreed. "But I still think Dr Krupp should have kept the kids here rather than putting them on a bus. This cafeteria is a good two metres above the buildings in front."

"She'll figure it out when she gets back to school," Marco said.

Just then, Tomás's satellite phone rang, which was odd, because the only person who ever called him on it was John. He took it out of his coat pocket and answered. "*¿Qué pasa?*"

"Chase?" John asked.

Tomás shook his head gravely. "No."

"How about if we upload all your raw footage and let them edit it at the station?" Richard suggested.

"Here we go," Mark muttered to Cindy.

"I heard that," Richard said. "I'm not trying to steal anything from you. You'll get all of the credit. Our viewers want to know what happened during Hurricane Emily. We have an obligation to tell them. I'll make sure you get the video rights after we air it."

"Fine," Cindy said. "But we need to get moving. I don't know what they're off looking at, but when John's finished he'll want to get back on the road."

They climbed out of the back of the van.

"Palm Breeze Middle School," Richard said. "What's John looking at here?"

"Who knows," Cindy said. "At one point last night he and Tomás got down on their bellies to see how a road disintegrates in a Category Five hurricane."

"What's the matter with him?"

Cindy laughed. "John's a little different."

"Who was it?" John asked.

Tomás put the satellite phone back into his pocket, then launched into a long explanation in Spanglish.

"More bad news." John turned to Marco. "That was Tomás's brother."

"Arturo?"

John nodded. "He was calling from Mexico City. He drove ahead of the show to set things up for the next date. Unfortunately, the show didn't show up."

"Where are they?"

"He doesn't know exactly. No one is answering their mobile phones. He thinks they're outside a city called Puebla."

"How late are they?"

"Twenty-four hours."

"How far is Puebla from Mexico City?"

"It's only seventy miles, but that's not the problem. There's been an earthquake in Puebla. A big one. The city's a disaster area. And it gets worse." John glanced at Tomás. "Twenty-five miles east of Puebla is an active volcano called Popocatepetl. Tomás's family lives in a small village on the side of that mountain."

07:23 AM

"At least it's starting to get light out here," Nicole said.

"And the wind has dropped even more," Chase added. "We might just live through this storm."

"You had doubts?"

Chase smiled. "You didn't?"

They had just waded across the gap. The water in the deepest part had been up to their waists. The semi would never have made it across.

"After we get the generator filled, will you try to reach your dad?" Nicole asked.

"If the phone works," Chase answered, opening the door.

"Dark," Nicole said.

"I wonder how long they've been out of gas."

They stepped inside and closed the door behind them.

"Hello?" Nicole called.

The only thing they heard was Pet pulling on her chain.

"You think they're out looking for us?" Chase asked.

"Hector's in the barn!" Rashawn's warning echoed through the metal barn.

"Where?" Nicole shouted back.

"Don't know. I'm up on the flier platform. I don't know where Momma Rossi is either. I think she's hiding down there somewhere. She can't answer back because it'll give her hiding place away. At least I think that's the situation."

"Stay where you are," Nicole said.

Chase sliced his headlamp through the darkness. "How did Hector get in here?"

"I don't know, but we need to get the lights on. We need to find Momma Rossi," Nicole said.

"You think she's hiding like Rashawn said."

"I hope so. Let's get gas in the generator."

Chase hesitated. "Rashawn is safe up there," he said. "And Momma Rossi might be fine too. The weather isn't too bad. Maybe we should go back outside and wait for help. At least that way *we'll* be safe from Hector."

"No," Nicole said.

"I knew you were going to say that, but could you just think about it for a second?"

"I'll think about it in the bunkhouse," Nicole said.

"OK."

Chase was glad to see that the bunkhouse door was closed, which meant that Hector could not have sneaked inside. They slipped through, securing the door behind them, then hurried past the apartments to the shop.

"How long will the generator run?" Nicole asked as he filled the tank.

"Several hours. Depends on how many lights we turn on out in the barn. What's your plan?"

"Hector can't get up to the platform where Rashawn is hiding. She's safe. We have to find Momma Rossi and make sure she's OK, then we have to contain Hector."

Chase put the lid back on the tank, pulled the choke out,

and pushed the start button. The generator started purring. He turned to Nicole. "Could you be a little more specific about your plan?"

"I need to show you how to use that tranquillizer gun," Nicole said.

When the light over Pet's ring came on, Rashawn's first instinct was to climb down and join Chase and Nicole in the bunkhouse, but two things held her back. One was Hector. The other was Poco. She couldn't take him with her.

"Dodging a leopard while carrying a monkey is a very bad idea," she said firmly.

She couldn't leave Poco behind, though. There were no edges on the platform. He might roll off, and, with a broken arm, probably wouldn't survive the fall.

"Even if he's lucky enough to land in that catch net," she said, peering over the edge of the platform into the darkness, trying to find Momma Rossi's hiding spot, or a spotted leopard slinking in the shadows. She saw neither. The only thing moving below was Pet.

"Hector can't take that big ol' elephant down. But if she starts to have her baby, he might be able to..."

The satellite phone rang from its spot on the window sill.

No one could reach it.

"No answer?" Marco sounded sick with worry.

"No answer," John confirmed. "How soon do you think we'll be there?"

"Fifteen minutes if we don't run into a snag."

John stared through the windscreen. The rain had all but stopped, the wind had dropped, and the storm surge seemed to be receding, but the damage had already been done. Palm Breeze was ruined. It would take months, if not years, to recover from Hurricane Emily. There would be a lot of work.

"But not for us," John said.

"What?" Marco asked.

"Sorry," John said. "Just thinking out loud." He turned and looked at Cindy and Mark. "Do either of you speak Spanish?"

"Nope," Mark said.

"*Un poco,*" Cindy answered. "A little."

He hadn't yet told them about Tomás's conversation with his brother, Arturo. Or the change in plan.

07:30 AM

"Two darts," Nicole said. "Two chances."

"At fifty feet," Chase said.

"Or less. The darts aren't very accurate past fifty. Aim for a big muscle like the meaty part of his hind leg."

"How long does it take a leopard to cover fifty feet?"

"About as long as it took Simba to jump into the truck over your head."

"That's pretty quick."

"I can do this on my own," Nicole said. "I mean it, Chase. There's no reason for us both to risk our hides."

"I think I have a little more experience with big cat attacks than you do." Chase smiled. "Now."

"Ha," Nicole said. "Here's how we'll handle it. If I think he's going to pounce, I'll fire the shotgun. It will sound like a nuclear bomb inside the barn."

"Louder," Chase said. His ears were still ringing from when she shot the ostrich.

"Hopefully the sound will be enough to get him to back off."

"What if the nuclear explosion doesn't work?"

"I guess I'll have to shoot him."

"How many bullets do you have?"

"They're called shells," Nicole corrected. "And I have plenty."

248

The only gun Chase had ever fired was his father's nail gun.

They headed to the door with Nicole in the lead. Before they stepped into the barn, she unhooked a fire extinguisher from the wall and handed it to him.

"Good idea," he said. "We can put Hector out if he catches on fire."

"Funny."

"Seriously. What do you want me to do with this?"

"Big cats are cautious," Nicole said. "Simba backed off when I fired the shotgun because he'd never seen or heard one before. It probably wouldn't work a second time. I doubt Hector has seen a fire extinguisher in use. It'll stop him in his tracks."

"Once," Chase said.

Nicole nodded. "Once."

They stepped into the dark circus barn.

Rashawn heard the door open and saw Chase's and Nicole's headlamps.

"What are you doing?" she shouted. "I told you Hector's in here."

"Have you seen him since we left?" Nicole shouted back.

"No."

"Momma Rossi?"

"Not a sign."

"Stay where you are. We're going to find her. Keep your eyes open. If you see Hector, tell—"

"Don't worry," Rashawn said. "You'll be the first to know. By the way … Poco is alive. I have him up here with me."

"Maybe Hector isn't as aggressive as we think," Chase said hopefully.

"Don't count on it," Nicole said. "Momma Rossi? I hope you can hear me. Chase and I are coming to get you. I have the shotgun. Chase has the tranquillizer pistol."

"I hope Hector doesn't understand English," Rashawn shouted from her perch.

"Funny," Nicole said.

"I hope she's right," Chase said.

"Watch for eyeshine," Rashawn yelled. "Yellow eyes."

"Yellow eyes," Chase repeated. "I hope we don't see them."

"I hope we do," Nicole said. "Before they see us."

They moved away from the safety of the door. With each footstep into the huge barn Chase's anxiety grew. Every shadow looked like an enraged leopard.

"We'll stay in the middle of the barn so we have time to react," Nicole whispered. "I'll look to the right, you look to the left."

"What about our backs?" Chase asked.

"We'll go slow and make sure we don't walk past him."

This didn't seem like a very good plan to Chase, but he kept it to himself. "Do you have any idea where Momma Rossi might be hiding?"

"I'm pretty sure she isn't in a very secure place, or she would have answered us by now," Nicole said.

"Which means that Hector knows where we are because we're talking," Chase said.

"Hector knows where we are because we're *here*,"

Nicole said. "Our job is to distract him so he doesn't find Momma Rossi. We're the mice."

"Mice with guns," Chase said.

"And a fire extinguisher," Nicole added.

07:43AM

"This is as far as we go," John said.

The group was standing in front of the van, looking at water gushing through a wide gap where the road to the farm used to be.

"We're only a couple hundred yards from the front gate," Marco said. "The fence is down. Looks like if we follow this stream up on this side, we'll end up near the barns."

"That might save us from wading across," John said.

"Wait a second," Richard protested. "Are you suggesting that we head out on foot?"

"How else are we going to get to the farm?" John asked.

"There's a leopard running around."

"That's probably not all that's running around," Marco said.

"I appreciate your letting us use the van," John said. "You can wait here or you can drive back to the shelter." He looked at Cindy and Mark. "That goes for you two as well. You might want to stay here until it's safe."

"Safe?" Mark said. "Since when have you been worried about our safety?"

"Good point," Cindy said.

John grinned. "I know a lot about big storms, but I don't know anything about big cats – except that they scare me."

"John Masters scared?" Cindy said. "This I've got to see. I'm going with you."

"Me too," Mark said.

Richard sighed but joined them as they filed past the fence into the soggy paddock.

As they climbed, John tried Chase's phone again.

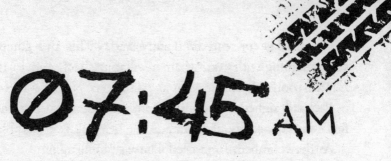

07:45 AM

"The sat phone!" Chase said.

"It's probably your dad," Rashawn shouted down. "He's called a couple of times."

The phone continued ringing. Chase wanted to run through Pet's ring and answer it, but that would surely draw Hector's attention. He and Nicole continued their slow walk down the centre of the barn.

"Where is he?" Chase asked.

"He's on his way here. And he found Nicole's dad."

"Thank goodness. Is he OK?" Nicole shouted.

"Yes. He's with Chase's dad."

The phone rang five more times, then went silent.

"Maybe we should wait for them," Chase said.

"On the way and getting here are two different things," Nicole said.

Chase knew she was right. They were midway down the centre of the long barn. Getting back to the bunkhouse door would take just as long as continuing on to the elephant ring. The only difference was that Hector wasn't behind them.

"Hopefully," Chase said.

"What?" Nicole asked.

"Nothing. Let's get this squeeze play over with."

"Guys?" Rashawn called out quietly.

Her change in tone stopped both Nicole and Chase in midstep. They swung their headlamps back and forth frantically, trying to see what she had seen. Nicole tracked her headlamp's beam with the shotgun. Chase held up the fire extinguisher in one hand and the tranquillizer pistol in the other while turning a complete three-sixty.

"Look at Pet," Nicole said.

She was standing perfectly still with her ears flared and her trunk in the air. "What's she doing?"

"She's looking up," Nicole answered.

They tilted their heads back. Ten metres above them was a series of catwalks, and slinking down the one directly above them was a leopard.

"How did he get up there?" Chase asked.

"He climbed up on these bales of hay," Momma Rossi said, rushing out from behind the stack. "That's why I couldn't answer you."

Hector was less than six metres away from Rashawn.

"Shoot him," Chase said.

"I can't," Nicole said. "He's too close to Rashawn."

"Use the ladder, Rashawn!" Chase shouted.

"No time," Momma Rossi said. "Jump!"

07:46 AM

"Are you kidding?" Rashawn shouted. "I can't even see the net in the dark!"

"Relax your body," Momma Rossi called up to her. "Land on your back."

"That's easy for you to say! Sorry, ma'am. I don't mean to be rude, but it's true!" Rashawn looked along the catwalk. Hector stalked towards her in the flickering headlamp lights.

She turned her back to him, got down on her knees on the edge of the platform and scooped Poco into her arms.

"This is stupid," she said, then rolled off the platform into the air.

Rashawn felt her stomach lurch into her throat. She couldn't tell if she was falling backwards, frontward or head first.

Hector leapt for the platform just as Rashawn dropped into the darkness below.

Momma Rossi reached the net before Rashawn's second bounce. "Roll!"

Rashawn was horrified to see that Hector was three metres away from her, trying to regain his footing. She rolled.

Nicole yanked the pistol from Chase's hand and ran under the net. He rushed forward to help Rashawn.

"Take Poco," Rashawn said.

He gently took the little monkey from her and stepped back as she did a backwards somersault off the net.

Pop.

Hector jumped up in the air, snarling.

Nicole came out from under the net. "I think I got the dart in."

"He's not too happy about it," Chase said.

"What dart?" Rashawn asked.

"Tranquillizer dart," Nicole explained.

Hector was trying to pull the dart from his hind leg with his teeth.

"His claws are snagged in the net," Rashawn said. "He's getting tangled up."

"Perfect," Momma Rossi said. "Let's put the cat in the bag before he gets untangled."

"What about the tranquillizer?" Rashawn asked.

"It takes a few minutes for it to take effect," Momma Rossi explained.

"Hector can do a lot of damage in a few seconds," Nicole added. She looked at Momma Rossi. "Do you want to fold it up like we do in the show?"

"Yes, but we'll have to do it a lot quicker," Momma Rossi said.

"What are you talking about?" Chase asked.

"Watch," Nicole said.

"Can I borrow your headlamp?" Momma Rossi asked.

Chase handed Poco to Rashawn and took the headlamp off. Once Momma Rossi had the headlamp over her grey hair, she and Nicole went to the far end of the catch net and took up positions on opposite corners.

"Ready?" Momma Rossi called out.

"Yes."

"On three. One . . . two . . . three!"

The end of the net dropped to the ground. They picked up their corners and hurried forward, pulling the net over the top of the struggling leopard. When they had the net halved, they brought it back, quartering it, and so on until the net was about a metre wide. They flipped the ends up and stood back, panting and admiring their work.

"Leopard in a cube," Rashawn said.

"He's already starting to slow down," Nicole said. "We should be able to unwrap him and haul him to the cat cage in a few minutes."

"How's Poco?" Momma Rossi asked.

"The thirty-foot drop doesn't seem to have hurt him," Rashawn said, placing Poco gently into his owner's small hands.

"How are *you*?" Nicole asked Rashawn.

"It wasn't nearly as bad as I thought it would be. But I don't want to do it again. Ever."

"I guess the drama's over," Momma Rossi said.

Chase looked at his watch. Had it really been just twenty-four hours since he'd stepped into Palm Breeze Middle School?

Pet trumpeted, and they all turned to her ring. The drama was not over.

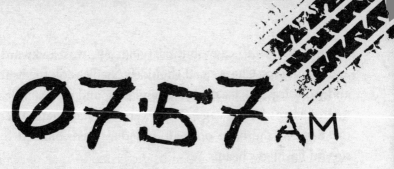

07:57 AM

Momma Rossi and Rashawn had rushed back to Pet's ring. Chase waited with Nicole to help her carry Hector to the cat cage. They started carefully peeling away the net.

"How will you know he's out?" Chase asked.

"Gentle prodding," Nicole said.

She found a broom and unscrewed the handle. Each time they pulled a layer off, she tapped Hector on the head and waited. If there was no reaction, they removed another layer.

"One layer left," Nicole said.

They could see Hector clearly now through the fine mesh. His eyes and mouth were open. Nicole touched him several times around his ears and muzzle, waiting for a reaction.

"I think he's down for the count," she said.

They pulled the last layer off. Hector didn't move.

"Now what?" Chase asked.

"We pick him up and carry him to the cage."

"Have you ever had one wake up while you're carrying it?"

"I've never picked up an immobilized cat before."

"That's encouraging."

"But I've seen it done a half a dozen times. I've never seen one wake up."

"Let's hope your perfect record isn't broken this morning."

Hector wasn't heavy, but carrying him was awkward, and painful for Chase's bad shoulder. Nicole took the head and front legs, Chase took the hind legs, and they shuffled their way to the big cage. They were halfway there when the door to the barn opened, and they were blinded by several flashlight beams.

Marco was the first to reach them.

"Dad!" Nicole shouted.

"I'd give you a hug, but I see you have your hands full. Is he dead?"

"Tranquillized."

John, Tomás, Cindy, Mark and Richard joined them.

"You OK?" John asked, staring at the leopard.

"We're fine," Chase said.

John grinned. "Guess you had an eventful night."

Chase returned the grin. "You might say that."

"Need a hand?"

"Yeah, my shoulder got banged up."

Tomás stepped forward and took Hector all by himself. "Where?"

"Follow me," Marco said.

John introduced everyone as they followed Tomás and Marco.

"We'll put him into one of the holding cages," Marco said, sliding open a guillotine door. "It will be easier to deal with him in here after the drug wears off."

Tomás laid Hector inside on a bed of straw.

"Is that you, Marco?" Momma Rossi hollered from the other end of the barn.

"Yes, Momma," he hollered back, then looked at Nicole.

"Sounds like your grandmother isn't any the worse for wear." He closed the door.

"You'd better hurry," Momma Rossi called. "I think your elephant is about ready to have her calf."

08:15 AM

Everyone had gathered around the elephant ring, waiting. Mark had started his camera rolling.

"It's kind of dark in here," John observed. "We have some spare generators in our trailer. Tomás and I could go and—"

"Not a good idea, Dad," Chase said.

"Why not? The weather's fine now."

"That's not the problem," Chase said. "There's a lion locked in the trailer."

"What?"

About halfway through his explanation about how Simba had got into the Shop, Pet gave birth.

The calf emerged with a whoosh of fluid, hitting the hay-covered floor hard enough to break the pinkish embryonic sac. The tiny calf started kicking immediately. Pet whipped around. For a moment it looked as if she was going to step on the calf, but then she nudged it gently with her foot. She reached down with her trunk and pulled away some of the sac from its wrinkled grey skin.

"I had no idea elephants had that much hair when they were born," Richard said.

"I didn't either," Cindy said.

The calf struggled to get up, but couldn't seem to get its long legs under its body.

"Is it a male or female?" Nicole asked.

"We won't be able to figure that out for a while," Marco answered.

"It looks strong," Rashawn said.

"And more important," Momma Rossi said, "Pet looks calm."

Marco nodded. "You're right. I haven't seen her this tranquil in weeks. She might just take care of this calf." He looked at Nicole. "What do you think we should name it?"

Nicole thought for a minute. "If it's a girl, I think we should call her Emily." She looked at Chase. "What should we call it if it's a boy?"

Chase smiled.

"Storm."

Ø8:42 AM

The calf finally managed to get to its feet and take a few wobbly steps.

Tomás had pulled several bales of hay around the ring for everyone to sit on. Chase shared a bale with his father. Rashawn sat with Tomás. Richard with Cindy. Nicole was squeezed between Marco and Momma Rossi. Mark was not sitting. He was darting around the ring, videotaping Pet and her calf.

"Tell me about your shoulder," Chase's father said.

Chase described their desperate run across the crumbling levee road the previous day.

His father shook his head in wonder. "We saw you."

"What are you talking about?"

"Your headlamps on the other end of the washed-out road. Of course we didn't know it was *you*. Mark caught it on video."

Chase rubbed his sore shoulder. "You wouldn't have been able to reach us. By then, the levee was gone."

His father nodded. "We'll have to get your shoulder checked out."

"I need to go to the dentist," Chase said, showing him his broken front tooth.

"We'll take care of that too," his father said, then looked across the ring at the calf.

Something wasn't right. His father wasn't asking the *questions*. After every storm there was a debriefing. They would go over the disaster in minute detail, point by point, discussing what they had done, and what they should have done. His father was exhausted – they were all exhausted – but that had never stopped him before.

"What's going on?" Chase asked.

His father looked at him with sad eyes. "Earthquake. A big one in Mexico. It's near Tomás's family. Nicole's mom and the circus are in the same area. They're off the grid. We can't reach them by phone."

"Does Nicole know?"

"I doubt that Marco has had time to tell her, or his mother."

The calf took some tentative steps underneath Pet. It put its tiny trunk over its head and opened its mouth.

"It's nursing," Nicole said happily.

"What are we going to do?" Chase asked quietly.

His father stood up. "We're going to Mexico."

ERUPTION

THE ONLY EASY DAY WAS YESTERDAY...

Chase Masters sat on a hay bale next to his father, John. His broken front tooth hurt, his shoulder ached, and he was exhausted but oddly content.

Not many people survive a Category Five hurricane, a bus sinking, a lion attack, a leopard capture, a torrential flood ... oh, and a four-metre alligator. *He shook his head in wonder.* And now we're heading to Mexico?

His father was staring at the elephant and its calf as they paced around the ring. Rashawn was scooping grain out of a fifty-gallon barrel. The Rossis were examining Momma Rossi's injured monkey, Poco. Cindy and Mark were reviewing the video footage Mark had just taken.

His father stood up and stretched. "I guess we'd better get moving. We have a lot of work to do before we head to the airport." *He looked at Chase.* "Nine thirty?"

Chase looked at his watch.

"Exactly," *Chase said.*

09:30 AM

Nicole, Marco and Momma Rossi started arguing.

"Let's give them some privacy, Chase," John Masters said quietly. "Cindy, Mark – you too."

"We'll go out back and shoot some B-roll of the damage," Cindy Stewart said.

"Always thinking of your next story!" Cindy's cameraman, Mark, rolled his eyes. "That's why you're in front of the camera, and I'm behind it. Where did Richard go? Doesn't the Number One News Anchor in Saint Petersburg, Florida, want to take over this story too? I can see it now: 'Hurricane Emily: A Journey Through the Aftermath with Richard Krupp'."

"He headed home to see if his family is OK," John said. "That's why he came with us to Palm Breeze."

"Yeah, yeah, and to steal our hurricane footage," Mark said as he followed Cindy out of the door.

"I guess I'll go to the bunkhouse to rustle up some food," Rashawn Stone said. "I worked up an appetite dodging that leopard. Can I borrow your satellite phone, Mr Masters? I'd like to see if I can get ahold of my daddy."

John handed her his phone.

"We'll meet you at the truck," Chase told Nicole as he and his father headed to the far door.

Nicole stopped arguing with her father and grandmother

just long enough to holler, "Remember Simba's locked in there!"

"Funny girl," Chase's father said. "I have no intention of getting the generators out of my truck until that lion is out of my rig. How big is he?"

"Big enough," Chase said, shuddering at the thought of seeing Simba again. He looked back at Nicole. The Rossis presented a strange sight. They stood at the edge of a dimly lit circus ring, an elephant with a newborn calf rattling her chains behind them. Nicole wasn't that tall, but she stood at least half a metre taller than her father and grandmother. Marco and Momma Rossi were little people.

Outside the circus barn, it looked as if the world had been tipped upside down and shaken out on to the ground. Tomás was walking around the paddocks, talking on his satellite phone while he picked through the storm debris.

It was a beautiful Florida morning – warm, a slight breeze, not a cloud in the sky. If it weren't for the debris scattered everywhere, it would be hard to believe that Hurricane Emily had swept through a few hours earlier, grinding the community of Palm Breeze into splinters.

"Looks like you picked the best building to take shelter in," Chase's father said.

The circus barn was the only building on the property with minimal damage.

"It was luck," Chase said.

"Fate," his father said.

"What's the difference?"

His father shrugged.

"What now?" Chase asked.

"Tomás is talking to Arturo in Mexico City. We'll meet him there tomorrow and head south."

"What about Nicole?"

"She's welcome to come if she can talk her dad into it, but I wouldn't hold my breath. We're not going down there on vacation. I can't guarantee her safety, and neither can you."

"Nicole can take care of herself. I wouldn't count her out. She's tough."

"After what you, Nicole and Rashawn lived through last night, I have no doubt about that." His father continued, "You don't have to come with us. I'm sure Mr Rossi would be happy to put you up. There's plenty to do here, and he could use your help."

"You want me to stay?"

"No, but you've been through a lot over the past twenty-four hours."

"So have you."

The all-night trip to reach the Rossis' farm had cost John Masters two trucks and nearly his life. On the way, his partner, Tomás, had got a call from his brother, Arturo, in Mexico City. Arturo had driven a load of animals south of the border for the Rossi Brothers' Circus, but the circus hadn't been there to meet him and he'd been unable to reach them by phone. Arturo thought the show was stranded in the mountains outside of Puebla, close to the village where Tomás's wife and children lived. While Emily had been smashing Palm Breeze, a 7.5 magnitude earthquake had been crushing Puebla.

"It's your call," Chase's father said.

Chase wanted to say that he'd go if Nicole went, but whether she went or not was out of his control and, he had to admit, out of the question. He was going to Mexico.

"I'm in."

His father nodded.

"What about the reporters?"

"They're going too."

"Why?"

His father avoided Chase's gaze and looked towards the debris-ridden path. "I'm not exactly sure," he finally said. "I guess we got close during the hurricane. Extreme danger does that to people."

Chase had seen how Cindy Stewart looked at his father, and how his father looked at Cindy. As far as he knew, his father hadn't been on a single date since Chase's mother and little sister had died two years earlier. Chase didn't object to his father's new relationship, if that's even what it was. *It just feels a little sudden*, he thought. Less than forty-eight hours ago, his father and Tomás had headed off to Saint Petersburg to look for work. A few hours later, he'd seen his father on television being interviewed by Cindy about disaster preparedness. Then she showed up with his father at the Rossis' farm. Now she and her cameraman were going to Mexico with them? Chase was having a hard time wrapping his mind around it.

"Cindy's making a documentary," his father said.

"About what?"

"Hurricane Emily, for one thing. The earthquake in Mexico. Natural disasters..." His father hesitated. "And me, I guess."

"You?"

His father knew a lot about natural disasters and was an interesting guy. *But a documentary about him?*

"She was curious about me getting struck by lightning," his father said.

Chase was surprised to hear that his father had told someone he'd just met about the lightning strike. As far as he knew, his father had never told anyone. It had happened a year ago, in the back yard of their home. Chase had seen a blinding flash, and the next thing he knew, someone was giving his father CPR. His father was in a coma for two days. When he woke up, he sold everything they owned, including their home. Then he bought a semi-truck to carry building supplies, and a fifth-wheel to live in. He and Chase and Tomás hit the road, running after storms, charging desperate victims a fortune to repair the damage. Chase looked at the gold lightning bolt earring in his father's earlobe.

Did he also tell her the bolt was made from his wedding band?

"It might help us to have a news crew from the States," his father continued.

"How so?" Chase asked.

"For Mexico to get aid, they need to get the word out about the earthquake. The news here is going to be about Hurricane Emily twenty-four-seven. Natural disasters compete with each other for money and airwaves. I think the officials in Mexico might be more lenient about letting us into restricted areas with a reporter and a cameraman on board. They need to get the word out."

His father was probably right. Chase and his father didn't watch a lot of television, but when they did, it was always weather and disaster related. They were well versed in the tragedy and politics of natural disasters.

"Just the opposite of here," Chase said. "How did you get past the roadblocks?"

"Tomás found a way around them."

"He always does."

Tomás – short, strong and quick – hurried across the paddocks towards them, stuffing his sat phone into his back pocket. He had been working at Chase's father's side for over twenty years, and during that time, neither had mastered the other's language. They spoke in what could only be called Spanglish. Tomás was talking nearly as quickly as he'd been walking, but Chase was able to pick out a few words: *quads*, *compound*, *lion*, *generator*, *steel*, *winch*, *elephant*, *welder*, *dentist*...

The word *dentist* did not usually give Chase a jolt of joy, but today was different. He had snapped off one of his front teeth when the school bus sank. The broken tooth was killing him. The only way he could stand the pain was by keeping his upper lip wrapped around the jagged edge.

When the conversation ended, Tomás nodded and trotted off.

"Wait!" Chase winced as air hit his tooth.

Tomás stopped and looked back.

"Does he understand there's a lion in the semi?"

His father laughed. "Yeah, he understands." He waved Tomás on his way. "He's going to build a bridge across that gap."

The night before, during the worst of the storm surge, a river of water had roared between two of the barns, scooping out a deep furrow. Chase and Nicole had managed to wade across the gap twice. They had trapped Simba in the semitrailer on the other side of the gap. Most of Chase's father's tools were in the semi, including the three industrial generators they needed to power up the Rossis' farm.

Chase and his father walked over to the gap. It was littered with debris, most of which, the day before, had been the Rossis' farmhouse.

"Is that a dead giraffe?" his father asked in shock.

"Gertrude," Chase said.

"Horrible," his father said.

Chase had already seen the dead giraffe and had paid his last respects. What now interested him was the storage container sitting crossways between the two barns. He stepped over Gertrude's neck to get a closer look.

"What is it?" his father asked.

"Momma Rossi was convinced Hurricane Emily was going to hit the farm. She has..." Chase hesitated. He didn't want to tell his father that Nicole's grandmother was a psychic, but she had certainly been right about the hurricane. "She was right."

"Lucky guess," his father said.

It was more than luck, Chase thought. "I loaded that container with boxes of Rossi Brothers' Circus memorabilia and other valuables. I caulked it and bungeed a tarp around it. The tarp's gone, of course, but it looks like..."

His father examined the container's seams and its door. He climbed underneath and checked the undercarriage.

"You did a heck of a job, Chase. It looks like it rolled down here. Where was it parked?"

"Behind their house. Well ... where the house used to be."

"A house can be rebuilt," his father said. "But the stuff inside the container is irreplaceable. You saved the Rossis' past."

Chase flushed. Praise was something his father did not give out easily, or often.

"If we have time, we'll try to pull the container out of here with the tractor." His father looked at the barn to their right. "What's in this one?"

"More animals," Chase answered. "Ostriches, zebras, parrots and a bear named Brutus."

"Let's go check it out. Might be room to park the container inside."

"That's probably not a good idea until they get Brutus back into his cage."

"The bear's loose in there?"

"The last time I looked, yeah. Along with the ostriches, except for the one Nicole had to shoot after it broke its legs running into a wall."

His father shook his head. "You had a much more interesting night than I thought."

More terrifying than interesting, Chase thought, but didn't say it. "Why's Tomás building a bridge?"

"I thought it might be easier to get the lion out of the semi by backing it right up to the cat cage in the circus barn. Once we have the cat out of the bag, I can hook up the three generators in tandem without moving them out

278

of the truck. We'll have enough power to run anything we need, including the arc welders."

"Why do you need the welders?"

"Because Marco told me that he doesn't have an elephant-proof barn. We're going to make it elephant-proof before we go to Mexico."

"When does our flight leave?"

His father smiled. "What time is it?"

The Internal Clock Game. Chase's father did not wear a watch. Since the lightning strike, he hadn't needed one. He always knew exactly what time it was – to the minute.

Chase looked at his watch. "You tell me."

"Ten-oh-two."

"Exactly."

"That gives us ten hours before we have to leave for the airport to catch the red-eye to Mexico City."

11:46 AM

The Rossis came out of the barn, followed by Rashawn, just as Chase, John and Tomás were pounding the final nails into their bridge. Nicole was smiling, which could mean only one thing. She was going to Mexico.

"Against my better judgement," Marco began. "And because I've been outvoted two to one." He glanced at Nicole and Momma Rossi. "Nicole can go to Mexico with you if you'll have her. I'm hoping you'll say no."

Chase's father stood up and slipped his hammer into his tool belt. "Sorry," he said. "But it's your call, not mine."

"I had a feeling you were going to say that." Marco looked at his daughter and his mother. "When you see my wife in Mexico, tell her the reason I sent Nicole down there is that my mother is absolutely convinced that Nicole has to go, or bad things will happen. As if an earthquake isn't bad enough."

Chase's father climbed out of the ditch and looked at Momma Rossi. "What kind of bad things?"

"We need to check on the animals," Momma Rossi said, and walked towards the second barn without answering him.

As they followed, Chase's father stopped him. "What was that all about?"

"Momma Rossi, well … I don't know how to say it exactly. She can see things."

"She's psychic?"

"You'll have to ask her."

Food and security were all it really took to get the animals back where they belonged … along with some repairs. Chase's father and Tomás fixed the bear cage while Marco kept Brutus away from them by pounding a metal rubbish-bin lid with a stick. Next they fixed the ostrich pen while Nicole, Rashawn and Chase corralled the birds into a corner by spreading their arms so the birds wouldn't run around and smash into walls. When the ostrich pen was repaired, Marco dumped some chow into their troughs. The ostriches couldn't get inside the pen fast enough. Brutus proved to be more of a challenge. He wasn't hungry, having eaten a good portion of the ostrich Nicole had been forced to shoot the night before. Marco was about to use the tranquillizer gun on him, when Momma Rossi walked in to see how things were going.

"No need for that," she said. "Brutus, get in that cage right now!"

Brutus looked up at her, with black feathers dangling from his mouth, but he didn't leave the bird carcass.

"Fine," Momma Rossi said, and rushed him. It was hard to say who was more startled, Brutus or everyone in the barn watching. She slapped him on the rear end. He bellowed in protest and nearly knocked Marco down in his desperation to get into his cage.

"Now, why didn't I think of that?" Marco said, shaking

his head in dismay. "I can just see the headline now. 'Old Woman Killed by Bear After Surviving the Storm of the Century.'"

"You didn't think of it because you didn't raise Brutus from a cub. I did. He and I have an understanding."

"You raised me from a cub too," Marco said. "But I'm liable to bite you if you ever try to swat *me* on the butt."

Momma Rossi raised her hand. "Let's give it a try and see what happens."

"I wouldn't if I were you, Dad," Nicole said.

"You're probably right."

Ø1:15 PM

A truck bearing the logo of the Palm Breeze Wildlife Refuge pulled up as they were walking over to the third barn to check on the lions.

"Daddy!" Rashawn threw her arms around the man who had just stepped out of the cab. He returned the hug, then picked her up and swung her around in a circle. Mr Stone was a giant and looked strong enough to swing Brutus around too.

He reached over to shake Chase's hand. "You must be Chase. Rashawn tells me that if it hadn't been for you, she wouldn't have survived the storm."

"We helped each other," Chase said. "If we hadn't, none of us would have made it through Emily."

"However it went down, I'm grateful," Mr Stone said. He gave Rashawn another hug and looked at Marco. "The name's Roger Stone. I manage the refuge down the road. I'm here to help in any way I can."

"Marco Rossi." Marco shook the tall man's hand. "Right now we're getting the animals contained. Four lions to go ... five if you count Simba, but he's already kind of contained." Marco nodded at the semi.

"Rashawn told me about that on the phone," Roger said. "I don't know much about lions, but I've handled a lot of bobcats and pumas over the years."

They walked to the third barn, which had partially collapsed. The young lion and three lionesses were in the outside pen, which was in pretty good shape. The men made a few quick repairs to the chain-link fence and pulled the debris off the wire before going inside. The holding areas were completely destroyed, except Simba's cage.

"If the lions had been inside, they would have been crushed," Marco said.

"Or they would have escaped," Nicole added.

"Lucky," Marco said.

"Fate?" Chase asked his father.

"You'll have to ask Momma Rossi."

02:20 PM

Tomás jumped into the semi, pulled it across the new bridge, then backed it into the first barn. Pet trumpeted. Her calf took shelter between her legs. Hector the leopard growled and hit the bars of his holding cage. Even Poco, the injured squirrel monkey, weakly protested as the rig backed up towards the cat cage. Momma Rossi cradled Poco in her arm, trying to comfort him. Inside the trailer, Simba was silent. No roaring. No slamming into the walls as he had done the night before.

"You sure he's in there?" Marco asked.

"He's in there," Nicole said.

Chase wasn't as certain. Simba was being awfully quiet.

Tomás aligned the trailer perfectly with the section of cage they had removed. Marco had rigged a rope to the truck's door latch so it could be pulled from outside the cage, from the top of the trailer.

"Who wants to do the honours?" he asked, holding the end of the rope and a long pole.

"I'll do it," Roger said. "But you'll need to tell me what I have to do."

"Pretty simple. Get on top of the trailer, pull the rope to release the latch, use the pole to swing the doors open and try not to fall inside the cage with Simba."

285

"I'll pay particular attention to that last part," Roger said.

"I'll work the holding-area door," Marco said. "Hopefully, Simba's hungry and will dash inside to get the meat."

Simba was out of the truck and into the cage before Roger was able to push the truck door all the way open. The cat roared, and rushed the bars of the circular cage, shaking the entire structure.

"He jumped over your heads last night?" Chase's father asked.

"Yeah."

"I would have had a heart attack."

"I think I did," Chase said, feeling his legs go weak at the memory.

Simba strutted to the centre of the ring and let loose one final roar that echoed through the barn long after it had ended. He shook his black mane as if he was shaking off his rage, then caught the scent of the meat.

"That's it, old man," Marco said. "Dinner time."

Simba growled, then sprinted into the holding area. Marco closed the guillotine door behind him.

"The animals are contained," Marco said with a sigh of relief.

It took them the rest of the day to elephant-proof the barn.

07:45 PM

Roger Stone had offered to drive them to the airport in the refuge's touring van. When he returned with the van, he had a couple of extra passengers: Rashawn's mom and two-year-old brother, Randall, who was a miniature version of Rashawn.

"Where's elephant?" he asked. "Show me elephant."

"I guess I'd better stick here with Randall," Rashawn said, laughing. "He'll throw a fit if we try to get him back in that van."

"There isn't enough room in the van for all of us anyway," Mrs Stone said. "I'll stay here too. It takes two people to take care of Randall."

Chase and Nicole gave Rashawn hugs goodbye, promising to stay safe.

Chase and his father were the last ones to get into the van. Momma Rossi took John's hand and fixed her dark eyes on him.

"What?" John asked.

"That lightning is still looking for you," Momma Rossi said.

He gave her an uncomfortable smile. "It already found me."

She returned his smile. "It's going to find you again, Lightning John."

Before he could ask her what she meant, she hurried after Rashawn and Randall into the elephant barn.

John looked at Chase. "Did you tell her about the lightning strike?"

Chase shook his head. "No, nothing. But I like the name."

"I'm serious."

"I didn't tell her," Chase said. "Momma Rossi just knows things."

WEDNESDAY
10:00 AM

The high-pitched whine of the dentist's drill sent shivers down Chase's spine. He had slept soundly on the flight to Mexico, but he was awake now.

Wide awake, Chase thought.

The dentist asked him something in Spanish, which he didn't understand – not that he would have been able to answer anyway. His mouth was stuffed with clamps, spreaders, gauze, surgical-gloved fingers and a nasty-sounding suction hose. He nodded, hoping the dentist hadn't just asked him if he wanted a gold tooth. The next sensation was almost as bad as the drill. It felt as if the dentist were pounding the cap on with a ball-peen hammer. The man finally finished, smiled, said something else Chase didn't understand and started extracting the hardware from Chase's mouth. When he was done, he smiled again and handed Chase a mirror. To Chase's relief, his new front tooth was porcelain and a pretty good match to his other front tooth.

Nicole was waiting for him in the reception area.

"Let's see."

Chase smiled to show her, but he really wasn't sure if she

289

could see the new tooth. He really wasn't sure if he'd even moved his mouth – his face was numb from his upper lip to the top of his forehead.

"Looks good," Nicole said.

Chase paid the dentist in cash. Before they'd left the Rossis' farm, his father had given him a pile of money. Chase had always wondered what his father did with the money he made repairing storm damage. Apparently, he kept it in cash – in large-denomination notes – inside his go bag along with the emergency supplies. They all carried go bags now, including Cindy and Mark, as well as new satellite phones so they could stay in touch without relying on cellular towers.

"What did you learn?" Chase asked. He had given Nicole his laptop to keep while he was in the dentist's chair.

"A lot," Nicole said. "And none of it's good. Half of Puebla has been turned to rubble. Thousands of people are dead or missing. All the roads are impassable. They're using helicopters to get rescue workers in and the injured out, but it's very slow going. And to top it off, Mount Popocatepetl is smoking."

"Mount what?"

"Po-po-cat-uh-petal." Nicole pronounced it slowly. "It means 'smoking mountain'."

"It's erupting?"

"Steam and ash, but nothing serious yet."

"This just gets better and better," Chase said. "What about your mom?"

Nicole shook her head. "No word. Their last performance was in Puebla, Monday night. Normally, they would have struck the show right after the final act and hit the road when the traffic was light. They were supposed to meet Arturo here in Mexico City yesterday to pick up the animals he was hauling down. The show is supposed to start tonight, and they aren't here. This is the first time in a hundred years that the Rossi Brothers' Circus has missed a performance."

"So they're stuck in Puebla, or just outside it."

Nicole gave him a worried nod.

"Don't worry," Chase said. "We'll find them. Where are my dad and Tomás?"

"Out getting supplies. Arturo's at the fairgrounds just down the street. We're supposed to meet everyone there."

10:35 AM

Arturo was an exact copy of Tomás, only younger and with a small chimpanzee on his lap. Nicole picked the chimpanzee up and gave it a hug. It seemed happy to see her.

"How was dentist?" Arturo asked.

Chase smiled and showed his new tooth.

"*Bueno*."

Chase pointed at the chimpanzee. "What's his name?"

"It's a she, and her name is Chiquita."

Chiquita wasn't alone. There were two camels, a black bear, a tiger and a good-size crowd of people gawking at the animals. Arturo had roped off the area to keep the spectators at a distance.

"You should charge an entrance fee," Nicole said.

"I'm thinking about it. They are here from morning until darkness. I have to pay children to bring me food."

Chase looked at Arturo's old sleeping bag and rumpled clothes in the back of the truck. Since meeting Nicole, he had thought more than once about becoming a circus roustabout when he got older. This sight took some of the romance out of the idea. Sleeping in the back of a truck without being able to leave to get food did not sound like much fun.

"I take it you're not coming with us," Nicole said.

"The only way I could go would be to take the animals with me. But of course that won't work. I'll wait here in case your mother shows up while you're out looking for her."

"The clowns will be happy to see Chiquita," Nicole explained to Chase. "Chiquita and her twin brother, Chico, are part of their act. Chiquita was under the weather when the show headed south, so we held her back. But you're all better now, aren't you, Chiquita?"

Chiquita gave her a hoot and a high five.

Two brand-new white 4x4 trucks pulled up, equipped with crew cabs, roll bars, auxiliary lights and power winches. Strapped down in the bed of each truck was a quad. The sides of both trucks were stencilled in red:

M.D. Emergency Services

The *M.D.* didn't stand for *Medical Doctor*, but sometimes the authorities thought it did and Chase's father didn't correct them. It helped get them into restricted areas. *M.D.* stood for *Masters of Disaster*. His father's little joke. But his father wasn't joking now. He climbed out of the truck all business. He didn't even ask about Chase's tooth.

"The new sat phones have GPS. Keep the phone with you at all times. I also got these." He handed Bluetooth earpieces to Chase and Nicole. Cindy, Mark and Tomás already had theirs in. His father's Bluetooth flashed just above his lightning bolt earring.

That lightning is still looking for you, Momma Rossi had said. Chase wondered if the bolt had found his father while

293

he'd been at the dentist's. John Masters looked completely charged – and clearly *in charge*. Chase smiled. *Lightning John is a perfect name for him.*

"The phones are synced to each other and will act like walkie-talkies," his father continued. "If you answer, you'll be able to hear everyone, and everyone will be able to hear you. Just tap the Bluetooth if you want to listen in. Mark and Cindy will ride with me. Chase and Nicole will ride with Tomás. When we get closer to Puebla, we'll decide our next step. And one more thing." He gave each of them a small zippered case. "Respirators in case we run into ash up on the mountain. Put them in your go bags. Any questions?"

No one had any questions. Or if they did, they didn't ask out loud. Mark was filming the whole thing. *That's a question killer*, Chase thought. *Who wants to ask a dumb question with the camera rolling?*

Tomás gave Arturo a hug and got into his truck. Chase and Nicole climbed in after him. Chase looked back as they drove away. His father was already getting into his truck behind them. Arturo was waving. Chiquita had her hand up too.

"Was your dad in the military?" Nicole asked as they pulled on to the highway.

"Navy," Chase answered. "But it was before he married my mom."

"What did he do in the Navy?"

"I never asked him, and he never talks about it. Why?"

"He seems ... I don't know. Organized, I guess."

"He's certainly organized. Most contractors are."

"Circus people are organized too," Nicole said. "But your dad's *extra*-organized. We've been here less than five hours and he's mounted a full-scale expedition inside a foreign country."

"Mexico is hardly a foreign country."

"Look at this truck and all this special gear. He had to get a car dealer out of bed at the crack of dawn to get these trucks."

Chase looked around the cab. It smelled new. The only things that weren't new were the laminated photos of Tomás's eight children and his wife, Guadalupe, duct-taped to the dash. Above them was Tomás's plastic statue of Saint Christopher, patron saint of travellers.

He's also invoked against lightning, Chase thought. *Not a problem today. There isn't a cloud in the sky. People are driving, shopping, going about their day as if—*

"Popocatepetl," Tomás said.

The "smoking mountain" was smoking. A plume of white steam rose three thousand metres above the nearly six-thousand-metre peak.

"I didn't realize it was so close to Mexico City," Chase said.

Nicole turned and said something to Tomás in what sounded to Chase like pretty good Spanish. Tomás responded, and they continued speaking rapidly as the volcano loomed larger in the distance.

When they stopped talking, Chase asked Nicole about her Spanish.

"Circuses are international," Nicole said. "The acts are from all over the world, but most of our roustabouts are Hispanic. I was asking Tomás about his family. They live in a village called Lago de la Montaña, or Lake of the Mountain. I guess people call it Lago for short. It's on the east side of the mountain just below the rim."

"So, not a good place to be right now," Chase said.

"No," Tomás said.

They drove on in silence.

12:00PM

"Noon," his father said over the Bluetooth.

Chase looked at his watch. "Exactly."

"Pull over where the road splits."

Tomás pulled the 4x4 on to the shoulder. Everyone got out.

"We haven't seen another car in half an hour," Chase's father said. "My guess is nobody's getting in or out of Puebla, at least not on this road. And I don't like the look of that plume. We need to split up so we can cover more ground. I'll continue towards Puebla and see what we're up against. Tomás will head up to Lago and make sure his family's OK."

"Then I want to ride with you, to Puebla," Nicole said to John.

"I figured that." He looked at Cindy and Mark. "One of you needs to go with Tomás and Chase."

"I'll do it," Cindy said. "Mark needs to shoot video. I'm extra baggage."

Except for Tomás and Lightning John, we're all extra baggage, Chase thought. He would have preferred to travel with Nicole, but he understood her wanting to go to Puebla, where her mother and sister might be. And he understood his father's reason for going to Puebla right away. The plume – what they could see of it now so close to the mountain – had turned from white to grey in the

297

last half hour. Tomás had told them that didn't necessarily mean the volcano was going to be a problem. The steam and ash were common. But Chase could tell he was worried about it.

Nicole and Cindy went to pick up their go bags.

John waved Chase over to the guardrail to talk to him alone.

"You OK with Nicole going with me?"

"You OK with Cindy going with me?" Chase asked.

His father grinned. "Actually, I am. Take care of her, and take care of yourself."

"What do you want us to do when we find Tomás's family?"

He looked up the mountainside. "It's up to Tomás, but I'd get them out of here. I just really don't like the look of that plume."

"Do you know anything about volcanic eruptions?"

"A little. I was in a bad eruption in Indonesia before you were born."

"When you were in the Navy?"

His father nodded.

"Why were you in Indonesia?" This trip down to Mexico was Chase's first time out of the country, but apparently it was not his father's.

"I was sent there to help rescue some people."

"From an eruption?"

"Not exactly. Look – let's talk about this another time. We need to get moving."

"Sure," Chase said. *Just another thing he doesn't want to talk about.*

He walked over to Nicole. "Don't do anything I wouldn't do."

She burst out laughing. "It can't be worse than the hurricane," she said.

Chase looked up at the grey plume. He wasn't so sure.

12:22 PM

"The bridge is out," John said.

There were three army trucks parked on their side of the bridge and no vehicles on the Puebla side. He slowed to a stop, then consulted his GPS.

"I'll go talk to them," Nicole said.

"I'll go with you," Mark said.

"Ask them when the bridge went out," John said, pulling a topographical map from the glove box to compare to the map on his phone.

The bridge had spanned a deep gully a hundred metres across. A third of the bridge was now gone. Nicole asked the soldiers when it had collapsed, but they didn't know exactly. They'd been sent from Mexico City right after the earthquake hit. When they called in and reported that the bridge was out, their commander told them to stay put until they were relieved. The sergeant asked if Nicole had any spare food or water. She sent Mark to see what Mr Masters could spare.

"Did you see any circus trucks drive up to the other side? Or did you pass any circus trucks on your way up here?" Nicole asked in Spanish.

The sergeant shook his head. But he had heard about the circus. His cousin had gone to see it in Puebla. He'd been planning to take his family when the circus performed in Mexico City.

"That may not happen," Nicole told him. She went on to explain her connection to the circus and gathered as much information from the man as she could.

A few minutes later, Mark and John walked up with a box of food and water and handed it to the soldiers. Nicole filled them in. "The sergeant thinks my mother and sister and the rest of the circus probably started out of Puebla, found they couldn't get far on the ruined roads and turned back. So maybe they're safe." *Or stranded somewhere on the road – or worse*, she thought. She continued aloud, "He says there are several roads and trails through the mountains, but they're only passable with four-wheel drive."

"I think I've found a way around the bridge," John said. "Ask him about the volcano."

"I already did," she told him. "He said the same thing as Tomás. He isn't worried about Popocatepetl either. He told me the mountain lets out steam all of the time, and it's nothing serious. He's guessing the earthquake opened a fissure in the crater, but it will close up in a couple of days. It always does, he said."

John gave the sergeant his phone number and asked him to call if he heard anything about the circus or warnings about the volcano. Back in the truck, he showed Nicole and Mark the map, moving his finger along the road he was planning to take.

"It looks more like a trail than a road," Mark said.

"It is a trail," John admitted. "It swings back around to the highway on the other side of the bridge. If it's wide enough and not too steep, we should be able to make it."

"If it's still there after the earthquake," Mark said.

John put the truck into four-wheel drive. "If the trail's not there, we'll make our own."

Mark rolled his eyes. "Here we go again."

"What are you talking about?" Nicole asked.

"When we ran out of roads during the hurricane, Lightning John here and his sidekick, Tomás, decided to redefine the meaning of *off-road vehicle*. At one point we were stuck on a train trestle. I can't tell you how much fun that was."

John smiled. "Lightning John, huh? I gather Chase told you? It's not the worst nickname I've had." He bumped the truck off the highway and headed into the trees.

12:33PM

In some ways Popocatepetl reminded Chase of Mount Hood. The dense blanket of evergreen trees, the steep and winding logging roads, the small patches of snow surviving in the shade. Before the lightning strike – before everything changed – his family had owned a cabin on Mount Hood. They had spent almost as much time at the cabin as they did in their regular home. His father had even been a volunteer in the Mount Hood Ski Patrol. Chase's best memories were from their time on the mountain. His worst memory was too.

"So tell me something about Chase Masters," Cindy said. She was sitting between him and Tomás.

"There's not much to tell," Chase said.

Cindy laughed. "You sound like your dad."

"You sound like a reporter."

"Guilty as charged. It's in my blood. My parents are both journalists."

"Where do they live?" Chase asked.

"Southern California. In the same house I grew up in."

"So you know about earthquakes."

"I've been in my share of quakes, and of course I've covered them for television."

"How about volcanoes?"

"The only volcano I've covered is Mount Saint Helens in

Washington. I did a story about it the last time it acted up. It blew some steam and ash for a few days, then went back to sleep. I hope Popocatepetl does the same."

Chase hoped so too, but his TGB was telling him otherwise. How often had his father said, "The gut barometer is never wrong, so always listen to your TGB." His father believed that everyone had a TGB. It worked like a real barometer, but instead of hanging on a wall, it was in your solar plexus. "When you feel the bottom drop out of your gut, you'd better go on full alert," his father always said. Right now Chase's gut was somewhere between his knees and his ankles. He hoped the feeling of hollow dread was an aftereffect of the novocaine. *Or maybe I'm just hungry*. He hadn't eaten anything since the aeroplane. He pulled an energy bar out of his go bag and offered half to Cindy.

"No, thanks. Let's get back to Chase Masters."

"Like I said, there not much to tell. I was born and raised in Oregon. Two years ago, my mother and sister were killed in an auto accident. One year ago my father was struck by lightning in our back yard. When he came out of the coma, he sold my uncle his share in their construction company, and we hit the road. I go to school while my father and Tomás charge people a lot of money to put their property back together."

"I was sorry to hear about your mom and sister," Cindy said. "I can't imagine how difficult that's been."

"Thanks."

"As far as your father charging people a lot of money to fix things, I suspect he's spent most, if not all, of his profit on this little excursion. If he didn't have the cash, we'd be back in Florida, worrying about Tomás's and Nicole's families instead of down here trying to find them."

Chase shrugged. She had a point, but his father was not a psychic like Momma Rossi. He hadn't been charging people because he knew that one day he would have to save Tomás's and Nicole's families.

"I can see you're not convinced," Cindy said. "It's hard for men like your father to give up their training."

"What training?"

"His SEAL training."

"As in sea, air, and land? The Navy SEALs?"

"That's right."

"My father was not a Navy SEAL."

"Chief Petty Officer John Sebastian Masters."

"Sebastian?"

"Don't tell me you didn't know your father's middle name."

"I knew the initial," Chase said, which sounded weak even to him. "Did he tell you he was a Navy SEAL?"

"No."

"Then how—"

"You don't really think that I would pick your dad as a documentary subject without doing some research first?"

"I guess not," Chase said. *How could I not have known something so important?*

"My little brother – well, not so little any more – is a Navy SEAL. We lived close to Coronado, California, where SEAL Team One is based. I can't remember a time when my brother didn't want to become a SEAL. His bedroom was plastered with SEAL paraphernalia and Navy recruiting posters. Your father was younger in the photo, of course, but I recognized him from one of those posters. I called my brother to verify it. He said John Sebastian Masters is the real deal. Your dad's exploits in Asia are the things of SEAL Team One legend."

Chase's father's voice echoed in his head. *I was in a bad eruption in Indonesia before you were born... I was sent there to help rescue some people...* Chase still couldn't believe he hadn't heard any of this before now. His mother had to have known his father had been a SEAL.

"What kind of operations?" Chase asked.

"My brother wouldn't tell me, the little creep. He said they were classified."

Chase looked over at Tomás. He had both hands on the steering wheel and was looking straight ahead as if he wasn't paying the slightest attention to their conversation. Did he know about his partner's past?

"What did my dad say when you asked him about being a SEAL?"

"I didn't ask him."

"Why not?" If they weren't driving up the side of an active volcano, he'd be on the sat phone with his father right now demanding an answer.

"Good question," Cindy said. "I guess I was waiting for him to say something about it, but the fact that he didn't tells me even more about him than if he had."

"How so?"

"I know a lot of ex-SEALs. They're a proud bunch and delighted to talk about their accomplishments. Then along

306

comes someone like your dad, who doesn't even tell *you* about it. I assumed that you knew. I probably shouldn't have said anything."

"I'm glad you did," Chase said. "And don't worry. When I ask him about it, I'll figure out a way to do it without pointing at you."

"I'd appreciate that." Cindy looked out the windscreen at the darkening sky. "The only easy day was yesterday," she said.

"What do you mean?"

"That's the SEAL motto."

Chase hoped it wasn't true.

12:52 PM

"Stop the truck!" Nicole shouted.

"Why?" John asked.

"Because I need to puke," Mark said.

"I'm serious," Nicole insisted. "I saw something!"

John put the brakes on, and Nicole was out of the cab before the truck came to a complete stop.

"I'm serious about puking," Mark said.

"Take care of it *outside* the cab while I find out what Nicole is up to."

The trail they had been following was slippery and narrow. They had already got stuck twice, but both times John had managed to get the truck loose without using the winch. He caught up to Nicole fifty metres into the woods, on the downhill side of the trail.

"What did you see?"

"I'm not sure." Nicole scanned the thick trees. "It was just a glimpse of something or someone."

"We're at least a mile above the highway and several miles from the nearest village. It's not likely that anyone would be wandering this far above the—"

The ground shook. John grabbed Nicole and pulled her down to the base of a tree, shielding her from the dead branches raining down. The tremor sounded like a freight train barrelling right past them. John counted the seconds.

When he reached nine the tremor stopped, followed by complete silence, as if the forest were holding its breath, waiting.

"You OK?" he asked.

"I think so." Nicole sat up and brushed the pine needles out of her black hair.

John looked up the hill and shouted, "Are you alive, Mark?"

"Barely!" Mark shouted back. "Oh, no..."

The ground had started shaking again.

The truck continued to shake *after* Tomás had stopped. Saint Christopher and two of Tomás's children fell off the dash. Four cracks appeared in front of the truck, as if a giant, invisible cat paw had scratched the road.

"Whoa," Chase said.

"I think that was the second tremor," Cindy said. "We couldn't feel the first one because the truck was moving."

Tomás put Saint Christopher back on the dash and replaced the photos of the two children. Everyone got out of the cab to take a closer look at the cracks.

"Not too bad," Tomás said. "We can get around them."

All at once, each of their satellite phones starting ringing. Chase was about to hit talk when he remembered the Bluetooth in his ear and tapped it instead.

"Are you guys OK?"

Chase jumped when he heard his father's voice directly in his ear.

"We're fine," Cindy said. Chase could hear her speaking out loud and in his ear at the same time. He walked a short distance away to avoid the echo. "There are some cracks in the road, but Tomás thinks we can get around them. Where are you?"

"About twelve miles from the bridge overland. An hour and a half by road. The bridge was out. We're trying to get around it and drop back down to the highway. It's tough going, but we're making progress."

"How's Nicole?" Chase asked.

"Shaken," Nicole answered in his earpiece.

Chase laughed. It was going to take him a while to get used to the fact that everyone was listening in.

"Nicole thought she saw something in the woods, so we stopped. Lucky we did. The truck slid about five feet during the last tremor. I'm going to have to winch it back up on to the trail."

"Don't worry about Mark," Mark chimed in. "He was crushed by the truck, but it means more food for all of you."

It was Cindy's turn to laugh. "Did you get video?"

"Of my death? Yeah."

"Good. Seriously, are you OK?"

"I'm fine. I was on the other side of the truck when it slid off the trail. And the camera *was* rolling. So were my bowels."

"Too much information, Mark."

"Don't worry. I didn't get any footage of that. You did hear that I said *trail* instead of *road*, right?"

"I heard."

"Lightning John is up to his old tricks, blazing trails like Meriwether Lewis. Why are we down here again?"

"We won't know until it's over," Cindy said.

"Perfect."

"We'd better get going," John interrupted. "We have to winch the truck back up, contact Mark's next of kin, then bury him."

"I think the mountain is going to take care of that for you," Mark said.

Lightning John laughed and ended the call.

01:06 PM

"Landslide," Tomás said. When he spoke in English, it was usually in one-word sentences.

"A huge landslide," Chase said. A five-metre pile of boulders and uprooted trees covered the road.

"How far is Lago?" Cindy asked.

"Nine or ten miles."

They got out of the truck. Chase started to climb the pile.

"What are you doing?" Cindy called after him.

"Checking to see how far it goes."

"Be careful."

"Yes, Mo – uh … ma'am. I'll be fine." *Did I almost say mom?* He scrambled up the loose scree as if he were trying to get away from the idea. *What's up with that?* He reached the top and looked at the debris pile. It was extensive. Fifty metres, maybe more. It would take a road crew a week to move it. A dangerous job. They'd have to start at the top of the slide and work their way down. *If the pile shifted, or if there was another earthquake…* Chase suddenly realized the precarious position he was in and quickly climbed back down.

"What's it look like?" Cindy asked.

"It's a mess. We're not getting past it, and no one from Lago is either. We were lucky we weren't driving by when this let go. I couldn't see very far beyond the slide, but there might be more slides up ahead. We're going to have to go around."

Chase looked at Tomás to see how much he had understood. Apparently, he'd understood enough, because he'd switched on his sat phone and was consulting the GPS. When he finished, he showed the screen to them and traced the alternate route he wanted to take. All of it was off-road.

"It might be best if we unload the quad," Chase said. Tomás nodded. "I can ride up ahead of you and make sure the path is clear."

"Crank the steering wheel to the left," John told Mark. "Keep your foot off the brake. When I tell you, give it a little gas. But don't let the wheels spin. If it starts to slide, we'll lose the truck. In fact, we should unload everything in case we do lose the truck. That way we'll still have the quad and our supplies."

"How many people can ride on the quad?" Mark asked.

"Two."

"But there are three of us."

"If we lose the truck, there won't be because you'll be inside the truck." John pointed down the steep hill. "Wherever it ends up."

"Maybe Nicole would like to do the truck thing."

"I'd be happy to," Nicole said.

"Except I told her dad that I'd try to keep her safe," John said.

Mark pulled his phone out of his pocket. "Wanna call my dad?"

313

John smiled. "Give me a hand unloading the quad."

"I'm going to look around," Nicole said. "I know I saw something."

"Don't wander too far," John said. "And take your go bag with you."

Nicole walked back to where she thought she had seen something. *Whatever it is*, she thought, uncertain why *it* was so important. *Mr Masters probably thinks I'm insane.* She had seen *it* out of the corner of her eye past Mark's head on the passenger side. By the time she'd leaned forward, *it* had vanished into the trees. She scanned the forest for a familiar landmark. *There!* An old tree blown over by the wind or downed by lightning. She walked towards it. Halfway there, she saw a movement behind the splintered stump and stopped. She knew better than to walk up to a wild animal in the woods, if that's what it was. She waited and watched. In the distance she heard the truck start and John shouting instructions to Mark. *It* moved again. A humanlike face peered out from behind the stump. *It* was Chico, Chiquita's twin brother. He was baring his teeth in a fear grimace. She didn't blame him. Earthquakes were scary. So was being lost in the woods and separated from the show. She couldn't imagine what was going through the young chimp's mind, but she knew exactly what was going through her own.

Chico's bizarre appearance here meant that her mother and sister had to be nearby. It also meant that animals had escaped from the circus trucks, and the show was almost certainly in trouble. Nicole sat down on the ground and averted her gaze to make herself appear less threatening. If it had been Chiquita peeking out from behind the stump, Nicole would have walked up to her with open arms, calling her name, but she didn't know Chico that well. If she walked towards him, he was liable to run away. The only thing to do was wait for him to get over his fear and approach her.

If only I had some food, I could... She remembered the go bag. Very slowly she slipped the small backpack off her shoulders. Chico watched her suspiciously but didn't run. He showed a little more of his body as she unzipped a side pocket and pulled out an energy bar.

"Hungry?"

Chico stepped completely out from behind the stump.

"Me too." Nicole started to unwrap the bar. Chico took a tentative step forward. "You recognize my voice, don't you?"

Chico gave her a quiet woot.

"That's what I thought." Nicole took a bite out of the bar, then held the rest out to him. "You want some?"

"*Woot.*"

"You're going to have to come and get it, because I'm not bringing it to you. And you'd better make it quick. This train's about to leave the station."

Chico took a couple steps forward.

"I know you're scared. It's creepy when the ground shakes. Scared me too. But you're lucky you weren't at the farm during the hurricane. Now, *that* was terrifying."

Chico started knuckling his way towards Nicole, then froze, looking at something behind her.

"It's OK, Chico. Don't run off." Nicole turned her head. Mark was fifteen metres away with his camera.

"Is that a chimpanzee?"

"No, Mark, it's a baby Sasquatch."

"Funny. Can I get a little closer?"

"No. You need to back off. Preferably all the way to the truck."

"I'm filming. You look just like Jane Goodall. This will be great for our—"

"Mark. You. Need. To. Get. Out. Of. Here. Now."

"I guess I'll get out of here," Mark said.

Nicole turned back around, half expecting Chico to be behind the stump again or, worse, completely gone. But he was still there, looking past her, watching Mark's retreat.

"Where were we?" she said. "Oh, yes … food." She pulled more of the wrapper away from the bar. Chico took another couple steps forward, reaching out for the treat. "No snatch-and-run for you. You're going to have to eat it here." She patted her lap.

"*Woot.*"

"That's right."

Reluctantly, Chico climbed into her lap. Nicole broke off a small chunk of energy bar and handed it to him.

"I wish you could talk and tell me what happened. Where are my mother and sister?"

"*Woot.*"

02:15 PM

Chase stopped the quad and waited for Tomás and Cindy to catch up. They had dropped below the slide and had managed to get past it without mishap.

Now the hard part.

He looked up the hill. It was a half-mile climb back up to the road, with no guarantee there wouldn't be more slides blocking their way to Lago. Chase's eyes stung and his mouth was dry from what he thought was dust. As the truck bounced towards him through the trackless forest, he saw that Tomás had his wipers on. The windscreen was streaked with a grey slurry the colour of cement.

Not dust. Ash.

Tomás and Cindy got out of the truck. Tomás opened the crew cab door and pulled out a roll of toilet paper.

"*Azufre*," Tomás said.

Chase looked at Cindy. "Toilet paper?"

"I think *azufre* means 'brimstone'," Cindy explained. "He's talking about volcanic ash. I have no idea why he has the toilet paper."

Tomás popped the hood, removed the air filter and shook out a cloud of grey ash. He wrapped the filter in toilet paper, put it back in, then did the same to the air filter on the quad. He handed the toilet paper roll to Chase.

"Wrap every ten miles or the quad, it will stop."

"Sure." Chase put the roll in his go bag and pulled out his respirator.

"You need something for your eyes," Cindy told him.

Tomás ran to the back of the truck, rummaged through the toolbox and came back with a pair of eye protectors and a roll of duct tape. He covered the perforated sides of the glasses with tape and handed them to Chase.

"Thanks."

"*De nada*."

"I think you should stay down here with the truck while I go up and check the road to see if there are any more landslides." Chase took the sat phone out of his pocket. "I'll call you if it's clear."

Tomás nodded.

Cindy looked doubtful.

"There's no point in driving the truck up to the road if it isn't clear." Chase took his helmet off so he could put on the mask and the glasses. He had to leave the Bluetooth in his pocket because the helmet wouldn't fit over it.

"I just don't like the idea of us splitting up."

Chase put his helmet back on. "I've been driving a quad since I was five years old."

"But not during an eruption. I'm worried about this ash."

Chase was too. He looked up through the trees. It had got darker in the last hour, and the grey against the sky was not a thundercloud.

"It won't take me long." Chase swung on to the quad and started up the hill towards the road.

*

Nicole walked up to the truck with Chico in her arms. The young chimp was happily munching his third energy bar.

"I told you there was a chimp," Mark said.

"So you did," John said.

"Chico," Nicole said. "Chiquita's twin brother."

"Where does Chico ride when the circus is travelling?"

"In the clown truck."

"Semi?"

Nicole nodded. "Two drivers. They haul most of the wardrobe for the show, portable dressing rooms, props. The clowns follow the semi in campers and trailers."

"What are the chances of Chico's getting loose on his own?"

"Just about zero. When he's not performing, he's in a harness with a leash."

"No harness," Mark said.

"They take it off when they put him in his cage."

"Then we can assume the clown truck has had an accident," John said. "What other animals would the circus be transporting?"

"Lions, tigers, bears, camels, elephants and dogs."

"Dogs?" Mark asked.

"Thirty-two of them. Mostly poodles. Teacup up to standard. It's the show's most popular act."

"How far can a chimp travel in a day?" John asked.

"I don't know. What worries me is, why did he travel anywhere?"

02:46PM

Chase made it back up to the road, but it hadn't been easy. It was going to be even harder for the truck, but if anyone could get it up there, Tomás could. The road was covered with a centimetre of fine grey ash. Sweat dripped down the back of Chase's neck from his helmet. He took it off, pulled down his respirator, took a long drink of water, then rinsed the ash off the safety glasses. The glasses had helped, but the stinging ash was still finding its way into his eyes. He put the Bluetooth back into his ear and hit redial on the sat phone. Cindy answered first.

"Are you on the road?"

"Yes. A lot of ash up here. I'm going to drive down a mile or so and make sure there aren't any more landslides. So stay put. I'll give you a call when I know."

"What landslides?" His father's voice was in his ear.

Chase had forgotten again that everyone could listen in. He told his father – and everyone else – about the landslide and their plan to get around it.

"How much ash is up there?" his father asked.

"Half an inch on the road. But it's not falling. It's kind of swirling around in the breeze."

"Same here," his father said. "There might have been an eruption *and* an earthquake. You need to get up to Lago. The sooner we get off this mountain, the better."

Chase could tell by the tone of his voice that his father's gut barometer was on high alert. Chase's TGB was too. The afternoon light filtering through the suspended ash was ghostlike. *I wonder if this is what it would look like after a nuclear explosion*, he thought.

"Are you wearing your respirator?" his father asked.

"Yeah. And some eye protection Tomás rigged up."

"Keep a lookout for circus animals," Nicole said.

"What?"

"I found Chico wandering around in the woods."

"The chimp?"

"Yes. He was scared to death. I don't know if any other animals escaped. Or if they did, whether they're anywhere near you. But it's possible. We looked at the map, and Chico was three miles from the highway."

"What other kinds of animals are you talking about?"

"Lions and tigers and bears, oh my," Mark said. "Along with some other less aggressive things."

Chase switched over to the phone's GPS screen. He was probably less than five miles from the highway as the crow flies. *Or as the tiger runs.*

"The only easy day was yesterday," he said.

"What did you say?" his father asked.

"I gotta go."

Chase ended the call, pulled the Bluetooth from his ear and put on his gear before getting back on the quad. He continued down the road, smiling. *Let* him *think about what* I *said for a change.* But the smile didn't last long. He rounded a corner and put on the brakes so hard, the quad nearly flipped. Sitting in the middle of the road was a grey poodle the size of a small domestic cat. At least, Chase thought it was a poodle, from the way its fur was cut.

And very few wild animals have blue bows tied to their ears.

The poodle was holding up its right front paw as if it were injured. If Chase hadn't slammed on the brakes, he would have run right over the tiny dog. He got off the quad, squatted down and called the dog to him. The poodle didn't move.

"You probably think I'm an alien," Chase said. He took off his helmet, glasses and respirator. "Is that better?" The poodle still didn't move. "Apparently, it isn't better. Look. We're on an active volcano. We need to get—"

The ground started shaking violently. Chase dropped to the ground and covered his head with his arms, wishing he'd kept his helmet on. The upheaval and deafening roar seemed to go on for ever. When it finally stopped, Chase was still shaking even though the ground was still. As he struggled to catch his breath, he felt something rubbing against his thigh. He glanced down. The trembling poodle looked up at him. Chase picked up the dog and settled it in his lap. He started to pet it and discovered that the poodle was not grey. Its white fur was covered in ash.

03:04PM

John Masters felt the steering go and hit the brakes. The truck slid sideways for six metres before it slammed against a tree, crunching the passenger door. The ground continued to shake for a couple more seconds, then stopped.

Chico had his arms around Nicole's neck so tightly, he was nearly choking her. "That was a bad one," she said.

Mark rubbed the bump on his forehead. "I'm getting a little sick of these earthquakes!"

John was getting sick of them too, but this last one had felt a little different. "That might have been an eruption."

"Perfect," Mark said.

"Are you OK?" Nicole asked Mark.

"Just a small concussion. But thanks for asking."

"I'll check the truck." John put on his respirator.

"I'll go with you," Nicole said.

John shook his head. "You two stay here. No use in all of us going out into the ash."

With difficulty Nicole managed to peel Chico's arms from around her neck. They were less than half a mile from the highway. She hoped there was nothing wrong with the truck.

We're so close! she thought.

Her phone and Mark's rang simultaneously. Nicole put hers on speakerphone so she and Mark could listen together.

"Is everyone OK?" John asked.

"Tomás and I are fine," Cindy said. "We're waiting to hear from Chase."

"I'm fine," Chase said. "Tomás and Cindy, the road looks clear, so you can start making your way up here. Are you listening in, Nicole?"

"I'm here."

"Does the show have a dog act?"

"Yes. Why?"

"I think I have one of the performers in my lap. It's the size of a big squirrel."

"White?"

"It was, but now it's ash grey. It has blue bows in its ears."

"Pepe," Nicole said. "What's he doing all the way over there? Why is he loose? Why is he by himself?"

"I have no idea. I'm just glad it was Pepe in the middle of the road and not a lion, tiger or bear."

"Oh, my," Mark said.

"Funny," Chase said. "I'm going to head up the road with Pepe and find out where he came from, or get to Lago, whichever comes first. Are you on the highway?"

"No," Nicole said. "We just hit a tree. I'm not sure if we're going anywhere."

"The truck's fine," John said. "Just a little dented. We'll be back down to the highway within half an hour unless we have another earthquake, or eruption. Everyone stay in touch." He ended the call.

Chase picked up Pepe and looked at the little poodle's paw. The pad was split, but the ash in the wound seemed to have stopped the bleeding.

"I'm sure that's sore, but I think you're going to live."

Chase had never owned a dog. His mother had been allergic to both cats and dogs. He'd always wanted a dog, but not under these circumstances. He got on the quad and put Pepe on his lap.

"Let's go see what's up the road."

A few minutes later, he saw two men. They had rags wrapped around their heads to keep the ash out. Chase slowed down so he wouldn't stir up too much ash. He stopped the quad about six metres away, removed his helmet and respirator, then walked up to them, carrying Pepe in the crook of his arm. When he reached them, Pepe started growling. The two men looked at the poodle as if they didn't know what it was. At first Chase thought they might be with the circus, but judging from Pepe's reaction, they couldn't be roustabouts. They'd know the dog, and Pepe would know them.

They must be from Lago. Chase smiled, wishing Cindy was with him so she could talk to them.

"*¿Hablas inglés?*"

The men shook their covered heads.

"I'm afraid that's about the extent of my Spanish," Chase said.

One of the men pointed at the quad.

"Yes." He turned his head to look at the quad. "I came up the road on—"

Chase's eyes rolled up in their sockets, he fell to his knees and his world went from ash grey to pitch black.

Ø3:33PM

John pulled the truck on to the highway with a satisfied sigh.

"Not too bad," he said.

"Yeah," Mark said. "We only almost died twice."

"We'll go to the bridge. If we don't find them, we'll turn around and head back to Puebla. But first I'm going to rewrap the air filter."

This time Nicole and Mark got out with him to stretch their legs. Nicole wandered over to the edge of the road, carrying Chico. Suddenly, she screamed.

John and Mark ran over to them. At the bottom of the ravine was a stream. A smashed semi-trailer marked with the Rossi Brothers' logo lay across it. Scattered around the trailer were four dead elephants.

Nicole had turned away from the terrible sight. "Rosy, Hannico, Me-Tu and Hugo," she said quietly. "Hugo is ... was ... the father of Pet's calf."

Mark turned his camera away from the carnage as well, and put his arm around Nicole.

John was equally horrified, but he did not turn away. He looked up the road towards the bridge and saw where the shoulder must have broken off and fallen into the ravine. He ran back to the truck and grabbed his climbing rope and harness.

"What are you doing?" Nicole asked.

"I'm going down to check it out. How many people ride in the tractor?"

"Two. But there might be a third riding in the sleeper. Do you think they're still in there?"

"We'll see," John said, though from the look of the wreckage, he was certain no one had got out. The real question was, were they still alive? "What do your mom and sister drive?"

"They have a truck camper."

John was relieved to hear that. "Can you drive a quad?"

"Sure," Nicole said.

"I want you and Mark to head up to the bridge and see if anyone else has had an accident or is stranded." He pointed at the ravine. "The circus logo on the side of the trailer is pointing away from the bridge, which means they were heading to Puebla when they went off the road. They'd probably turned around when they saw the bridge was out."

"What made them go off the road?"

John pointed up the road. "Looks like they were in the right-hand lane coming around that curve. Maybe another quake. Or maybe the elephants got scared and rocked the trailer, and the drivers lost control. You can see where the asphalt fell away. If you find something, let me know. If I find someone alive down there, I'll call you." He looked at Mark. "I need you to use your eyes without the camera."

"No problem," Mark said.

"Is your head OK?"

Mark smiled. "The only time you have to worry about

my head, or any other part of my body, is when I'm not complaining."

John returned the smile. "That's what I figured." Back in his SEAL days, he'd had a team member just like Mark, a guy by the name of Raul Delgado. Raul used to constantly whine and complain, but when it was crunch time, he was the best operative they had. John had heard that Raul was now Commander Delgado, head honcho of SEAL Team One.

As Mark and Nicole off-loaded the quad, John rigged his ropes. It had been fifteen years since he had rappelled into a ravine, but he found his hands working the line and harness as if it were yesterday.

The only easy day was yesterday. Where had Chase heard that? It couldn't be a coincidence.

When he'd left the SEALs and married Emily, John Masters had put all that behind him. It wasn't until the lightning strike that it had all come back. He had even thought about re-enlisting.

But where would that have left Chase?

Chase came to with a hammering headache, ash and bile in his mouth and something tickling his face. His eyelids fluttered open. The thing tickling his face was Pepe's tongue. He didn't move as he tried to put together what had happened. He'd been talking to the two guys with the rags wrapped around their heads. One of them had pointed at the quad. Chase had turned to look and the lights had gone out.

He sat up very slowly, but not slowly enough. He threw

up. He thought his head was going to explode. He felt the back of his skull and discovered a hard lump the size of a chicken egg.

He looked up the road. The quad was gone. He felt around his neck. The respirator was gone. So was his helmet and his go bag and... He felt his pockets. They were turned inside out. They had taken the sat phone and everything else.

In a disaster, desperate people do desperate things.

One of his father's warnings.

What was I supposed to do? Blow right by them without stopping?

He wished he had now.

Pepe barked.

He looked down at him. "Yeah, yeah, I know. You had them pegged. I should have listened to you."

Pepe barked again.

"I'm not picking you up. If I bend over, my head might roll off my neck."

Pepe did a backwards flip.

"Nice trick. I'm still not picking you up."

Chase looked at his watch. He had been out cold for five minutes.

Ø3:38 PM

John dropped over the edge as soon as Nicole and Mark took off on the quad. It was an easy rappel, but being among the broken elephants was much worse than seeing them from the road. Swarms of flies covered the carcasses, rising in a black mass as he made his way to the tractor. The respirator kept the dust out, but not the stench of rotting flesh.

He walked past the colourful trailer, which was now nothing more than a pile of twisted metal. The tractor was on its side several feet from the trailer. The fuel tank had ruptured, coating the tractor with slick diesel. One of the men had been ejected through the windscreen and was lying six metres from the tractor. Two other men were seatbelted in the cab. Both were just as dead as the man on the ground.

He looked up at the road. He could see more clearly now how it had happened. A good portion of the outside lane had collapsed.

It must have happened at night, John thought. *They came around the corner, thinking the worst was over, then the world dropped out from under them.* Looking at the shattered bodies, he could not help but think of another accident on another mountain thousands of miles away. His wife and daughter, Emily and Monica, both killed

331

on impact, while he had walked away without a cut or a bruise. Unscathed. Safe. Why? He shook the memory off, as he had so many times before. He was about to climb back up to the road, but a glint of metal further off in the trees caught his attention. He reached it with some difficulty. It was a second semi, smaller than the elephant truck but equally destroyed. Two dead men crushed in the cab. It was impossible to get to, or even see into, the sleeper behind the men. He called out and listened. There was no reply.

He looked up at the road again. He could barely see it from this position, which is why they hadn't seen the second truck from the road. He walked over to what was left of the trailer to see what they had been hauling.

Cats.

The ground was littered with lions and tigers. Some were still in their cages. Others had been thrown out on to the ground. He counted seven lions and three tigers. All dead.

Heartbreaking.

He did a thorough search of the area to make sure he hadn't missed anything, but when he finished, something was still nagging at him. He returned to the cat trailer and counted again.

Seven lions. Three tigers.

He called Nicole to find out how many cats the show had. She didn't answer.

Probably can't hear above the noise of the quad.

He called Mark. Again no answer.

He counted the cats for the third time, then he counted the cages.

Ten cats. Eleven cages.

He called Nicole and Mark again, and again there was no answer.

He climbed back up to the road as fast as he could.

The tiger watched the man climb the rope. The man had climbed down the rope faster than he was going up. The tiger had seen this countless times before in the big tent, from the humans who swung and walked the rope in the air. This man was not like the ones in the big tent. He did not sparkle and glitter in the light. And he was a new man. The tiger had not seen him before. The tiger had thought about coming out of hiding as he watched the man wander among the dead, but had waited instead. Since the fall in the dark, everything was new. Nothing was as it had been. The ground had shaken. The sky rained dust. The tiger was afraid of this new world, but also intrigued by it. And hungry. He heard the truck door close and the engine rumble and the tyres move along the asphalt above. He waited until the sound faded away, then came out of hiding. He walked to the stream and drank. A movement to his right caught his attention. A deer bounding up the steep bank to the road. He knew deer, but not like this. At the farm during the long days of stillness with no man in the ring snapping the whip, making him do things, he was sometimes given deer to eat. But this deer was full of life. It moved with strength and grace up the mountainside. The tiger was hungry. It followed the deer.

Nicole drove the quad slowly down the left lane of the highway, with Chico clinging to her front, and Mark clinging to her back.

"Not so close to the edge," Mark reminded her for the twentieth time. "I'm not wearing a helmet."

"A helmet won't do you much good if we plunge over the side."

"Thanks for reminding me. And that's exactly what I'm afraid of. Scoot over!"

"If I get too far over, we won't be able to see into the ravine."

"Then at least keep your eyes on the road. I'll watch the ravine and tell you if I see anything horrible."

It was hard for Nicole to imagine what could be more horrible than four dead elephants and a smashed circus truck. The image would be tattooed in her memory for ever. If they hadn't stopped where they had, they probably would never have seen the elephant rig. She dreaded seeing her mother and sister's crushed camper, or any of the other circus rigs, but she felt compelled to keep peering over the edge. Chico had got away from the clown rig. Pepe had got away from the dog rig. She hoped they weren't the only survivors.

She eased the quad around a sharp curve and nearly fell off the seat. There were at least thirty cars, campers and Rossi Brothers' Circus trailers blocking the highway. She throttled the quad to full speed and came to a sliding stop in the midst of the vehicles.

"Thanks for that experience," Mark said.

Nicole jumped off the quad and ran towards a tall, thin man wearing a red wig, oversize floppy shoes and clown make-up.

"Doug!" she shouted.

"I can't believe this!" the clown shouted back. He threw his long arms around her and Chico, who seemed as happy to see Doug as Nicole was. "What are you doing here? How did you get here?"

A crowd gathered around them. Mark unwrapped the bungee cord securing his camera to the back of the quad and started videotaping.

"Where are my mom and sister?"

"Mexico City. I'm sure they're worried sick…"

"They're not in Mexico City. We were just—"

"Maybe they got stuck at the village."

"What village?"

"The Lake of the Mountain. It's up near the rim of the volcano."

"Lago?"

"Yeah, I think they called it that. It's Arturo's village."

"Why would they go up there?"

"The orphanage. Your mom took the dog act, Chico and a few clowns to … Wait – how did you get your hands on Chico?"

"This isn't getting us anywhere," Nicole interrupted. "You go first. From the beginning."

"All right." Doug took a deep breath. "The day before yesterday, a priest shows up at the matinee in Puebla with a half dozen kids from an orphanage. He could only bring a few of the kids because he doesn't have a way to transport them all." Doug smiled. "You know your mom, she's a sucker for kids. So she offers to do a free show for the orphanage. You know, a mini show. Some clowns. The dog act. Ponies for the kids to ride. The priest invites them to spend the night. Your mom and her crew take off for Lago halfway through the big show. She wants to get up to the village at a decent hour so they can get some sleep, get up early and do the show. She wants to get over to Mexico City by early afternoon. The priest offers to lead them to Lago, which he says is kind of hard to find in the dark.

"We finish the last act, strike the big top, and decide to drive straight to Mexico City. Maybe get there at three in the morning and have a day off to do laundry, look around, you know... Anyway, we're driving down the highway in a caravan and everything's fine and then suddenly it feels like the world's coming apart. We pull over, wait it out, gather our wits and take off again. We get maybe a quarter of a mile up the road and run into this gigantic landslide. We try to get ahold of your mom, but all the phones are dead. We turn around and come back here because it's a good place to pull the rigs off the road. The elephant guys decide to go back to Puebla. Because we were heading straight to Mexico City, they hadn't bothered to load up with hay and grain. The cat guys decided to go with them. Don't ask me why. They leave with a promise to find out if there's another way to Mexico City. No point in all of us going to Puebla until we find out.

"By noon the next day, we still haven't heard from the elephant crew or the cat guys, so we send a car to Puebla to find out what's up. They don't get very far either. They run into a landslide bigger than the one in front of us. They drive back and tell us what's up. One of the tumblers crawls over the slide in front of us and finds out the bridge up ahead is out. We can't go forward. We can't go backwards.

We're stuck between a rock and a hard place. Then the ash starts coming down, so we set up tents to keep it off us and our new friends." He pointed to some of the people standing around. "Not everybody here's on the show. We took in the locals who got stranded with us. A couple of us are clowning to entertain the kids and keep the grown-ups' minds off the situation."

"I was wondering why you were clowning," Nicole said.

"The concession trucks are with us, so we have plenty of food. There's a stream down in the gully running along the road. We've been hauling water up, so we aren't going to die of thirst any time soon. I figure we can last a couple of weeks if we don't get sick of hot dogs before then."

"I wouldn't drink that water," John Masters said. No one had noticed him pull up.

Nicole looked at him with hopeful eyes.

John shook his head. "They didn't make it. How many cats does the show have?"

"Eleven," Doug answered. "Seven lions and four tigers."

"One of the tigers is missing," John said, then explained what he had found upstream.

04:06 PM

"Stop!" Cindy shouted.

Tomás slammed on the brakes.

"There are no tyre tracks in front of us," she said in Spanish.

Tomás looked through the windscreen and nodded. He pointed at her sat phone.

Cindy looked down at the phone's screen. "No satellite signal."

Tomás put the truck into reverse and turned it around. A couple miles down the road, they found the disturbed ash. They got out for a closer look and found the tyre tracks going back in the direction Chase had come from.

"Footprints," Tomás said.

"And animal prints," Cindy added.

"*Muy pequeño.*"

"Very small," Cindy agreed.

They got into the truck and followed the tracks all the way back to the slide. There was a man sitting on the rubble, wearing Chase's respirator and helmet. Sitting next to him was Chase's go bag. Tomás was out of the truck in a flash. The man got up and tried to run away but fell. Tomás yanked him to his feet, slapped the helmet off his head and tore the respirator off his face.

"I think his leg is broken!" Cindy shouted.

Tomás either didn't understand or didn't care. He dragged the blubbering man over to the edge of the road. The quad was smashed against a tree ten metres below them. Lying next to it was another man.

"¿*Muerto?*" Tomás asked.

"*Si*," the man said. He looked at Cindy. "My friend is dead."

"So you speak English," Cindy said with absolutely no sympathy for him. "Where is *our* friend?"

"We left the boy on the road."

"Alive?"

"Yes."

"He had better be."

Tomás marched the man to the truck and pushed him into the bed, ignoring his protests.

"We go," he told Cindy.

Cindy ran to the passenger door and jumped in. She was afraid that in his present mood, Tomás would leave her behind.

Tomás stepped on the gas, but they didn't get very far. A hundred metres down the road, the right front tyre exploded.

Chase walked up the road in the direction of Lago with Pepe at his feet, stirring up tiny puffs of ash with each dainty step. He was no longer limping.

Where are Tomás and Cindy? What's taking them so long?

It had been over an hour since he had told them it was clear.

Maybe Tomás found a better way up and is in front of me. But where are the tyre tracks?

The only tracks in front of him were the thieves' boot prints reminding him how stupid he'd been. The pounding in his head had diminished to a dull thud, but his anger had not. He came around yet another curve in the winding ash-covered road and stopped. In front of him was a crack in the earth that ran across the road and up the mountain as far as he could see. White steam billowed out of the crack. It was as if the ground had been unzipped, leaving a gap ten metres across. In the middle of the gap were two upended trucks with the Rossi Brothers' Circus logo painted on their sides. One truck had a camper on the back. The other truck had been pulling a trailer, which was now a twisted wreck. Scattered around the smashed trailer were at least a dozen dog crates. The wire-mesh doors were all hanging open. Chase looked inside one of the crates and saw what looked like dried blood. There was a second trailer just off the road. Inside were four dead ponies.

Pepe barked.

"I hear you," Chase said. "You were lucky to get away with an injured paw." He looked at the trucks. The passenger's and driver's doors were open, just like the crates. "Looks like everyone got out." He scratched Pepe's ears. "This explains how you got up here, but it doesn't explain *why* you were up here, or where everyone went."

The trucks formed a bridge across the gap, which the circus people must have used to get to the other side.

And there's no doubt the thieves used the same bridge to get to my side, Chase thought. He was still angry, but looking at the steam coming out of the crack, he couldn't really blame them. The mountain was coming apart. The two men had been in a panic, with a long, dangerous walk ahead of them. He just wished they had left the go bag with the sat phone and his water. He was thirsty and he was sure the others were wondering why he hadn't checked in or answered the phone.

Chase looked down the road where he had come from. The curve was sharp. With the ash flying around, there was a good chance Tomás wouldn't see the crack before he crashed into it. Chase had to warn them. He thought about walking back and flagging them down. But what if they didn't drive up the road? What if something had happened to the truck? A flat tyre, mechanical breakdown, getting mired in the soft ground... The possibilities were endless.

He looked up at the sky. It was getting darker, and it wasn't just the ash. The sun was getting lower. It would be pitch dark in a couple of hours. He couldn't wrap himself in toilet paper like they had the air filters. His eyes were swollen, his throat was sore. He needed water. He needed shelter. And he needed both of them soon.

You're no good to anybody if you're dead ... including yourself.

Another of his father's favourite sayings. He wondered if that one was a Navy SEAL deal too. The SEAL motto Cindy had told him about was certainly holding up. The only easy day *was* yesterday. The hardest thing they'd done the day before was move a lion and slap a bear on the butt, and it was Momma Rossi who had slapped the bear.

"Guess I better get my own butt in gear," Chase said.

Pepe barked and ran into one of the crates.

"I'm not carrying you in one of those, but I will carry you across the junkyard bridge so you don't fall into the steaming crevasse." He squatted down. "Let's go."

Pepe gave him another bark, but didn't budge.

Chase got an idea. He reached into the crate and pulled Pepe out.

"I need this."

He picked up Pepe's crate and a couple others, then jogged back down to the spot where the curve straightened out. It was roughly thirty metres from the crack. He came back and picked up a few more crates, then returned for a third and fourth load.

"Fifteen crates," he said. "We're going to build a pyramid."

Chase set out five crates in the middle of the road, then four on top of the five, then three on top of the four, then two on top of the three, topping it off with Pepe's crate, which was the smallest.

Pepe did a backflip and landed on the first tier.

"Nice," Chase said. "But this isn't a circus prop. It's a stop sign. The truck will have to slow down as it's coming around the curve. Tomás will stop when he sees the crates, or he'll run into them. Either way, he won't fall through the crack."

Pepe stared at him.

"I can't believe I'm explaining this to a poodle."

He picked Pepe up and started towards the crack in the earth.

04:21PM

"I'm sorry about your friends," Mark said.

"Thanks," Doug said. "I guess this is the end of the Rossi Brothers' Circus. No cat act. No elephant act." He looked off into the distance. "Maybe no owner. We all knew it was coming, but we had no idea it was going to end this way."

Doug was smiling, but it was clear from his voice and the expression beneath the greasepaint that he was anything but happy. When he'd heard about the elephants and cats and his friends, he had nearly collapsed. John and Mark had to help him into the tent where he could sit down.

John was out trying to make a phone call, Nicole was in the opposite corner of the tent talking quietly to the other circus people, leaving Mark to look after the bereaved clown. He didn't mind. He liked clowns.

"What's the deal with the camera?" Doug asked.

Mark explained the last forty-eight hours as best as he could.

"The Rossis lost their house!" Doug said. "We didn't even hear about the hurricane. Does Mrs Rossi know?"

"I don't think so. We haven't been able to get in touch with anyone down here to let them know."

"You're making a documentary about this John dude?"

"I'm just the camera guy. My producer, Cindy, is making the documentary. But it's a safe bet you'll be in it."

"Clown on a volcano," Doug said.

Mark smiled. "Something like that."

"Might be my last performance."

John came into the tent, looking worried. Nicole saw him enter and ran over to join Mark and Doug as he walked up to them.

"I spoke to Cindy, but the conversation was garbled. The ash is playing havoc with the satellite signal. She said she completely lost the signal for a while. From what I understood, a couple of men jacked Chase's quad and he's missing. Tomás found the thieves. They had totalled the quad, and one of them is dead. The other guy has a broken leg. To top it off, Tomás had a blowout, which caused some other damage to the truck besides the flat. Cindy's walking ahead trying to find Chase while Tomás tries to fix the truck. It sounds like the ash is a lot worse up there than it is down here."

"What do we do?" Nicole asked.

"*We* do nothing," John said. "You and Mark are going to stay here. I'm going back up to find Chase."

"I'm going with you," Nicole said.

John shook his head. "You'll be safer here. I'm not going back the same way we came. That would take too long. I've figured out a way of going over the top. Or close to the top. I'll get the truck up as far as I can, then head out on foot or on the quad to Lago. There's only one road going in. If I get there before Tomás and Cindy, I'll backtrack along the road."

"I'm still going with you," Nicole said.

"Sorry," John said.

"My mother and sister are in Lago. It's the reason I came all the way down here."

"It's why Cindy and I came down here too," Mark said. "Who's to say it's any safer here than it is up at the village? Stranded is stranded."

"Are you saying that you want to go too?" John asked.

"Not particularly, but Cindy would probably kill me if I didn't." Mark smiled. "Besides, you're lucky. Bad things happen all around you, but you always come through without a scratch. You're the Teflon man. Nothing seems to stick to you, so I'm sticking *with* you."

"You're forgetting that if we have to use the quad, there's only room for two people," John said.

"If it comes to that, I'll flip you for it," Mark said.

"What about my luck?"

"I'll take my chances."

"What about us?" Doug asked.

"I spoke to the authorities in Mexico City. They know you're stranded here. There's a road crew on the way to repair the bridge and clear the slide."

"How long is that going to take?" Doug asked.

"Too long," John admitted. "But I think I have that covered as well. A friend of mine in the States is trying to get permission to bring a rescue team in with choppers. As soon as they get the OK, they'll mobilize quickly. It won't take them more than a few hours to get here."

"How'd you arrange that?"

"My friend is in charge of the outfit."

"A military outfit?" Nicole asked.

"Definitely military." John looked at Doug. "The best

thing you can do while you're waiting is to set up a landing zone. You'll have to move some of these trucks. They'll fly in and ferry you to the other side of the bridge, where you'll be driven to Mexico City."

"What about the animals?" Doug asked.

"That's up to Delgado."

"Delgado?" Mark asked.

"Commander Raul Delgado of the US Navy SEALs." John smiled. "He reminds me of you, actually. Constantly whining and complaining, but he's the best operative I know. His priority is going to be getting the people out of here, not the animals, but you never know with Raul. He's done some crazy things in his life. He might like the idea of evacuating lions and tigers and bears." John looked at Nicole and Mark. "Time to go."

It was time for Chase to go. He put the dusty poodle down his shirt and started across the junkyard bridge. The short crossing turned out to be a lot harder than he was expecting. The wrecks were hot with steam and slick with ash. And Pepe's sharp nails scratching his stomach and chest as the little dog tried to get out wasn't helping matters.

"Knock it off! Unless you want to fall off into the bottomless pit."

Chase knew it wasn't bottomless, but it was deep. He couldn't see the bottom. He got down on his hands and knees, afraid he would slip off if he stayed on his feet. As he crawled on to the camper roof, the pile suddenly shifted with a loud screech. He froze and held his breath.

This is it.

The screeching stopped. The twisted metal held. Chase breathed.

Forward or backwards?

He looked behind him. The distance was just about equal.

Dead centre.

He didn't like the sound of that.

In the middle. Halfway. Better.

Pepe had stopped struggling. It was as if he sensed the danger. Whatever the reason, Chase was grateful. It would make his next move easier.

Whatever that move is going to be.

There wasn't enough room to turn around safely. He'd have to crawl backwards to get to where he'd come from. The other problem was that when the camper shifted, the top had settled at a steep angle. He was hanging on to the edge to keep himself from slipping into the crack.

"Just go!" he shouted.

He crawled forward, feeling the pile tremble every time he put a hand or a knee down. The far side seemed like it was a football field away.

If there's another earthquake... If the crack widens... If I slip...

Chase knew better than to think this way. *Fear brings disaster from the inside out.* His father had told him this a thousand times. *Focus on the moment. Concentrate on survival. Think about what's right, not what's wrong. Take advantage of it.*

Chase wished his father was there to explain what was "right" about this. After what seemed like an eternity, he finally reached the other side of the junkyard bridge, but he was far from safe. The edge of the road was a metre above him. He would have to stand on the tilted truck hood, reach above his head and pull himself up. He got to his feet very slowly, looking for something solid to grab on to if the pile started to go. The camper rocked back and forth. Pepe began struggling again.

"Can't have that."

He reached into his shirt and pulled him out.

"Sorry."

He tossed the poodle up over the ledge. Pepe landed with a soft thud and a whimper. A second later, his head appeared over the edge and he started barking indignantly.

"No need to thank me," Chase said.

He reached up and grabbed the overhang of broken road. Pepe licked his fingers.

"That's not helpful."

He pulled himself up, relieved to have his feet off the unstable camper, and even happier to have climbed on to the road. He lay on his back, catching his breath, with Pepe perched on his chest.

04:47 PM

Tomás pulled the truck over and Cindy got in. She told him about her broken conversation with John Masters. Tomás told her about the conversation he'd had with the broken-legged thief in back while changing the tyre and repairing the undercarriage.

The man had said that he and his friend were working in Lago when the earthquake hit in the middle of the night. There had been a great deal of damage to the houses, and people had been killed, but he didn't know how many or who.

Cindy looked at Tomás's children smiling in the photos taped to the dash. Tomás wasn't showing it, but she was certain he was sick with worry.

Tomás explained that the village priest had returned to Lago just after the earthquake with a van full of orphans, three circus clowns, a dozen performing dogs and two very small women.

"Mrs Rossi and Nicole's sister, Leah," Cindy said.

Tomás nodded.

Mrs Rossi, Leah and two of the clowns had been badly injured. A few miles from Lago the road had opened up, swallowing the Rossis' camper and the other vehicle. The priest and orphans had been right in front of them and had missed falling into the enormous crack by centimetres. Because that road was the only way in or out, Lago was completely cut off. The two men had decided to head out on foot. They were both from Puebla and wanted to find out how their families were. They were surprised to see Chase drive up on the quad. The man with the broken leg claimed he had no idea that his friend was going to hit Chase in the head and take the quad.

"Do you believe him?" Cindy asked.

Tomás shrugged.

Neither of the men had ever driven a quad. When they reached the landslide, his friend took the quad off-road and it flipped. The man in back crawled up the bank because he didn't know what else to do. He had been expecting to die there.

"He may yet die," Tomás concluded in English, "if Chase is unwell."

Cindy took her phone out, hoping to reach Nicole with the news about her mother and sister. The signal was gone again.

John drove the truck up the mountainside at an impossible angle.

Mark was holding on to his precious camera with white knuckles. "You know," he said, "these tyres don't have suction cups."

"But we do have a roll bar," John said. "If we flip, we should be OK."

"Comforting," Mark said.

"Do we have a signal yet?" John asked.

Nicole tore her eyes away from the tops of the trees and glanced at the satellite phone she was carrying. "No."

"Maybe it will get better when we get above the tree line."

"*If* we get to the tree line," Mark said. "Where did you learn to drive?"

"In the Navy."

"Figures."

"Lago de la Montaña," Chase said. Pepe looked up at him. "I'm not sure how you say it in poodle, but in English it means 'Lake of the Mountain'."

The last half mile of road had been steep. The small lake was above the tree line and fed by glaciers, which had now turned from white to grey. The village was on the opposite side of the lake. Looming behind it like a petrified tooth was the summit of Popocatepetl. A thick plume of grey ash and steam billowed from the peak into the darkening sky as far as Chase could see.

Pepe scampered to the edge of the water and started drinking. Chase joined him. The surface was covered with fine ash and what looked like white floating rocks. He picked one up. It was porous and as light as a feather.

"Pumice stone," he said.

Pepe picked one up in his teeth and tossed it into the air.

"Knock yourself out. It's not poisonous."

Chase kneeled, cleared an area of ash and pumice and scooped water into his mouth. He wasn't aware of just how thirsty he was until the icy liquid hit the back of his throat.

He put his head under water and came up gasping from the glacial chill.

"Whoa!"

Having his face clean made every other part of his body itch. He looked across the lake at the village. It had taken him so long to get this far, five minutes more couldn't hurt. He quickly stripped off his clothes, tossed them into the water to soak, then dived in. He thought his heart would turn to ice. He lifted his head above the water. His teeth chattered. Pumice stones bobbed around him like an armada of toy ships. Pepe ran back and forth along the shore, barking.

"Come on in! The water's fine!"

Pepe would have none of it. Chase stayed in as long as he could, which was less than three minutes. He waded back to shore, shivering. Facing the lake, he rinsed and wrung out his clothes as the air dried his skin. The wind had died down to almost nothing, which meant the ash was not blowing around as much, for which he was grateful. It meant he might be reasonably clean when he got to Lago. As he pulled on his underwear, he heard something behind him. He turned, expecting to see Pepe tossing more pumice around. Pepe was there, but he wasn't tossing volcanic rock, and he wasn't alone. He was sitting next to an old man and five children. Next to the old man was a wheelbarrow filled with sticks. The five children were carrying bundles of sticks in their arms and giggling. He didn't blame them. A second earlier, they had been staring at his shivering butt. He would have laughed too.

He quickly pulled on the rest of his clothes.

When he was dressed, the old man said something to him, which Chase didn't understand.

"*No hablo español. ¿Hablas inglés?*"

The old man shook his head.

Chase pointed at the village. "Lago de la Montaña?"

The old man nodded.

That was just about the extent of Chase's Spanish. He thought about mentioning Tomás's name, but realized he didn't know Tomás's last name.

I've known Tomás my entire life. How could I not know his last name? He looked at the five children. He did know what Tomás's children looked like, though, and none of them were here with the old man.

Why are children out gathering wood?

He would have to *see* why when he got to Lago because he didn't know how to ask.

Tomás eased around the curve, then stepped on the gas. He didn't see the dog crates until they were bouncing off the windscreen. He slammed on the brakes.

"What was that?" Cindy shouted.

Tomás shook his head.

They got out. The man in the truck bed moaned. Tomás checked on him before coming around to the front of the truck, where Cindy was pulling something out from under the bumper.

"Dog crates. Obviously from the circus, but why did they leave them in the middle of the road? And where are the dogs?"

Tomás squatted down and looked at the ground in front of the truck.

"What do you see?"

"Footprints."

They followed them to the crack.

"Chase put the crates there to warn us," Cindy said.

Tomás got down on his knees and pushed on the trailer to test its stability. It moved. He took the flashlight from his go bag and leaned over the edge with it. Cindy had seen him and John do the same thing on the levee road during the worst of Hurricane Emily.

After a couple of minutes, Tomás popped back up and said, "I will go first."

This implied that Cindy was going second. She wasn't sure she wanted to go at all. "What about our friend in the truck?"

"He will have to stay here."

"Maybe I should stay with him."

Tomás shrugged and jogged back to the truck. He drove forward and parked it as far to the right side of the road as he could. He came back with a coil of rope and Chase's go bag slung over his shoulder. He tied one end of the rope to the bumper.

"What are you doing?" Cindy asked.

Instead of answering, he handed her a webbed harness with a carabiner attached to it.

"What am I supposed to do with this?"

Without a moment's hesitation, Tomás danced nimbly across the wreckage to the other side of the crack. The trailer and camper were still wobbling and screeching as he pulled himself up to the road.

"Are you with the circus?" Cindy shouted across the fissure. "I can't do that!"

Tomás wrapped the rope around a tree, took up the slack and tied it off. He motioned for her to put the harness around her waist and clip the carabiner to the rope.

"You are crazy!"

Tomás pointed at his watch.

"I know you're in a hurry, but still . . . I can't do this. I'll stay here and take care of the man in the truck."

Tomás gave her another shrug and turned to leave.

"Wait!"

Tomás turned back.

Cindy snapped the carabiner to the rope. "Just go before you regain your sanity," she muttered to herself. She stepped on to the twisted metal and immediately dropped to her hands and knees. There was no way she'd be able to cross it like Tomás had. She began to crawl. Three quarters of the way across, she heard a loud rumbling coming up from the fissure. The wreckage started to sway. She looked up. The sides of the fissure were grinding back and forth like jaws. The metal dropped away as if the earth were swallowing it.

Cindy screamed.

05:16PM

The old man was kneeling, with his arms wrapped around three of the children. Chase was crouched down, his arms around the other two and the poodle. Pepe was whimpering. The children were crying. As the ground rumbled and rolled beneath them, Chase looked up at the volcano. The plume had turned darker and thicker, as if someone were stoking the fire beneath. A church bell rang from the village. He wondered if someone was pulling the rope or if the quake was causing it to toll.

Chase had glanced at his watch the moment they had dropped to their knees in the middle of the road. When the quake finally stopped, only thirteen seconds had passed.

The shaking terrified the tiger. He unsheathed his claws and gripped the earth so the ground would not drop out from beneath him. When it finally stopped, he continued to hold on for several seconds. He had lost track of the deer some time ago. Other scents were now pushing up the mountain. He lifted his head and listened. He heard the bang of metal in the trees below. He did not like the sound. It reminded him of the night before, when the world came apart and the other cats lay still. He moved away from the noise so it could not catch him.

John, Nicole and Mark were sitting upside down, pushing airbags out of their faces. Thirteen seconds earlier, they had been heading up the mountain on a steep incline. The trees had begun to thin out, making it easier for John to pick and choose his route. The truck had started to slip sideways and tip to the left. John shouted for them to lean to the right, but their weight wasn't enough to put the truck back on four wheels. The 4x4 rolled over in slow motion and landed on its roof. Then it started to slide, spinning like a windmill, banging off several trees before coming to a jarring stop against a boulder.

"Everyone OK?" John asked.

"I'm fine," Nicole said.

"It seems to me that we were in this exact same position a couple of days ago," Mark said.

"Not the exact same position," John said. "That time we were on our side."

"Oh, yeah, that's right. On a train trestle!"

"Are you OK?" John repeated.

"Couldn't be better," Mark said. "Can we do that again?"

John unhooked his seat belt, righted himself, and kicked out the windscreen. The three crawled out of the truck and looked it over. The quad had been smashed into several pieces.

"Guess we won't have to flip a coin to see who rides," Mark said.

John didn't hear him. He was already headed up the mountain.

Cindy dangled over the steaming chasm, suspended by her waist. Eternal blackness loomed beneath her. There was no sign of the wreckage she'd been crawling on a moment before. The earth had swallowed it. She reached up and grabbed the rope, not trusting the harness alone to hold her. The rope bowed under her weight. She was three metres below the road's jagged edge. Was Tomás OK? Would the rope hold? Did she have the strength to pull herself up if it did?

Tomás's respirator-covered face appeared over the edge. He shined his flashlight down on her. Cindy could see only his eyes, but he looked as relieved to see her as she was to see him.

"Rope fraying. Stay still. I pull you up."

His face disappeared before she could ask him to explain.

Fraying *is not a word you want to hear when you're hanging from a rope*, Cindy thought, tightening her grip. As a television reporter, she had been in a lot of frightening situations, including Hurricane Emily, but this was by far the most terrified she had ever been. Her heart slammed in her chest. Tears poured from her eyes. She couldn't breathe. She tore the respirator off and dropped it into the void. She took a deep breath and started to choke. Something bad was in the air. *Sulphur? What's taking Tomás so long?* The end of a rope dropped down. She looked up.

"Tie to harness," Tomás shouted through his respirator. "Tight."

She fumbled with the line.

"Hurry!"

Cindy was doing the best she could. The respirator had not worked well against the foul air, but she realized now that it had been better than nothing. *What was I thinking?*

I've got to get out of this hole! With fumbling fingers she managed to get the line through the carabiner and tie it off.

"Secured!" she shouted.

She began to pull herself along the rope, but found that Tomás was pulling her faster than she could move her hands. Within seconds he had her over the ledge and on to the road. He dragged her away from the crack and gave her a bottle of water. Her mouth and throat were raw from breathing ash and toxic steam, but she washed her face and rinsed her eyes before taking a drink.

"The village is not too far." Tomás helped her to her feet. He took his respirator off and handed it to her.

Cindy shook her head. "You keep it."

"Please. I insist."

Reluctantly, she put it on. Tomás took his shirt off, wet it down and wrapped it around his nose and mouth.

They continued up the road towards Lago.

06:01PM

Brittle pumice popped beneath Chase's feet as he walked down the centre of the road towards Lago. He had taken the bundles of sticks from the three smallest children. They in turn had taken Pepe and were handing him back and forth as they walked. As they drew closer to the village, they passed piles of rubble beside the road. At first Chase thought the piles were discarded building material or village rubbish. But when the old man and the children stopped at one of the piles, crossed themselves and bowed their heads, he knew he was wrong. The piles had once been houses. People had died beneath the debris. The group stopped three more times before entering the village.

Lago de la Montaña was much bigger than Chase had expected, and the damage also was much worse. The cobbled streets had buckled. The houses and buildings on both sides had all collapsed. The village was in ruins. The initial earthquake had struck at night while people were sleeping. Chase looked in dismay at the mounds of adobe brick and wood, knowing that some of the people, if not most of them, had died in their beds.

They arrived at the village square. It looked like a refugee camp, with dozens of people cooking, cleaning and hovering outside crudely constructed shelters. The old man pointed at the church.

"Padre," he said. "Inside."

One wall of the church had collapsed, but the roof was intact. Popocatepetl's plume rose high above the steeple. The church's front door was open, and people were sitting on the stairs with blank, exhausted expressions. No one seemed even remotely interested in Chase's sudden appearance in the village.

Hopelessness. Defeat. He thought he had seen the look before in emergency shelters and on the faces of people standing outside what were once their homes, but this was different.

These people have given up. They are waiting for doom.

Two men came out of the church, carrying between them a body wrapped in a blanket. Everyone followed their progress across the square to the right of the church with dull eyes. The men lay the body on the ground among dozens of others.

The old man said something to the children. The one carrying Pepe handed him to Chase. Then they started distributing the sticks to the shelters for the pitiful fires.

Chase set Pepe on the ground. They had come to Lago to find Tomás's children, but he didn't know exactly where to start. Pepe decided for him. The little dog ran up the steps through the open doors of the church. Chase ran after him.

Dull light filtered through the cut-glass windows and the collapsed wall. Candles and oil lamps were scattered along the floor. Dark shadows flickered throughout the nave. It took a few seconds for Chase's eyes to adjust to the dark. The pews had been rearranged and turned into hospital beds. All of them were full. A murmuring of pain filled the church. Above the pitiful sound, Chase heard a high-pitched barking up near the altar. He wasn't sure why – Pepe wasn't his dog – but he felt responsible. He started to weave his way through the pews towards the front. It was a sad sight. The people lying on the makeshift beds were badly broken. Those who weren't hurt were helping those who were. Chase couldn't say it was exactly cheerful inside the church, but the mood was certainly more hopeful than it had been out on the square.

When Chase was halfway across the church, a man stepped out in front of him. He was wearing a black cassock dusted with ash, and a white clerical collar.

"Padre," Chase said.

"Yes. Are you with the circus?"

Chase shook his head, relieved to hear that the father spoke English. "My name is Chase Masters."

"I'm Father Alejandro, but you may call me Father Al, or just Al, if you like."

"I think I'll stick with Father Al," Chase said.

Father Al smiled. "And you say you are not with the circus."

"No, I just got here."

"The road is clear?" Father Al asked excitedly.

"No ... sorry." Chase explained how he had got to the village and why he had come.

"I'm sorry about the men who robbed you. I know who they are, but they are not from here. They came from Puebla a few days ago to work in our bottling plant."

"Bottling plant?"

"*Agua* ... water. The lake is glacial. Very pure. Montaña

water is sold all over Mexico. Our other industry comes from the volcano itself. Perhaps you saw some of our product as you walked here."

"Pumice stone?"

"Yes. Plentiful." His expression turned serious. "Of course after this, I don't know what we will do. The village is in ruins. Many people have died. Others have left."

"Where did they go?" Chase asked. "How did they leave?"

"On foot in the middle of the night after the big earthquake. You climbed across the wreckage?"

"Yes."

"It is stable?"

"No. They couldn't have gone that way, and I didn't see anyone on the road coming up here besides those two men."

"I hope they are safe. You say you are here to check on a family?"

"The family of my father's partner, our friend. He's somewhere behind me. I'm sure he'll be here soon. His name is Tomás."

"That is a very common name. What is his last name?"

Chase flushed. "I don't know, but he's married to a woman named Guadalupe and they have eight children."

Father Al laughed. "That would be Tomás Vargas! The eight are not exactly his children, and Guadalupe is not exactly his wife. You say he's on his way up here?"

"I expect him any time," Chase said, hoping that nothing had happened to Tomás and Cindy.

Father Al gave him a broad smile. "That is wonderful

news! Tomás has very clever hands. The generator is out. It is our only source of electricity. We tried to fix it but failed."

Tomás does have clever hands, Chase thought. *If anyone can fix the generator, Tomás can.*

"What do you mean, the children aren't exactly his children?" Chase asked.

"Yes," Father Al said, "I should explain. The eight children are orphans. Tomás pays all of their expenses, including their education if they decide to go to the university. Guadalupe runs the orphanage for the church. She and Tomás have been friends since they were children. They were both raised in the orphanage."

Chase had known none of this, but he wasn't completely surprised by the revelation. Tomás was a man of few words. It was probably just simpler for him to say that they were his kids and Guadalupe was his wife. It made no difference. He obviously loved them or he wouldn't be down here. Neither would Chase's father.

"Are the kids OK?"

"Oh, yes. We lost no one in the orphanage. In fact, two of those children were with me at the circus in Puebla. The orphanage is behind the church. It's the only building in Lago with virtually no damage."

"Then all the houses have been searched?"

"Yes. We started right after the big earthquake. Most of the people here were pulled from the rubble of their homes. Many of the people in the square have been up for two days straight looking for survivors. They are exhausted. I called the search off just two hours ago so they can get some rest. We will resume the search tomorrow when it's light, although I fear we've found all we are going to find." Father Al sighed. "Alive, anyway.

"The mother and daughter who run the circus are badly injured, I'm afraid. They are in the orphanage, where we set up our first hospital. As you can see, it has overflowed here, into the church. The three clowns and the dog trainer who came with them are bruised but fine."

"The Rossis are here?"

"So you know them. Leah and her mother."

"That was their camper?" Chase said.

"Unfortunately, yes."

"I've – we've been looking for them, too. The people I was travelling with before, I mean. I knew those vehicles belonged to the circus. I just didn't know who was driving them." Chase was shocked. He wondered if his father had heard about this, or Nicole.

"The uninjured circus people are outside the orphanage, resting. Like the villagers in the square, they have been up for two days searching for survivors."

"The orphanage..." Chase said slowly. "I walked into the village with an older man and five children. Were they from the orphanage?"

"Gathering wood?"

Chase nodded.

Father Al smiled. "We have been giving the children small jobs like gathering firewood to keep their minds off the tragedy and the volcano."

"What about the volcano?" Chase asked.

Father Al shrugged. "I have lived in Popocatepetl's

shadow for over thirty years. This is the worst of the eruptions and it might be the end of Lago de la Montaña, but there is nothing we can do. The injured are not strong enough to walk off this mountain, and they outnumber those who are well, so we cannot carry them. It is up to God."

Chase understood Father Al's reasoning, but he had been taught his entire life that there is always something you can do. "So you're saying it's fate," he said.

Father Al shook his head. "Not fate. *Faith*. Come with me. I will take you to see the Rossis."

07:05 PM

John, Nicole and Mark stepped above the tree line just after sunset. In front of them, Popocatepetl's plume shot up into the night sky, hundreds of metres above the summit.

"It looks close enough to touch," Nicole said with awe.

"It's further away than you think," John said. "It just looks close because of its size."

Mark started videotaping.

"It would be a lot easier for you if you weren't lugging that camera," John said.

"Do you see all the colours in the plume?" Mark asked, totally ignoring the suggestion. "We couldn't see them during the day, but at night it's like the Fourth of July."

"Lightning," Nicole said.

"I see it," John said.

Crackling white and gold bolts exploded through the plume like electrified spider's webs.

"Does lightning make you nervous?" Mark asked.

John stared at the powerful column, remembering what Momma Rossi had said. *That lightning is still looking for you... It's going to find you again...* Reflexively, his hand went up to his earring.

"It *should* make me nervous," he admitted. "But for some reason, it doesn't." Then he pulled his sat phone out as he said abruptly to Mark and Nicole, "Get your headlamps out of your go bags. We'll need them to see where we're heading."

He tried the phone. Still no signal.

Tomás and Cindy had their headlamps on. They had reached the lake and were drinking the cold water and washing the ash from their faces and hair.

"I'm worried about that plume," Cindy said in Spanish.

"The pressure is being relieved," Tomás replied in his native tongue. "It is good."

"What about the lava?"

"There will be lava on the summit, but it is not a problem. It moves very slowly and hardens before it can reach Lago. Mudflows from melting snow and ice, earthquakes and flying rocks are what we have to worry about. When I was young, a rock the size of a school bus fell on the village square. It was on a Sunday morning. Everyone was in church. No one died."

Cindy pointed across the lake. "Are those fires?"

Tomás nodded. "Campfires in the village square. It means people no longer have houses to return to. We should go."

Chase stood beside two small beds in the orphanage. They were children's beds, but the adults occupying them did not fill their length. On his left was Mrs Rossi. On his right was Nicole's sister, Leah. Mrs Rossi was unconscious. Leah was asleep. The village doctor had been tending to them when Father Al showed Chase into the girls' dormitory. The doctor finished his work, then turned to Chase and explained the extent of their injuries in English almost as good as Father Al's.

"Both women have broken ribs and severe concussions. Mrs Rossi has two broken wrists and there is some damage to her neck, but without an X-ray machine or CAT scanner here, I can't say how bad the injuries are. I have stabilized the women, but they need to be hospitalized. I have sedated Mrs Rossi, and of course they are both on pain medication." He looked at Father Al. "How are the patients in the church?"

"We lost Mrs Ruiz," Father Al answered sadly.

The doctor nodded. "The medical supplies?"

"Very low. We are down to the expired medications. We are boiling cloth in the square to make dressings."

The doctor looked at his watch. "I'd better check on the other patients."

"And I need to see how the food supplies are holding up in the square," Father Al said.

"I'll stay here," Chase volunteered.

"One of the circus people is over in that corner, sleeping," Father Al said, nodding towards the man.

Chase looked over. He hadn't noticed the man sprawled on the tiny bed in the dark corner, with his knees hanging over the end.

"I believe his name is Dennis," Father Al continued. "He's one of the circus clowns. They took turns caring for the Rossis while the others helped us search the rubble for survivors. The dog trainer even enlisted some of the poodles to help. The little dogs found three people we would have missed otherwise."

The poodles were being kept in a large pen on the orphanage playground. The circus people had been asleep when Chase tiptoed up to put Pepe in the pen with his friends. He thought the little dog might start barking and wake everyone, but Pepe trotted over to the pile of his fellow poodles sleeping in the corner and snuggled into them without a whimper.

"If there are any problems, I'll be in the church," the doctor said. "When the girl wakes up, she will be thirsty. You can give her water but not too much. There is a case of Montaña under the bed. It's also important that she and her mother do not move. I've only been able to splint and wrap the broken bones. Undue movement could cause further damage. In fact..." He reached into his pocket and took out some pills. "If the girl wakes up, give her two of these."

"What are they?"

"They're sedatives, but tell her they're antibiotics. She's been a little difficult. Hard to keep down. I was thankful when she finally fell asleep. The best thing for her now is to rest."

07:26 PM

John stopped and pulled the topo map out of his go bag.

"Are we lost?" Mark asked.

"Not exactly," John answered. "I just need to check on where we're going."

"What about the GPS?" Nicole asked.

"You need a satellite signal to use the GPS." John pulled out a compass.

"We *are* lost," Mark said.

"Not as long as we keep the plume on our right. We're about here." He pointed to a spot on the map. "Here's the lake and the village." He moved his finger. "They're above the tree line, so we should be able to see them from this vantage point if they have any lights on."

"If they have electricity," Mark said.

John nodded. "That's the tricky part. If the power's out, Lago is going to be hard to spot, especially with all this ash floating around. They'll be using candles and lamps and have fires going in their houses. It's warm up here because of the plume, but down in the village, I'm betting it gets pretty cold when the sun goes down. I realize the plume is entertaining with the colours and lightning, but we're going to have to concentrate our attention down the mountain to the left. If we miss Lago, we could end up circling the mountain clockwise. I'd prefer not to do that if possible."

"Circling the drain," Mark said.

John laughed. "I haven't heard that phrase in years. And you're right. If we miss the village, we'll be in big trouble."

They started off again, looking down the mountain rather than up at the plume. John took the lead, followed by Mark, then Nicole.

Being a competitive swimmer, Nicole had great stamina, but she was learning that walking sideways on a volcano was using muscles she didn't know she had. Her legs and joints were killing her. But what bothered her more than her aching muscles was that skinny Mark, who looked like he'd never seen the inside of a gym, was loping behind John Masters with the ease of a mountain goat. And what about John Masters? She wouldn't be surprised to see him start flying. All he seemed to need was a sip of water and something to do, and he was good to go. Seemingly for ever.

She was still terribly worried about her mother and Leah... *And now Chase*, she thought. *I can't believe he got robbed in this desolate place. I just hope Tomás and Cindy have caught up to him and that he's OK. What if he's alone in the dark, maybe injured, maybe even—*

She stopped suddenly, then took a step backwards and shined her headlamp down to make sure, hoping her eyes had been playing tricks on her in the dark. They weren't.

"Back here," she called out.

John and Mark were about ten metres ahead of her. Their headlamps turned in her direction.

"What is it?" John asked.

"Don't tell me you've found another chimp," Mark said.

"You'd better come look."

The men walked back to where she was standing. She hadn't moved an inch.

"Well?" John said.

Nicole shined her headlamp down. "On the ground."

"My God!" Mark said. "They have bears here?"

"That's not a bear track," Nicole said, her mouth suddenly dry. "It's a tiger track."

07:45 PM

Chase sat between Mrs Rossi's and Leah's beds, trying hard to stay awake. The last patient he had watched like this was his father. The doctor and nurses had begged him to go home, but he had stubbornly refused. The only time he'd left his father's hospital bed was to go to the bathroom. He'd even eaten his food in the chair next to the bed, willing his father to come out of his coma.

Mrs Rossi and Leah were pretty, like Nicole. The same black hair. The same complexion. With their eyes closed, he could only guess at the colour, but he bet they were brown. Except for their height, it was obvious they were all related.

Leah began to stir. Her eyes fluttered open.

He smiled. *Brown.*

"Who are you?" Leah asked.

The blunt question startled him. He should have been thinking about what he was going to say in the event that she woke up.

"My name is Chase Masters."

"You're American."

"Yeah."

"What are you doing down here?"

"I'm a friend of Nicole's."

"My sister, Nicole?" She started to sit up and winced in pain.

"You'd better stay down."

"OK. Is there any water?"

Chase took a bottle of Montaña water out of the case beneath the bed. As he unscrewed the cap, he looked at the colourful label. It featured the lake, the church, and, looming behind them, an erupting Popocatepetl. He gave Leah a sip.

"That's better," she said.

"Oh . . . the doctor wanted you to take these." He handed her the two pills.

"What are they?"

"Antibiotics." He was off to a great start with Nicole's sister. He told himself that it was for her own good, but that didn't make him feel better about lying to her.

She popped the pills into her mouth and washed them down.

"You say you're a friend of my sister's?"

"We came down to look for you after we heard about the earthquake."

Leah's eyes went wide. "Nicole's here?"

"Not here, but she's . . . uh . . . close." Chase had no idea where Nicole was. If they hadn't heard about the Rossis being in Lago, they were probably in Puebla by now.

"I must be dreaming," Leah said.

Chase tried to explain, but it was difficult because he didn't want to tell her about the hurricane and losing her home. She had enough to worry about. When he finished his abridged story, she asked for another drink of water and seemed to be thinking about what he had told her. She turned her head and looked at her mother.

"How is she?"

"She's … uh … sedated."

Leah nodded. "We need to get her to a hospital. What are the chances of us getting out of here?"

"Not real good at the moment. There's only one road in and it's impassable."

"Then how did you get here?"

"I climbed over the trucks jammed in the gap. I wouldn't want to do that again."

"I bet. So your friend Tomás is from here, and you two split up."

"Right. We ran into a landslide, and I went ahead on a quad to find a way around the slide." He hadn't mentioned that he had got hit in the head and had everything stolen, including the quad. "Tomás is Arturo's brother."

"Our Arturo?"

Chase nodded.

"And Nicole is with your dad on the way to Puebla."

"Or on their way back here if they got word that you and your mother are in Lago." He hadn't mentioned Cindy and Mark. That was way too complicated, and he wasn't sure he understood why they were here himself.

"I'm still confused," Leah said. "Actually I'm shocked. It's not like my dad or my grandmother to let Nicole miss school and her swimming. Weekends are out too. She's a lifeguard at the local pool."

Chase hadn't known Nicole was a lifeguard, but he wasn't surprised. He wished he'd never started this conversation. His mother would have called it a *trie* – not quite the truth, but not exactly a lie. *Nice trie*, she used to tell him.

"I know most of Nicole's friends," Leah continued. "I don't think I've ever met you."

Here we go, Chase thought. "I just moved to Palm Breeze."

"Why would your dad drop everything and come down here to help us?"

"Actually he came down here to help Tomás and his family. It just turned out you were down here too. I guess it was fate."

"Fate, huh?"

Chase shrugged.

"What does your dad do for a living?"

"He..." Chase hesitated. "He rescues people."

"That's a job?"

"He used to be a Navy SEAL." Chase wasn't even sure this was true. "Look, your dad said you'd be shocked when Nicole showed up down here. He said to tell you that Momma Rossi was convinced that Nicole had to come with us or bad things would happen."

Leah smiled for the first time. "You should have started with that," she said. "What else did Momma Rossi have to say?"

"Not much," Chase answered, relieved, and wanting badly to keep the smile on Leah's face. "She was a little distracted because of Pet's calf."

"Pet had her baby! Tell me about it!"

Chase described the birth, leaving out anything having to do with the hurricane. Leah's smile broadened with each detail.

"Dad must have been frantic!"

Chase was certain Marco Rossi had been beyond frantic, considering he'd been trying to get back to the farm for Pet's labour during a Category Five hurricane. "He was pretty excited," he said.

Leah's smile turned into a yawn. "Excuse me," she said. "I don't know why I'm so tired. I've been sleeping for hours."

Chase knew exactly why she was tired and hoped she would fall back asleep before she asked any more questions he couldn't answer without *trie-ing*.

"He's definitely in front of us," Nicole said.

"He?" Mark asked.

"The tigers on the show are all males."

They had followed the tracks for at least thirty metres.

"The question is how far ahead he is." John squatted down to take a closer look at the tracks. "Pugmarks are a little out of my expertise."

"Pugmarks," Mark said. "It would be nice if you guys spoke English."

"*Pug* comes from the Hindi word for 'foot'," Nicole said.

"Hindi, as in India, where man-eating tigers are from?" Mark asked.

"He's not a man-eater," Nicole said.

"Not yet," Mark said.

"What are the circus tigers like?" John asked.

Nicole looked at the plume. The lightning was still crackling in the black funnel. Out of his cage, in the dark and the wind of Hurricane Emily, the big lion, Simba, had been a completely different cat than he was on the show. Ferocious, aggressive, terrifying. Nicole shuddered.

"They're fine in their cages," she said. "But out here the tiger will be confused, hungry. He may be injured."

"In other words, we're in deep trouble if we run into him," Mark said.

"It would be best if we didn't," Nicole agreed. "Although at some point the circus is going to have to try to get him back. We can't leave a tiger running around Mexico."

John looked ahead into the darkness. "Where do you think the tiger is going?"

Nicole followed John's gaze. "I doubt even he knows."

08:02 PM

"I assume none of these houses are yours," Cindy said quietly in Spanish. They were on the final stretch of buckled road leading to the village square.

Tomás walked between the ruins with uncharacteristic slowness, scanning the rubble with his headlamp. "Our home is not here, but these are the homes of my friends. I have seen Popocatepetl erupt many times in my life. There is always damage. This is the worst I have seen."

"Why would anyone live this close to an active volcano?"

"Because it is where we have always lived. The lake provides the water. The mountain provides the floating stones. It is a good place. There is no place that is completely safe."

Cindy couldn't argue with him, but she still thought living in the shadow of an active volcano was tempting fate.

They reached the square.

The only light came from the flickering fires next to where people were sleeping. It was cold. Thunder pealed from the flashing plume.

"A lot of people," Cindy said.

Tomás looked across the broad cobblestoned square at the crude campsites and shelters. "This is only half the people."

He looked beyond the fires and saw the patch of shrouded

bodies lined up in neat rows. Next to some of them, people were kneeling. He crossed himself and walked over to where the dead lay.

Father Al saw them approach and stood up from where he was comforting an old woman grieving for her son. He gave Tomás and Cindy a weary smile. "The boy said you would be here."

"Chase?" Cindy said.

"Yes."

"Is he OK?"

"He is fine. He is watching the Rossis in the orphanage. They are badly injured."

Tomás continued to stare at those who were now beyond injury.

Father Al put his hand on Tomás's shoulder. "None of yours are here," he said quietly. "The orphanage was spared. Guadalupe and the children are alive and well."

Tomás nodded stoically, but it was clear that he was greatly relieved. "The generator?" he said.

"Broken," Father Al said. "But it can wait. You and your friend need to rest. You've had a long journey.

"I will fix it now," Tomás said.

08:17 PM

Chase felt a hand on his shoulder and started awake. He turned around. Cindy was standing behind him with her finger to her lips, motioning for him to be quiet. He looked at the Rossis. They were both sound asleep. He stood up. Tomás was not with Cindy, but she wasn't alone. A girl, a few years older than Chase, was standing in the doorway. They walked over to her.

"This is Blanca," Cindy said. "Tomás's oldest daughter."

Chase recognized her from one of the photos on Tomás's dashboard. He gave her a smile and she returned it with a smile of her own.

"Guadalupe is down in the kitchen cooking. Tomás is with her. Blanca will watch the Rossis."

"I don't mind watching them," Chase said.

"Tomás needs your help with the generator."

Chase couldn't imagine Tomás needing help with anything mechanical, but he was pleased to be asked.

As they walked down to the first floor, Cindy explained what had happened since they had separated. Her voice got a little shaky when she came to the part about dangling over the abyss. He knew how she felt. If the pileup had given way when he was crossing it, he would be dead.

Fate, he thought. "So Nicole and my father are OK," he said.

"And Mark," Cindy said.

"Right." He had completely forgotten about the sixth member of their team.

"As far as I know, they are all good. Like I said, the connection was terrible. From what I gathered, they'd found the circus stranded on the road to Puebla. They can't go forward. They can't go back."

"Kind of like us," Chase said.

Cindy nodded. "He said something about elephants and cats getting killed. Apparently, a couple of circus trucks went off the road. I think the drivers died as well. He said *some* of the cats – or *one* of the cats – had escaped. It wasn't clear."

"What kind of cat?"

"I think he said it was a tiger. Your father was afraid he was going to lose the signal, so he was talking fast. He brushed over it like it was no big deal."

That's because he's never come face-to-face with a big cat in the dark, Chase thought.

"Did he say where he thought the tiger was?"

Cindy shook her head. "But just before the signal went dead, he said something about trying to arrange a rescue. I have no idea what he meant by that either."

"Did you tell him about me getting robbed?"

"Yes, and he was very concerned."

"Then he's on his way up here to find me," Chase said.

Cindy looked at him for a moment, then nodded. "I hadn't thought of that, but you're probably right. It's not going to be easy in the dark with essentially no way to get here."

"The only easy day was yesterday," Chase said.

Cindy smiled.

Mark stumbled and fell. He had been walking behind John and Nicole. They ran back and helped him to his feet. He was more concerned about his camera than he was about broken bones.

"I'm fine," he insisted, checking the camera. "I was focusing on the pugmarks, not paying attention to where I was stepping." He turned the camera on and looked through the viewfinder. Satisfied that there was no damage, he turned it off and asked John, "Why are you following the tiger? Aren't we in enough trouble? Things getting a little too dull for you?"

"I'm not following the tiger," John said. "I'm taking the easiest path across the mountain. Apparently, the tiger is doing the same thing."

"He's right," Nicole said. "Cats are generally lazy. This one's taking the path of least resistance."

"Really," Mark said. "Then why did he walk *up* the mountain instead of down?"

John laughed and looked at Nicole. "Mark has a good point."

"I guess," Nicole conceded.

"Here's the deal," John said. "We may bump into the tiger or we may not. It doesn't really matter. We don't have anything to defend ourselves with. We can't outrun it. Therefore the best thing we can do right now is to forget about the tiger. We need to concentrate on getting to Lago. That's our only option."

Mark looked down at the pugmarks. "Or we could walk in the opposite direction."

"You mean walk back down to the road?" John asked.

"Yeah."

"Suit yourself," John said and continued walking in the direction of the pugmarks.

"Mr Charm," Mark muttered.

Nicole smiled. "Are you really OK?"

"I'm fine. You're the cat expert. What do you do when you run into one in the dark during a volcanic eruption?"

"Cats generally go after the weakest or the slowest."

Mark looked at his camera. "This thing is going to be the death of—"

A lightning bolt struck the ground not six metres in front of them. Nicole and Mark were blown off their feet. They landed on their backs with the air knocked out of them.

Nicole raised her head and gulped for breath. The air was filled with the sharp acrid smell of ozone. She wasn't exactly sure what had happened. She sat up.

"Mark?"

"Yeah."

She could barely hear him. It was as if she had cotton stuffed in her ears. And there was something the matter with her vision. Flashes of bright light pulsated across her eyes, making it impossible to see more than a metre away.

"Did we just get struck by lightning?" Her own voice sounded a mile away from her.

"No," Mark said. "But it was close. Too close. Can you stand up?"

Nicole turned her head, surprised to see that he was right next to her.

"You sound a million miles away."

"Eardrums," he said. "We'll be OK in a little bit. Can you stand?"

"I think so."

She felt him take her hands and pull her to her feet.

"I'm having a hard time seeing," she said.

"That will come back too," Mark said, his voice sounding a little less muffled. "The flash was pretty bright. Blinded me too for a minute, but things are beginning to come into focus again."

"What about—" Nicole began.

"That's my next stop," Mark said. "I'll run up ahead and see how he's doing. He probably didn't even notice that we nearly got hit."

Nicole doubted that.

"Wait here," Mark said.

She wasn't about to wait there. She followed him.

Fifteen metres away, they found John Masters lying on the ground. His eyes were closed. He was pale. His right foot was turned at an unnatural angle. Nicole kneeled down next to him.

"He's not breathing," she said.

*

As Chase and Cindy reached the first floor, the air went still. They stopped and looked at each other.

"The rumbling is gone," Chase said.

Cindy nodded. "I hadn't really noticed the noise until now."

"I wonder what it means," Chase said.

They walked into the kitchen and saw Tomás standing at the window. He was holding two young children in his arms and looking out at Popocatepetl. Guadalupe stood behind him, stirring a delicious-smelling stew on top of a woodstove.

"The moon," Tomás said in English, giving Chase and Cindy a rare smile.

They joined him at the window. The full moon shined brightly next to the plume, casting an eerie light down the mountainside.

"Is it over?" Cindy asked.

Tomás nodded. "For now."

"How do you know?" Chase asked, hoping he was right.

"Experience," Guadalupe answered in surprisingly better English than Tomás spoke. "The worst is behind us. We will mourn our dead, then we will rebuild."

Tomás put the two children down and looked at the bump on Chase's head.

"I'm fine," Chase said.

"Good." He handed Chase his go bag. "We need to fix the generator."

Chase pulled his headlamp out and slipped it on.

The tiger stood listening in the stillness. He looked up at the moon until the ash cloud hid the light. He drank more

water. The people were close. He could hear them talking.
He was hungry.

08:22 PM

"Breathe!" Nicole shouted. She was on her knees next to John Masters, doing rapid and deep chest compressions with the heels of her hands.

"What can I do?" Mark asked, a look of panic and fear on his face.

"Nothing." She stopped the compressions, moved to John's head, tilted it back, filled his lungs with two quick breaths, then started the compressions once again.

Mark paced back and forth. John Masters's luck seemed to have run out. "What are the chances of getting struck by lightning twice?" he shouted in angry frustration. He looked up at the plume, expecting to see more lightning, but the flashes had been replaced by moonlight. The plume seemed to be breaking up, the wind blowing the ash cloud to the east.

And it's quiet, Mark thought. Popocatepetl's roar had stopped. The only thing he could hear was Nicole's rhythmic compressions as she tried to bring Lightning John back to life.

"Breathe!" she shouted again. "Please!"

Chase and Cindy followed Tomás out the back door of the orphanage. He led them over to a locked shed. He pulled a key ring out of his pocket and unlocked the double doors.

Behind the doors was an impressive collection of tools. Power tools, hand tools, compressors, a portable generator, a welder...

Chase smiled. *He has his own private tool stash. Visiting Lago only once a year, it must have taken him years to accumulate all of this stuff.*

Tomás started picking tools off the wall and shelves and putting them into a heavy-duty canvas bag. He looked at Chase and pointed to the portable generator and the dollied acetylene torch used for cutting metal.

Now Chase knew why Tomás had asked for his help. It wasn't to wield tools, it was to haul them.

"I can carry something," Cindy said.

Tomás offered her his go bag.

"Not a chance," she said. She grabbed the dolly with the heavy acetylene and oxygen tanks.

"Breathe!"

John Masters did. His mouth opened. He sucked in a loud gulp of air.

"You saved his life!" Mark shouted.

John stared up at them, disoriented and confused. "What happened?"

"Lightning," Nicole said.

"Again?" John said weakly. He tried to sit up but didn't get very far. He collapsed back on to the ground with a groan.

"I'm afraid I broke, or bruised, some of your ribs giving you CPR."

"Where'd you learn CPR?" John asked weakly.

"Lifeguard class, but I've never had to do it on a real person."

"Thanks," he said hoarsely. "Not for the ribs, but for sav—" He stopped in mid-sentence.

"What's the matter?" Nicole asked, concerned.

"Where's the sound?"

Mark smiled. "While you were taking your catnap, the volcano shut down."

"Catnap, huh?" John laughed, then winced in pain. "How long was I out?"

"You mean dead," Mark said.

"How long?"

Nicole looked at her watch in surprise. "Only four minutes or so," she said. Her arms ached from pushing on his chest.

John tried to sit up again, but it was no good. The pain was too bad.

"Just stay down, for crying out loud," Mark said. "Four minutes is enough to cause brain damage, but apparently it didn't in your case. You're *still* crazy. And Nicole didn't give you the complete diagnosis. Your right leg is broken, or at least twisted up pretty badly. Since you weren't breathing, we didn't think it was important."

"Well, I'm breathing now." John tried to raise his head to see his leg but failed. "Take a look at it."

Nicole and Mark looked without touching it. His right foot was at a right angle to his leg and swelling out of his boot.

"It's your ankle," Mark said. "It looks broken."

"I might be able to set it," Nicole said. "But I'd have to go back down to the tree line to get wood."

"Even if you set it, I wouldn't be able to walk." John laid his head back down and looked up at the sky. He laughed.

"I don't see anything funny about this," Nicole said.

"I'm laughing at your grandmother."

Nicole wondered if John Masters *did* have brain damage after all.

"She told me the lightning was going to find me again," John explained. "I guess she was right." He looked at Nicole. "She also told your father that if you didn't come, something bad was going to happen. I guess she was right about that too. I'd be dead if it weren't for you two."

"I didn't do anything," Mark said.

"I wouldn't say that," John said. "You kept us smiling. That's worth more than you know."

There was something different about John Masters. He wasn't the John Masters from half an hour ago, or even from the day before.

"Are you sure you're OK?" Mark asked.

Nicole was about to ask the same thing. He seemed to have lost his intensity. He looked like Chase's dad and sounded like Chase's dad, but he didn't act like him.

"Aside from my ribs and ankle?" John asked.

"Yeah," Mark said. "You seem ... I don't know ... cheerful, I guess."

John thought about it for a moment, then smiled. "I guess you're right. I do feel cheerful. It's been a long time."

"And you do realize that we are stuck on a mountain?"

John nodded. "If this ash went away, we could make a call and get some help. Tomás, Chase or Cindy might be at Lago by now. I hope they're there."

"The moon was out for a minute," Nicole said. "But the blowing ash has covered it again."

"Where's my go bag?"

It took a while for Mark to find it. The go bag had ended up six metres away from where John lay.

"It's totally hammered," Mark said. "Struck by lightning. Everything inside is burned or melted."

"Check your sat phones and see if there's a signal."

They checked and shook their heads.

"That's it, then," John said. "You two go ahead without me. Leave me one of your phones and a bottle of water. If you think about it when you get to Lago, send somebody up here to get me."

"Funny," Nicole said.

"That lightning bolt must have wiped out your short-term memory," Mark said. "There's a tiger wandering around. We can't leave you out here like some kind of roadkill."

"We can't stay here," John said. "Nobody knows where we are. Lago isn't very far."

"I don't feel right about leaving you here," Nicole said. "You're injured."

"I'll go," Mark said. "You stay with John."

"I'll go," Nicole said. "You stay."

"Stop!" John said, some of his former intensity returning. "You're not going by yourself, Nicole. And, Mark, you don't speak Spanish."

"I'm sure someone in Lago speaks enough English for me to make them understand that we need help."

"You're wasting time. No more debate. Give me your phone, Mark."

Mark fished his phone out of his go bag and handed it over. Nicole gave him a bottle of water.

"I still don't feel right about this," Nicole said.

"Just go," John said.

Mark set something down next to him. "What's that?" John asked.

"It's the camera. Keep an eye on it for me."

"Will do," John said.

He listened to them walk away.

Cheerful, he thought. *It's more than that. Content is more like it. That first bolt of lightning took something away from me. Maybe the second one brought something back. I'm so dense, it took not one but two bolts of lightning to square me away.*

He hoped Chase was OK. He was eager to see his son.

The tiger saw the lights and walked towards them. The smell of food was in the dusty air. It was time to eat. Time to drink. Time to find a safe place to rest with a full belly. He heard the human voices. Unfamiliar voices. He was nervous, but he didn't care. Hunger drove his fear away, and his paws towards the dancing lights.

09:02PM

"There!" Mark said, pointing.

"I see them," Nicole said. Down the mountain, maybe a quarter mile away, several small fires flickered in the dark.

They started down.

"I haven't seen any of those pugmarks in a long time," Mark said.

"I haven't either. He must have gone off in a different direction." Nicole no longer cared about the tiger. Her mother and sister and Chase were close.

The generator was inside the bottling plant, which had been badly damaged by the earthquakes. During the day, when the plant was running, the generator was used to run the pumps and filters and conveyor belts that produced their famous Montaña water. At night and on weekends, when the plant was idle, the generator was used to power the village.

The bottling plant was a lot more sophisticated than Chase had expected it would be. When Father Al had told him about their famous water, he'd had an image of villagers kneeling next to the lake, filling the plastic bottles one at a time, screwing on caps, and tossing them into the back of an old pickup truck. He couldn't have been more wrong. Aside from the church, the bottling plant was easily the largest building in the village. They had entered through a loading-dock door, which had been open when they arrived. Backed up to the dock were three relatively new trucks with the colourful Montaña logo painted on the panels.

A few of the ceiling tiles had fallen and there were thousands of plastic bottles, empty and full, strewn across the floor, making for treacherous walking with the portable generator he was carrying and the acetylene tanks Cindy was pulling. Tomás had tried to take the tanks from her, but she had slapped his hand and told him to quit being ridiculous.

The power plant was in a separate room at the far end of the building. When they got there, Tomás had Chase fire up the portable generator and set up some lights so he could see what he was doing. Tomás started by checking the electrical connections with his ohmmeter.

In the corner was an old sofa. Cindy plopped down on it, and within seconds she was sound asleep.

Chase watched Tomás's clever hands and mind at work, systematically examining the generator from one end to the other. He wondered if Montaña water had existed when Tomás was growing up in the orphanage. He doubted it. The bottled-water craze hadn't been around long. Forty years ago, when Tomás had lived in Lago, they probably really did just scoop water out of the lake.

A villager saw the two lights coming down the mountain and alerted Father Al. He and a small group of men met Nicole and Mark just before they reached the square.

Nicole quickly explained who they were and what had happened to John Masters.

"How far up the mountain is he?" Father Al asked.

"Two miles," Mark said. "Three at the most."

Father Al asked two of the men to go into the church and get a stretcher. "You say he was struck by lightning."

"Yes," Nicole said.

"And he lived."

"That's right," Mark said. "And that's not the first time he's been struck."

"A miracle," Father Al muttered, and crossed himself.

"Are my mother and sister here?" Nicole asked, almost afraid to hear his answer.

"Oh, yes," Father Al said. "They are in the orphanage, asleep. They have been injured."

"How badly?"

"Your mother is worse off than your sister, but if we can get her to a hospital soon, I think she will recover."

Nicole looked at Mark. He smiled. "Don't worry about it. I'll take them up to retrieve Lightning John."

"Thank you, Mark." She gave him a hug, then turned to the priest. "Where's the orphanage, Father?"

"Behind the church, but please try not to wake them. At this point, sleep is the best medicine. In fact, it is our only medicine until we get them to a proper facility."

Nicole smiled and started towards the square, but she didn't get far. She froze in mid-step.

"Oh, no!"

"What?" Mark hurried over and looked down. He swore.

Father Al joined them but didn't understand what they were staring at on the ground.

"There's a tiger in the village," Nicole said as calmly as she could. "We need to get everyone into the church until we find out where it is."

∅9:36PM

Tomás waved Chase over and showed him a handful of fuses. "In the shed," he said. "In a red box. Bring the box."

Chase smiled. He had always liked Tomás's way of communicating.

Clear and concise.

"I'll bring them right back."

He headed out of the generator room towards the loading dock, happy to have something to do, and hoping that the fix was as simple as a new fuse.

An odd sensation overcame him as he walked past the conveyor belt. He stopped. The hair on the back of his neck prickled. He felt the same unpleasant sensation he had felt not two days before. Something was watching him. He could feel its eyes on him.

It can't be.

He slowly moved his headlamp around the huge room. Bottles, boxes, equipment, and enough shadows to hide an elephant.

It's my imagination. I'm just tired. I'm having a flashback.

But he knew none of this was true. There was a tiger in the building.

Nicole had told him that the most important thing was containment, but he didn't think she meant to contain the animal in the same container you're standing in. At the farm, they'd had a shotgun and a tranquillizer. Now he had nothing.

Cindy and Tomás have less than nothing. They don't know the tiger is here.

He looked behind him. The light shined through the generator door. He looked in front of him at the loading-dock door.

Midway.

If he made a run for the generator room and slammed the door, the tiger could leave the building. There were people in the square. The church door was open. The orphanage door was open. The tiger could go wherever it wanted.

The loading-dock door was a roll-up with a pull chain on the side. If he managed to get there without getting mauled, the tiger would be between him and the open generator door. Cindy was sound asleep. And Tomás might not understand if Chase shouted for him to close the door. Besides, Chase knew him well. Tomás wouldn't close the door without an explanation. If he thought Chase was in trouble, he would step out into the open and take on whatever it was.

Not even Tomás's clever hands can stop a tiger.

"What are the chances of this happening twice?" he asked himself. "About as likely as being struck by lightning twice. Paranoia. I'm being ridiculous."

Just then he heard the crunch of something heavy stepping on empty plastic bottles. He turned his headlamp in time to see the flash of a striped tail disappearing into the shadows.

*

They managed to get everyone into the church without too much panic. Most of the villagers believed they were being herded inside because of the volcano.

It was crowded, with the injured taking up most of the pews. Father Al closed the double doors and started up the centre aisle to the pulpit. Nicole and Mark stood at the back.

"What about John?" Mark asked.

"I guess he's going to have to wait until we get this figured out. I doubt anyone is going to want to go outside with a tiger loose." She tried to spot Chase or Tomás in the dark church, but it was nearly impossible to see anyone in the candlelit room. "As soon as Father Al's finished, we'll look for Chase, Tomás and Cindy. Between the five of us, we'll be able to get John down here."

Father Al spoke in Spanish. Nicole translated for Mark.

"Thank you for being calm," he said, his deep voice filling the large church. "I believe that Popocatepetl has gone back to sleep. It was a terrible day. I am sorry for your losses. But right now we have another problem. I have asked you to come in here because we believe there is a circus tiger loose in the village."

Alarm and disbelief spread throughout the church. Father Al let them express their dismay for nearly a minute before holding up his hands to silence them.

"We believe everyone is in here, or inside the orphanage. We are safe as long as we stay inside and stay calm."

"How will we get the tiger?" a man shouted.

"We are working on that," Father Al said. "I'm going to

go over to the orphanage to talk to the circus people and find out what we can do about our visitor."

"The only circus people who are healthy are clowns!" another man shouted.

"There is an animal trainer among them," Father Al said.

"A poodle trainer," someone else shouted.

Some people wailed. Others laughed.

"This is not going well," Nicole said. She started towards the aisle.

Mark caught up with her. "What are you going to do?"

"I'm going to talk to the congregation," Nicole answered. She reached the pulpit and whispered something in Father Al's ear. He nodded and stepped aside.

Nicole waited for everyone to quieten down, which didn't take long. They stared up at her with curiosity and confusion. Public speaking had never been Nicole's favourite subject in school. Now she had to speak to over a hundred people in Spanish.

"My name is Nicole Rossi. My parents own the Rossi Brothers' Circus. There was a terrible accident on the road to Puebla. Two trucks went off the road. Five of my friends were killed, along with all of our elephants and our lions and tigers ... except one. He managed to escape. I am sorry for this. I am also sorry for the loss of my friends and the animals."

A tear rolled down her cheek. She paused and gathered herself before continuing.

"The clowns and the dog trainer have been with the circus for many years. During those years, they have seen many things and worked with many different animals. If the tiger is in Lago, we will find him and contain him before he harms anyone. You have my word."

She looked out into the dark church. No one said a word. She turned to Father Al and said quietly, "I need to talk to my friends."

"They are in the orphanage with your mother and sister," Father Al said. "I haven't had time to tell them about the tiger."

"I'll tell them," Nicole said. "I assume that Chase, Tomás and Cindy are over there too?"

Father Al went a little pale. He shook his head. "They are in the bottling plant, trying to fix the generator."

Chase needed to make up his mind. The rattling of the bottles was getting louder. Tomás was going to hear the noise and come out to investigate. Chase turned around very slowly and faced the generator door.

"Tomás!" he yelled.

The rattling stopped. He wished it hadn't.

Tomás appeared in the doorway, looking concerned.

"You need to close the door! The tiger is in here. I am going to make a run for the loading dock."

Tomás took a step out.

"No!" Chase shouted. "Stay where you are!"

Tomás hesitated.

A sleepy-looking Cindy appeared behind him. "What's going on?"

"The tiger is in the building. You need to close the generator door. I'm going to try to get to the loading dock and close that door so it doesn't escape into the village. You cannot come out until I tell you it's safe."

"But—"

"I'll be fine, and so will you if you stay where you are. Close the door. Now!"

Cindy quickly explained the situation to Tomás. After a long moment's hesitation, he closed the door slowly. Now the only light in the plant came from Chase's headlamp. What he had not told Cindy was that the dock door could be closed only by the chain from inside. He would have to pull the heavy door down, then find the small door to the side to get out.

The ground floor of the orphanage was chaotic. Poodles barking, children crying, people talking over one another.

"What are you doing here, Nicole?"

"Which tiger is it?"

"The elephants are dead?"

"Who was driving the trucks?"

"Enough!" Nicole said. "We need to find our friends and tell them about the tiger. Then we need to search the village to find out if it is still here."

"Yes, we will all go," Pierre Deveroux, the dog trainer, said. "We will walk in a large group with sticks or whatever we can find. It is unlikely the tiger will attack a group."

"Unlikely," Dennis the clown said.

Pierre shrugged. "Nothing is for certain, of course."

"Of course," Mark said.

Dennis smiled.

"If we can, we will contain him," Pierre said. "If we cannot, we will try to drive him from the village."

Chase ran towards the door, but he didn't get very far. He slipped on the bottles and fell.

This is it! American boy mauled to death by tiger in bottled-water plant in Mexico.

But that wasn't it. The big cat sounded like it was having the same difficulty negotiating the bottles strewn across the floor as Chase had.

The tiger roared in frustration.

Chase stood back up. He started moving forward again, but this time he went more slowly, trying to be careful about where he put his feet. He risked a glance behind him and wished he hadn't. The tiger was out in the open now and gaining on him.

Concentrate on the chain!

Chase wanted to head straight through the door and run off into the dark night, but it was too late for that. If the tiger followed him, he would never be able to outrun it. His only hope was the door, and the ruse Momma Rossi had used to confuse Hector the leopard back in Florida.

Chase lunged for the chain and grabbed it with his right hand, hoping the door hadn't been left open because it was broken. With his left hand he tore the headlamp off his forehead and tossed it back towards where he thought the tiger was. He was working in complete darkness now. The door began to close as Chase double-handed the chain down as fast as he could. The tiger growled. The light from Chase's headlamp flashed around the building, which meant the tiger had fallen for Momma Rossi's trick. The door clicked shut as it smashed into the threshold. The headlamp went out. The tiger had snapped the bulb.

All I have to do now is crawl a dozen feet to my left, find the small door in the pitch dark, and let myself out before the tiger pounces on me.

He started to crawl.

The tiger ran into the big metal door and let out another horrendous growl.

Chase tried to ignore the terrible sound as he felt his way along the wall. The building was made of cinder blocks. He felt the metal doorframe.

Doorknob. Four feet up from the ground.

He reached for where he thought the doorknob should be, but just then the door swung open. A hand reached through and pulled him to the dock. A second later, the tiger hit the door. The door held.

Gasping for breath, Chase looked up at his savior. It was Tomás. He helped Chase to his feet, then took a close look at him as if he were checking to see if Chase still had all of his limbs.

"You OK?"

"No," Chase said. "How did you get here?"

"Window," Tomás answered.

Chase started laughing. Tomás joined him.

And that's how Nicole, Mark, Cindy and the others found them.

"You two have a really twisted sense of humour," Mark said.

Nicole looked at the doors. She could hear the tiger on the other side. "Did you catch yourself another cat?"

"Sure did," Chase said. He looked at Tomás. "With a little help from my friend. Where's my dad?"

"Up on the mountain," Nicole said.

"Taking a catnap," Mark said. "Guess we should go up there and wake him."

10:47 PM

Chase was the first to reach his father.

"Hey, sport," his father said.

"What time is it?" Chase asked.

His father laughed. "You know what? I have no idea. Apparently, that last bolt knocked the ability right out of me. I guess I'll have to buy a watch now."

"You OK?"

"A couple cracked ribs and a badly sprained ankle."

"Mark said he thought it was broken."

"I bet you he's wrong."

Nicole and Cindy came up next, followed by Tomás, Mark and several men from the village with a stretcher.

His father's sat phone rang, startling everyone.

"Excuse me," he said, and answered it. "That's a negative. The cavalry just arrived. They're taking me down the mountain as we speak. Go ahead and evac the circus people. I'll get an LZ cleared up here and see you at the village at first light. Roger that. Out."

"Who was that?" Chase asked.

"That was SEAL Team One commander Raul Delgado."

"The only easy day was yesterday," Chase said.

His father smiled. "As it turns out, you might be right. I guess I have some explaining to do."

"Yeah, you do," Chase said.

"And I promise I will," his father said. He turned to Nicole. "Most of your people are on army trucks headed back to Mexico City. Delgado is going to move the animals next. Road crews should have the slide cleared and the bridge back up in a few days, and they'll be able retrieve their vehicles then. Delgado is leaving a couple men behind to keep an eye on things until they can return."

He handed Mark the video camera.

Mark turned it on and started filming.

THURSDAY
07:15 AM

Dawn filtered through the window as Tomás tightened the last bolt. He passed the ratchet to Chase, then wiped his clever hands with a rag.

"Fixed?" Chase asked.

"Maybe."

They had been in the generator room since they'd dropped Chase's father at the church to have his ribs and ankle looked at. When Chase wasn't handing Tomás tools, he was at the metal door peering through the safety glass. It was too dark to see the bottling plant, but he could hear the tiger prowling, slapping plastic bottles across the cement floor.

Tomás hit some switches and the generator came to life. The tiger roared.

Chase hurried over to the door. The tiger had his front paws on the conveyor belt and was looking up at the fluorescent lights.

Contained, Chase thought. *And bigger than he looked last night.*

He walked back over to Tomás.

"Everything good?"

"I think."

"I'm going over to the church to check on my dad."

Tomás nodded. "I will watch the generator."

"Don't open the door," Chase said, smiling.

Tomás laughed.

Chase climbed through the window. The sun was rising over the top of Popocatepetl. The slopes were covered with ash. A wisp of white steam curled up from the crater. The mountain was peaceful once again, but the memory of its violence was everywhere as Chase made his way to the village square.

He arrived just as the first chopper touched down on the cobblestones in a swirl of ash. His father was on crutches, waiting for it. Mark had his camera rolling. Cindy stood by him, jotting something down in a notebook. Chase stood at the edge of the square, out of the worst of the ash, and watched.

A big man in a black uniform jumped out, walked up to Chase's father, and saluted. John returned the salute.

Commander Delgado.

Chase shook his head. *I guess I had to see it to believe it,* he thought. *Dad really was a Navy SEAL.*

Several other men jumped out of the chopper, carrying stretchers and supplies. The last two men to climb out were not dressed in uniforms. One was tall and thin. The other was squat and heavy. They carried a large crate between them.

Circus roustabouts.

Nicole came out of the church alongside the stretcher carrying her mother. Leah's stretcher was right behind them. Chase waved, but Nicole didn't notice. She was talking to her mother. The men loaded the stretchers on to the chopper, and Nicole climbed in after them.

I should go up and say something. I can't just let her fly off. Chase started forward, but stopped. More stretchers were arriving. He didn't want to get in their way. He looked at his father, who was laughing about something with Delgado and Cindy. Mark was still filming. *Nicole wouldn't leave without saying goodbye.* Another chopper appeared over the lake and hovered, awaiting its turn. Two more stretchers were brought out to the first chopper. *Now or never.* He started across the square. Nicole jumped off the chopper before he had taken ten steps. He stopped again. She waved to someone inside and hurried out from beneath the rotors.

"Nicole!"

She ran over and gave him a hug.

"You're not going with your mom and sister?"

She shook her head. "I didn't want to take the space from someone who's injured. I'm taking the last chopper out with the poodles and the tiger." She raised an eyebrow. "You didn't think I'd leave without saying goodbye, did you?"

"Well . . ."

Nicole took his hand. "Let's go down to Lago de la Montaña. I haven't seen it yet."

Nicole and Chase walked along the shore, holding hands.

"So your mom's OK," Chase said.

Nicole nodded. "She woke up last night, wanting to get out of bed to check on the animals. It took three of us to hold her down. Leah wasn't much better. Rossis aren't very good at lying around. The doctor had been worried about spine or neck injuries, but he revised his prognosis after seeing her trying to get up. He suggested she stay in the hospital for several days. I predict it will be one day at the most. I talked to my dad. He's on the same flight we took to Mexico City. With any luck, he'll beat them to the hospital and try to keep them in their beds for a couple of days."

"Who's taking care of the farm?"

"The Stones. I talked to Rashawn. Pet and the calf are fine. The only problem they're having is with her little brother. He's so excited to be around the animals that Momma Rossi's threatening to lock him up in one of the cages so he doesn't hurt himself."

The second chopper took off and a third landed.

"Have they picked up the people on the road?" Chase asked.

"They're all at the fairgrounds with Arturo. As soon as I show up with the tiger, we'll head back to the States."

"Then what?"

Nicole shook her head. "I don't know. It could be the end of the Rossi Brothers' Circus. But you never know. We've been through bad times and the show still went on. We have all winter to see where we're at." She stopped and picked up a piece of pumice. "What about you?" she asked. "What are your plans?"

"I don't know. I haven't had a chance to talk to my father. It's up to him."

"You're welcome to come back with me to the farm. We could use your help and I. . ." She flushed and looked away. "So tell me about that tiger."

Chase smiled, but it wasn't about the tiger. He was pretty certain that Nicole felt the same way about him as he did about her.

"What's so funny?"

"Not a thing."

Chase leaned forward and kissed her.

09:30 AM

The last chopper had landed. They were standing outside the bottling plant.

"I guess it's tiger time," Nicole said. She looked at Chase. "So you think I can tranquillize it from the generator room?"

Chase nodded. "There's a small safety window in the door. It will have to be broken out to get the rifle through, but Tomás is there. He can break it out for you."

"All right," Nicole said. "Let's get this over with."

Commander Delgado looked at Nicole and scratched his stubbled chin. "I'll just come out with it," he said. "You can say yes or no. It's totally up to you. You're the expert. You're the boss. But I have always wanted to dart a big cat. Can I dart the big fella?"

Nicole looked at him and squinted her eyes. "What kind of shot are you?"

Delgado gave her a big smile. Chase's father smiled too. "Well, I'm a pretty fair shot, truth be told. But I'll be honest – I've never shot a tranquillizer rifle like this one."

Nicole looked at John. "What do you think?"

"He did fly out here and rescue your mom and sister and ferry all the circus people to the other side of the bridge."

"Don't forget the animals," Delgado said. "We took them too. Getting those camels on the chopper was no picnic, I can tell you. Although it was kind of fun."

Nicole handed him the rifle. "OK. You need to hit the large muscle mass in the hind leg. Seventy-five to a hundred feet max."

"I'm not going in there without you," Delgado said. "You need to guide me through it."

They disappeared around the corner, with Mark and Cindy close behind. That left Chase and his father alone.

"You're sure your ankle isn't broken?" Chase asked.

"Just a bad sprain. The crutches make it look worse than it is."

"And the ribs?"

"Those do hurt, but they'll heal."

"You won't be much good around here stove-in like you are."

"I'll supervise Tomás."

Chase laughed. "Like he needs you telling him what to do."

"Good point, but I'm still going to stick around. For a while anyway."

"Did they get that guy on the road with the broken leg?"

"The guy who hit you in the head and hijacked the quad?"

"Yeah, that guy."

"They got him, but it wasn't easy. No place to land. They had to rope him up."

"Good." Chase was in a forgiving mood.

"Are you heading out with Nicole and the tiger? I talked to Marco. He said he would be happy to have you stay on the farm a while. I'm sure Nicole would too."

Chase grinned. "I think I'd better stay here with you."

"What about school?"

"It'll be a couple of weeks before they get the schools going in Palm Breeze again."

"Then what?"

"You tell me," Chase said.

His father shook his head. "No, Chase, you tell *me*. When we're done here, we can go back to Palm Breeze. We can even go back home if you want."

"Oregon?" Chase was shocked.

His father held his gaze for a moment. "I'm ready, Chase."

Chase wasn't sure that *he* was ready. He'd put that possibility out of his mind a long time ago. And now there was Nicole to think about. "Are you sure you're OK? Did the lightning strike—"

"Knock some sense into me?"

"I guess. I mean you're acting like you did before—" He didn't finish the sentence. It was a subject they never talked about.

His father finished the sentence for him. "Before your mom and Little Monkey died?"

Chase hadn't heard his father use his sister Monica's nickname since the accident.

"I'm better, Chase. No more storm running. No more running from myself. It's my turn to follow you."

"The only *hard* day was yesterday?" Chase said.

"Let's hope so." His father smiled and put his hand out. "Do we have a deal?"

Chase shook his father's hand, happy to have him back, but wondering how long it would last.

"Deal," he said.

ROLAND SMITH

JUNGLE
HUNTERS

You thought they were extinct.
You were wrong.

DON'T MISS. . .

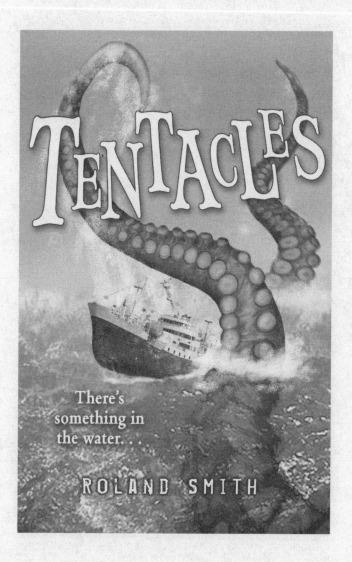

TENTACLES

There's
something in
the water. . .

ROLAND SMITH

LOOK OUT FOR. . .

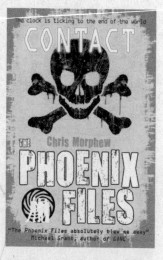

"*The Phoenix Files* absolutely blew me away"
Michael Grant, author of *GONE*